THE ALMOND IN THE APRICOT

THE ALMOND IN
THE APRICOT

Sara Goudarzi

DEEP VELLUM PUBLISHING
DALLAS, TEXAS

Deep Vellum Publishing
3000 Commerce St., Dallas, Texas 75226
deepvellum.org · @deepvellum

Deep Vellum is a 501c3 nonprofit literary arts organization founded in 2013
with the mission to bring the world into conversation through literature.

The author gratefully acknowledges Esther Morgan for permission to reprint the
poem "Hints for Outback Motoring," copyright 2001 by Esther Morgan, from *Beyond
Calling Distance*, published by Bloodaxe Books.

Support for this publication has been provided in part by The Moody Fund for the
Arts.

MOODY FUND FOR
THE ARTS

ISBNs: 978-1-64605-109-0 (hardcover) | 978-1-64605-110-6 (ebook)

LIBRARY OF CONGRESS CONTROL NUMBER: 2021947160

Cover Design by Marina Drukman
Interior Layout and Typesetting by KGT

PRINTED IN THE UNITED STATES OF AMERICA

To my parents; to Anthony

Beyond the edge of our universe, beyond infinity, beyond the gaze of our mechanical eyes, beyond our beliefs could lie pockets of space similar to but different from our world. Ours is but one of infinite separate and distinct cosmic islands. It's only when another world collides with our own that we realize we are not alone.

1. Siren

TOURAN

The basement smells wet. Other than random flashes of light coming through the small window, it's dark everywhere. I'm squatting on the cold concrete floor under a wooden table, covering my ears with my hands and wondering if our house will still be here tomorrow. Mom and Dad are sitting on chairs a few meters away. They're quiet. I don't like sitting on a chair. The table is like another roof. I told my parents it's like playing house, and they said it was okay. We all do different things when the lights are cut and the air raids begin.

It always starts with a siren; this is how the government lets us know we're in danger and that we should hurry to our shelters. For most of us, the basement is our shelter, the only place we could survive if they drop a bomb on our house. This morning, the siren sounded at 3:12 AM. I thought it was my alarm waking me up for school. But when I opened my eyes, the room was dark and the jays weren't squawking outside the windows yet. I pulled the covers over my head, but Mom's voice cut through the air: "Why aren't you up, Lily?!" She sounded panicky, like she always does.

"Coming," I yelled from under the blanket, trying to loosen my legs as fast as I could. I got out from under the warm covers, stepped on my favorite doll, the one I was playing with the night before, kicked her under the bed without looking down, and stumbled out.

Dad was outside waiting for us on the raised stone patio. In the corner of the yard, opposite the pool, steps took us to the basement, an unfinished room—originally for extra storage—with an attached bathroom. But for the past six months it's become our shelter. Mom even put canned food and dry bread in here. In case we're hungry and the bombing lasts more than the usual fifteen minutes. In case. We're always ready for in case.

Tonight the Milky Way looked extra brilliant with the electricity cut off in the city. Its luminous band, like a million bits of crushed diamonds, arched the darkness. Then the antimissile aircraft made the sky glow the color of blood.

As I squat under the table, the sound of the siren stops. The patchy thuds begin. It's the usual. First comes the loud sounds then the smell of raids. Dad says it's a combination of ozone and cordite. I don't know what those things are. To me, it just smells of war. Then I start praying, or my form of it. I mumble loud enough to cover up the noise outside my head. Dad doesn't hush me, so I assume it's okay to pray when we're down here. I don't know any real prayers, so I've made up my own. It's a kind of like begging, actually. Nothing I would want my friends at school to see. When the sun is out and I'm getting ready to go school, the whole God thing seems silly, just like Dad says. It's only when the raids begin that I believe.

I repeat my little prayer over and over again and promise, like I do every night, that I'll never not believe in God. "Really God, I promise I'll never think those awful things about you again. Just let this be over. Please let my family stay safe tonight. I'll be a better girl too, I promise. I'll start finishing my math problems before the day they're due, and I'll set my alarm clock on weekdays (because deep down, I actually do know that Mom's pet peeve is waking me up for school). If you let me grow up with my parents around, I'll do something good like become a teacher like Dad. Just please let my family and home be safe. Amen." I know you have to say *amen* to make all prayers official. It's like "sincerely" or "yours truly" at the end of a letter. You need to let God know that it's okay to stop listening to you and start listening to another begging child. There are a lot of us here wanting to make it out of the basement tonight. It's the polite thing to do. Really.

2. Everydayness and Sewers

NEW JERSEY

I whipped my silk robe around myself and rushed to the stove. Each of the round knobs was lined up at *off*, and the ignition ports were cold. Where else could that scorching smell be coming from? Milky, early rays were just making their way through the windows, finding the sparse lines in my living room. The television, maybe? I put a hand on the back of, and around, the enclosure. It was cold. Sniffing first the living room air, then the hallway and the bathroom, and finally the bedroom, I surveyed the entire home and came up empty. Nothing was burning. Yet that sharp, sulfuric electrical odor had roused me from a dead sleep.

That was the day everything changed. I'd woken up in that condo for five years. But that Thursday spring morning, a couple of weeks after my twenty-ninth birthday, I woke up scared, confused, and suspicious, frantically searching for something that I was sure existed.

That morning, I didn't know where I was.

But I went about the day as if I did, because that was the only way I knew how. Mr. Coffee percolated the powdered remnants of beans from Colombia while I inhaled warm water vapors in the shower to cleanse my insides and wash away the uncertainty that was beginning to take root.

Before long, dressed in a blouse and a pair of slacks with my wet hair twisted up with a brown clip, I stood by the answering machine, sitting on the island separating the kitchen from the living room and played my dead best friend's last message for the 103rd time. I stared beyond the machine at the ether that emanated the ringing voice of Spencer as clear as though he were standing there but as always couldn't get past the first three words *My not wife*. . . and sipped the remains of Mr. Coffee's masterpiece—my daily ritual.

By seven forty-five I was at my cubicle, one of sixty-three gray lidless boxes on our floor. I looked through my emails. The plans for the new developments were in. I walked over, retrieved them from our secretary's desk, and carried them through the leaden-hued corridor back to my work area, which seemed to have shrunk over the past few weeks. I seated myself at the desk, unrolled the plans, searched for my page—"Utilities"—looked at the grade of the land, and tried to imagine where the sewers would go.

Sewer design. To a very small group of people, or a party crowd for all of five minutes, it may seem fascinating. But really, even to those folks sewers quickly lose their allure. For me, it took about a year to exhaust my fascination with the underground maze of waste. That's when I realized the single most important point to grasp about designing sewer lines is that the shit must flow downhill. That's all one needs to know. Nothing else matters. Why it goes down and what happens at the end of its journey is not my concern. I only make sure it ends up there. Not too fast. Not too slow. But at a velocity determined by the masterminds of sewers: at least two feet per second. I hadn't acquired much new knowledge on the subject since that fact. And no matter how hard I listened to the news, no one ever made a breakthrough in my field. Sewers had already been mastered.

For the next few hours, my entire upper body was spread over the plans. With a pencil, eraser, and ruler in hand, I moved east and west, north and south, looking for contours on paper that connected points with the same elevation, figuring out where the little hills and valleys of the development were. Then, I calculated the length and slope of each sewer pipe. Just like that, with little lines drawn here and there, I hooked each house in the development up to the city sewer under the streets. I'd be lying if I said there was no gratification in the small act of designing something that made people's new homes work: those looking for the promise of new beginnings, taking in the smell of just-sanded wood and fresh paint, standing among empty walls, full of potential. But that feeling, which always brought me so much pleasure, had begun to sound like some excuse for what I did and wore off as I remembered, once again like I had the previous three months, that every cube around me was doing something similar. The world would go on no matter who occupied the one I sat in.

My office phone started ringing. It was barely noon.

"Lunch?" I could hear Tina's crisp but low voice in stereo, through the receiver and through the air from two cubicles away.

"Couldn't come soon enough," I said. Every morning, I waited for lunchtime to arrive, and every afternoon for evening to begin showing its dark head. Then I waited in my car on my forty-minute commute on a flat, two-lane, state highway to get home. I did a lot of waiting.

Within minutes, Tina was towering over my desk in a lightweight beige trench coat. Her wavy dark blond hair, hitting just below her jaw and sparkling under the fluorescent office lights, was parted on the side and lightly tucked behind her small porcelain ears, showing off an elongated neck. She is not what one would call beautiful—her slightly larger than normal forehead is connected to her nose with little differentiation, and her thin lips are bracketed by two deep lines marking where her smile has ended for nearly thirty years. Nonetheless, people notice Tina because she is striking. Her five-foot-nine-inch height, slender fingers, and jacked up cheekbones demand a quiet attention. She headed toward the door, and I followed, watching her long skinny legs move inside her trademark wide-legged slacks with what seemed like so little effort. I envied her fluidity, something I didn't feel I possessed. It wasn't so much a physical limitation on my end, but somehow I felt as though we moved through different airs and the one I lived in was denser than hers.

"What're you working on today?" she said.

"A new development in Red Bank. Just twenty homes, not much to lay out. Need to check the numbers again. I'm nearly done."

We headed down the steps to the reception area of our four-story office building and into the great outdoors: a parking lot with hundreds of bright parallel white lines drawn on the charcoal-colored asphalt designating two-dimensional structures where each person's car would be bound for the day. Much like most of us occupying the building, the cars were more or less the same, their price range corresponding to similar makes and models. If one were looking for an entry- to midrange-level Toyota, Nissan, Mazda, Honda, or the like, this was a good place to take a tour.

"At least you're designing. I am just reviewing an old job," Tina said.

"Same shit!" I said, feeling a sense of freedom that comes with seeing a cloudless sky after several hours under office lights. Tina and I shared a love of disliking our job, but often we just pretended to for the fun of it or to have a running topic of conversation.

"Shiitake Corner?" she said as we both got into her Nissan sedan. And off we went to spend our hour of midday bliss watching Japanese chefs chop, throw, catch, and smile.

"I had a weird dream last night," Tina started once we settled at the hibachi grill table. "Shirley was typing my township report and I was leaning on her desk waiting to get it from her when the mayor showed up at the office. I ran to the conference room and locked the door because the report wasn't ready, but the mayor started knocking and wouldn't stop. I thought he was going to break the door. But get this, when I turned around I realized Brian was in the conference room."

"GIS Brian?"

"The one and only," she said of the ever-popular, married man that we all had not-so-secret crushes on. "At first I was yelling through the door to Shirley to speed up the typing, but once I spotted Brian I stopped and then he walked over, turned me so my back was leaning on the door, and we started making out. And then . . ."

"There's more?"

"The mayor punched through the door, pushing us onto the conference table. Then I woke up."

"Damn. Why do dreams have to always end right before the best part?" I chuckled and took my chopsticks out of their red paper wrapper. Flashes of blood-hued streaks in a dark sky appeared under my eyelids. With each visual spark, loud noises poked holes into my eardrums. A thunderous boom of an explosion, and I was back in the restaurant. It all lasted a fraction of a second but the familiarity of it left me disquieted. I broke apart the conjoined chopsticks and started rubbing them together to get the splinters out.

This would have been a good time to tell her, or anyone for that matter, that something wasn't right with me. How I hadn't felt like myself lately and that I had these moments with strange visions and sensations that were somehow familiar. And these dreams that had plagued me for days but which I'd realized that morning were more than ordinary. My brows drew close together as I got ready to release the words I was still trying to locate and arrange but kept quiet because, like everyone else, she'd want to coddle me and circle back to Spencer and use his death as an excuse for everything that troubled me, every task I didn't excel at, and every incoherent thing I said.

"Hello?" Tina waved her fork in front of my eyes, her smile lines deepening. "Are you starting a fire there?" With her face, she pointed in the direction of my hands.

I looked down and realized I was still mindlessly rubbing together the pieces of wood. I put them aside on the table, and the chef placed two bowls of steaming white rice in front of us, followed by bowls of fried beef, zucchini, onions, and mushrooms doused with teriyaki sauce. He smiled at us, shut down the grill and the fan, and left. We were the only two seated at the table and all became quiet for a few seconds.

"You got nothing?" she said. "About my dream?"

"Maybe you can get overtime for staying at the office when you're asleep," I teased.

She ignored my stupid comment and continued: "Did you hear that Charlie is thinking of giving you Mayfield Township?"

I shook my head. "How do you figure?"

"Steve's office door was open and I overheard him and Charlie talking. He wants you to run it—partly because he doesn't want to do it himself and also because he trusts you. Or so he told Steve. He said something like he'll decide for sure at your meeting today."

"Curious," I said, trying to feel pleased. But the undercurrent of anxiety from that morning, that smell, that feeling, wouldn't allow me to fully bask.

"No, *huge!* Everyone wants Mayfield." I couldn't be sure if I felt a tinge of envy in her voice. Tina and I were both senior-level engineers, started within a month of each other, yet I had a slight edge over her, my words always carrying just a bit more weight in meetings, and now I seemed to have the project she probably wished she had landed. Although I'd never let on, I secretly enjoyed this bit of advantage.

"Everyone wants to spend months outside inspecting sewers?" I faked a roll of the eyes, downplaying the whole thing.

"C'mon. You know what it'll do for your credentials." Her voice was on the edge of being high-pitched, but she managed to curb it before it outed her.

"Let's see if it'll really happen." I picked up and blew on a hot piece of zucchini.

"You're Charlie's pet," she said in a nonchalant way.

I didn't retaliate because I was tired and she was right. Instead I focused on mixing equal amounts of rice with other ingredients and then, with care and trepidation, put a bite of the mix on the chopsticks and slowly lifted it to my mouth. It was kind of a meditative act, to not use a fork, to use a utensil for which millions of cubic feet of timber were razed so that Tina, me, and billions of others could eat with little disposable sticks. A luxury that I could sit in a nice restaurant and use them to put food in my mouth, food that I often thought of as just lunch. But that day, I was sorry for the trees and for the engineer who designed those chopsticks. A job, like mine, that had reached the terminal point of innovation.

That afternoon my boss, Charlie, took me to the meeting at the offices of the Mayfield Township Utility Authority. They were about to become one of our biggest clients, and this was the day we'd propose our plan. The utility company was responsible for 160 miles of sanitary sewer, all requiring inspection and assessment, for which they needed a team of engineers. Once that was done, the results were to be entered into a mapping software connected to a GIS system so the utility company could pull up a sewer line's history with the click of a mouse.

I sat at the oval conference table next to Charlie and across from Tom, the head of the utility authority, and two of his colleagues. Tom eyed me as if I were an exotic creature, likely wondering how I got shuffled into a seat of honor among all these middle-aged men.

"Emma is one of our brightest engineers," Charlie said, apparently reading Tom's mind.

"Glad she's on our team, then." Tom gave me a reassuring look as if he approved of my presence—I was now a useful creature. I reciprocated with a grin and a nod.

Charlie unrolled a set of plans on the table. "I had our CAD specialist digitize the info you already provided us into a map with direction of flow for each line." He made everything sound so much more technical and impressive than it was. If Tom were familiar with our department's lexicon, he would know that *CAD specialist* meant Linda, the elderly woman who worked on our drawings. *Direction of flow* meant arrows on a map.

But Charlie had a way with clients. Since he took over the Environmental Division six years ago, the department had doubled its annual revenue, and the company made Charlie, who hadn't yet started to go gray, partner. Somehow, I think Charlie saw something in me that resembled him—although I wasn't the best engineer in the office, he almost always gave me direct access to clients. Like him, I knew how to work the customers, engage them in a laugh or two, and ask about the family—a finesse that somehow made me appear smarter than I believed myself to be. Or maybe I really was smarter than I thought. Either way, Charlie believed me to be something special, and as I'd learned early in my career, perception was reality.

Tom shot a general look in our direction. "What's your plan for inspecting the sewers?" Charlie's dark eyes turned in my direction through his small, rimless glasses, cuing me to begin.

"We can set up a crew of three that can open every manhole in the city over four to six months," I said without missing a beat. "They can inspect every line, smoke it out, throw dye in the manholes, and map the flow direction for all the lines we still need information on. Someone at the office can then enter the data the crew brings back into a GIS database specifically designed for sewers, which I can set up," I continued. "I have looked into several companies that make such software and can get you some options and prices. Then you can have all your information in one place when you need it."

After I had finished the pitch, even if it weren't for the extra nods Tom offered or the pride I saw in Charlie's small twinkling eyes, I knew I had secured the project. It was a solid plan, though one that most anyone in the department would have come up with but perhaps not packaged as neatly, and the steadiness in my voice, the lack of *ums* and *uhs*, left our new clients with a sense of confidence in my abilities.

On the ride back, Charlie told me what was already clear, that I could lead the project: "You have a year to complete the work and could dedicate your time exclusively to this—split between field and office work," he said. "Also, give me a list of three people you'd like to have on your team. I can't promise I can get them if they're already committed to other projects, but I'll try."

That evening, I parked the car between two white lines in the condo parking lot designated for my little Honda. Instead of heading to my unit, I started to circle the development on foot. For the first time in weeks, maybe thanks to the boost at work, I had enough energy to let the evening in.

Late spring was settling in, and the days were already longer, and although there was no sunlight left, the cobalt sky assured me there was still at least twenty or so minutes before day completely gave into night. I walked fast as if to catch the remaining rays and, when they were gone, stopped by the fence that wrapped around our development pool, standing as still as the water, watching the shadowy blue hole darken and drown the reflection of the surrounding buildings and trees. That night, the sky was clear and the flickering dots above were vivid. They were predictable, the stars. Their position, their luminosity, their distance—I knew it all too well. I looked up, at the expanse of the darkness, almost pleading to my best friend, Spencer, whom I somehow thought to be somewhere high above, where I could feel his presence.

The pool was a special place for us. It was there, three years ago, that he asked me to marry him. We'd just come back from a party and brought over a bottle of wine, climbed the short fence, and lay on a couple of lounge chairs under the moonlight.

"Wish I could go to the moon," I said half-coherently.

"Sweetheart, it's lonely up there."

"Not forever, just for a bit, and I wouldn't be lonely. I'd take you with."

"You would? How sweet you are, Emmabelle, to take me to a rock with hardly an atmosphere in the middle of who knows where."

"Oh, stop. Just pretend we can go and it'd be wonderful."

"Well, Emmabelle, if I were going to the moon—Luna, help me—and I could take just one person, woman *or* man, it would be you." Spencer grabbed the wine and took a swig from the dark green bottle and then ceremoniously held it up with his lean, long arms pointing to the almost full disc in the sky.

"It would?"

"Of course. You're my future ex-wife." He handed me the bottle and pulled himself up into a seated position so he could better fit on the chair.

"But I'm not even your present wife."

Spencer jumped up from his chair and picked a salmon-colored petunia from the edging and knelt in front of me: "Emmabelle, will you pretend to be my wife, for now and forever?"

I nodded and laughed all at once, drops of wine traveling from my throat into my nose. Spencer put the petunia behind my ear, and from then on we called each other husband and wife.

"Now, let's go to the moon, wifey."

A crisp light wind brushed against my wet cheeks, prompting a frigid current through my torso and limbs, bringing me back to the present, the aftermath of that horrific night last February.

Spencer's writing and hookups took him to Manhattan all the time. One night, after leaving a club in the East Village, he crossed Second Avenue at the wrong time, was hit by a blue Ford Explorer, and was pronounced dead at the scene.

3. Spring Blossoms

TOURAN

"Wake up, monkey." I open my eyes enough to see Mom's face, then roll to the side, as if doing so will make her go away.

"Lily, it's time to get ready for school." She pulls the covers off me. It's cold. The woman knows what she's doing. After eleven years, she's a pro.

"You need to get out of bed. It's six thirty. I'm not going to say it again."

I'm also a pro at knowing when she means it. This morning, things could get ugly fast. "But I'm so tired." I sit up on the bed.

"I know. The sirens are disrupting everyone's schedule. Maybe you can go to bed a little earlier so you can make up for lost sleep."

"I don't wanna go to sleep earlier than eight. It won't even be dark." My hoarse morning voice gets higher, pleading.

"No need to whine. Go wash your face and brush your teeth. I'll see you in the kitchen."

The yard smells like spring—a sweet bouquet of cherry blossoms fused with wet soil. It must've rained after the bomb was dropped. But the sky is now cloudless, and the sun will dry up everything fast. I shouldn't have listened to Mom and worn this stupid sweater—it will have to come off at school. I walk out of the yard and close the large door behind me. The sycamore trees on our street are just starting to grow some baby leaves the size of my thumb, really light green ones, like apple candy. Soon, the branches will be full of large leaves and can give us some protection in the summer. Without those leaves, in the winter, the sky is so open. Everything above is too close. Somehow, it feels safer under the canopy of full trees.

I ring the doorbell across the street from our house and a smiling Mimi, wearing a bright yellow dress, answers. "Morning!" She lets go of the heavy metal door behind her and it slams. Her eyelids are puffy as though she hasn't slept much. I almost ask her why but I know the answer so I say nothing. We start walking to school.

We've been friends since the third grade, when her family moved here from another part of town. Her father owns a clothing store and makes a lot of money—mine teaches high school. Her parents are different from mine in a lot of ways, in fact: they let Mimi and her older brother do the kind of stuff my parents give me a hard time about, like buying them Walkmans and letting them have the latest Nikes. Sometimes, I wish my mom and dad were more like hers.

"Hey. You do that science homework?" I ask.

She nods; her superstraight bangs fall right into place with each move. With that hair and those round, big eyes, Mimi looks like a cartoon character. "But it was hard."

"Yeah, I had to ask my dad for help. I didn't know that's how volcanoes work." I pull at the collar of my stupid sweater. It's already getting too warm. *Thanks for dressing me for the North Pole, Mom.*

Mimi picks a cherry blossom that's fallen from a neighbor's tree and smells it. I look up at the hundreds of pink buds peering over the wall of their yard. It's hard to imagine those things will become fruit in just a few months.

Mimi is holding what would have grown into a cherry. We turn the corner to the street where our school is.

"You hear that bomb last night? It was a loud one," she says.

"Yeah, it *was* loud."

"Freaked me out." She throws the blossom back on the asphalt. It's street garbage again.

"Not me," I say. "I don't get scared." It did seem close by and I was scared, but I like making Mimi think I'm brave. Maybe 'cause she's a lot shorter than me, even though we're both in the sixth grade, or maybe because she is cute as a button with her perfect hair and clothes. It's one of the only things she looks up to me for, and I let her.

"What're you guys doing for the holiday?" She means the three-day break coming up next week.

"I think we might go to my grandma's. They're like five hours away and my dad thinks they won't bomb there. You guys?"

"I think my aunt's house up north. Mom says it'll be quiet there."

The tall gray walls of our school pop up at the end of the street.

"Race you," I say.

We both start running before the words finish leaving my mouth.

4. pH 7.0

NEW JERSEY

When I saw Peter's silhouette leaning on my condo door, I realized I'd forgotten about our Friday night plans.

"There you are," he said without sounding upset, forever defying Newton's first law, where no external force could change his steady temperament.

"I'm so sorry. I forgot it's date nigh—. . ." Before I could finish stringing together the slew of apologetic words, he put his finger on my lip and kissed my cheek.

Inside, Peter pulled three gerbera daisies, each a different color, out of his messenger bag. Gerberas were one of my favorite flowers; on one of our first dates, we walked by a florist, and upon spotting them in the window I talked incessantly about how they were the perfect flower, with their symmetry and saturated colors. Since then, they'd become Peter's standard gift.

"That reminds me, I got you something last week and forgot all about it. Hold on." I walked to the bedroom and came back with a small black plastic bag and handed it to Peter. "Meant to put it in a nicer bag."

"What's this for?" Peter pulled out the vintage Victorinox Pioneer knife, feeling the weight of it in his hand.

"I saw it in an antique store's window. I know it's not the same, but it looks just like your grandfather's pocket knife and I know how much that meant to you."

"Emma, this must have cost a fortune." Peter ran his fingers over the spine of the knife and opened the blades. "It's in perfect shape and looks just like the one I lost." He put the knife in his pocket and gave me a tight, warm hug. The trace of his clean-smelling aftershave made me wish for the ocean. I stood on my tiptoes to kiss him, pushing his limp, platinum hair out of his face with my fingers.

"How was your day, Dark Angel?"

Spencer came up with that nickname for me because he said I looked like the lead actress of some television show I'd never watched. No one else called me that but Spencer. Since his death, however, for some odd reason, Peter had taken it up. Even "pumpkin" or "muffin" would've been better—at least it'd be ours. I didn't answer and just set the vase of daisies I'd just arranged on the kitchen island and handed Peter a bottle of Stella that I grabbed from the nearly empty fridge.

"You fight any evil in the sewer lines?" he continued as we settled on the couch.

I shook my head. "I will be leading a massive project."

"That's my girl."

"It's because I know how to speak to the clients." I smiled.

"And because of those dark piercing eyes." He pulled my head to his chest.

"I hear it's going to rain later tonight," I sat back on the couch.

"Oh, yeah?" Peter looked in the direction of the window to the left of the fireplace, trying to assess the weather.

"That's what they say."

"Guess so." He put his feet up on the coffee table.

"You teach today?"

"Sure. One expos and then I held office hours for a bit."

I grabbed the remote and without asking switched on the window of oblivion. *Sure* was one of Peter's favorite words, not an overly positive or negative statement. It was the epitome of middle ground, like Peter—not acidic nor alkaline, a perfect pH 7.0 of a human. That was part of his appeal when we first met at Rutgers two and a half years back. He was finishing his doctorate in English while I was taking a nonmatriculated night class in advanced wastewater treatment—it was for career development, or potentially for grad school.

One evening, I stopped to grab a tea at the student center and waited as he fixed his coffee at the cream-and-sugar counter. I watched the back of his head and hands meticulously pour a little cream into his cup, stir, add more cream, and then stir again to achieve the perfect shade of beige.

"Please, take your time," I joked.

He turned around. "I'm sorry—I didn't realize anyone was behind me." His smile revealed two deep dimples on the cheeks, partially hidden by straight hair that framed his face. He looked like a collegiate surfer, if there was such a thing, a rather handsome specimen packaged in jeans and a button-down. "Please, go ahead." He motioned me toward the counter with his Bermuda blue eyes, reaching for a cup cover.

"I can wait till you get it just right!" I smiled.

"Promise, I'm done." He threw out the stirrer, put the lid on the paper cup, and stepped aside but not away. We ended up walking out of the student center together, stepping on just-crisped autumn leaves.

"So what brings you to night school?"

"Sewage!" I smiled, staring ahead but feeling the weight of his gaze on me.

"You must elaborate."

"I'm taking a class so I can learn about things like anaerobic wastewater treatment. Too much detail?"

"Fascinating!"

"Is it?" I turned to face him.

"It's not every day I meet a lovely woman educating herself on the intricate workings of feces." If his words weren't clearly flirtatious, his perfectly symmetrical smile was.

I laughed, amused by the banter and attention. "What are you in for?"

"Graduate school. Life sentence!"

"Ha! No kidding. What field?"

"English—Melville!"

"American Renaissance." I stopped and looked at him, awaiting an impressed expression.

"You know your writers." It worked.

I was enjoying our little back-and-forth: "Not really, just a hazy remainder of a memory from high school English." Then I realized the time and looked at my watch for confirmation.

He was observant enough to take the hint. "So can I make it up to you by taking you out for a drink?"

"Make what up to me?"

"The coffee wait?" He winked.

"Yeah, maybe." I smiled and handed him my business card. "I have to run. Talk later?"

"Talk soon," he looked at the card, "Emma! I'm Peter by the way."

The next day I went to work, designed my sewers, and had lunch with Tina—an ordinary, uneventful day. At dinnertime I stopped at Spencer's. A regular and quiet get-together we both looked forward to. He was cooking, and we were both having cocktails when my purse rang.

"Don't recognize it," I said, flipping open the little blue Motorola. Then there was a beep—a message from Peter. "I had forgotten about this guy," I muttered half to Spencer, half to myself, dropping the phone back into my large black motorcycle bag, likely the nicest thing I owned. Spencer bought it for me at a boutique in Manhattan after he had received a rare and handsome check for a long feature he'd written for *GQ* magazine. Because, he said, every once in a while you need some finer things in life. Spencer's apartment was sprinkled with some of those finer things, most of which were treasures others sold in their front yards. Treasures that only eyes like Spencer's could spot: a walnut credenza sitting against a light khaki accent wall decorated with various-sized pieces of art and photos, a dark gray mid-century sofa under the old tall windows of his living room, and a lone wooden chair with a fuzzy covering diagonally touching the corner of his geometric rug. Even the less-than-finer things, like the forty-five-peso white and turquoise Falsa blanket I had brought him from Mexico, somehow looked elegant draped over the arm of the chair.

"Don't sound so excited," he yelled over the fan in his kitchenette.

"He's cool, I'll meet him."

Spencer turned off the fan, lowered the flame on his Cajun shrimp stew, came over, sat across from me at the dining table, and held my hand in both of his. "So, details?"

"I have no details yet—just that he's cute, blond, tallish, and a PhD student."

"Oh, I love a nerdy blond. Is he in your poop class?"

"No, met him last night at the student center. He's a literature guy. Melville."

"Well, I knew it was too good to be true." He let go of my hand, took a sip of his mojito, and looked away, feigning disinterest.

"Why is that bad?"

"It isn't, Dark Angel. I just see you more with a Paul Auster or Donald Barthelme scholar, not a specialist in a guy who wrote a chapter on cetology." Spencer faked an exaggerated yawn, stood up, lightly touching his lips to the top of my forehead, and walked back to the kitchen. I watched him move around the stove, tasting the stew from a wooden spoon, then wipe his hand on his apron with precise movements.

"I don't even know what that means," I finally said. Unlike Spencer, who took his reading and writers very seriously, I wasn't caught up on the literary trends. "Besides, I'm with no scholar at all right now."

"But you do have a beautiful husband," he said, wiping the sweat off his forehead with a paper towel.

"I sure do," I smiled, insides cracking, knowing that in reality, though I could have a choice of husbands, the one who would be the rightest of all could never be mine, a feeling that paled in comparison with the anguish of not having him around.

"Now, tell me what you will wear on this date. We'll have to work with what we have. Or do we?" Having always put tremendous pressure on himself to be funny and fabulous at social events, Spencer was a master at knowing how to get one party-ready. And I happily let him Eliza Doolittle me into date-readiness.

"Jeans . . . and a top?" I picked up the place card he'd made and set on my dish. It was a piece of white printer paper he'd cut into a small rectangle with the words "DA" written on it, and a heart drawn by hand. Not Spencer's best work of art, but for us, he kept things low-key. Still, I was charmed and grinned before putting it down. He made every effort to make me feel like the only person who mattered.

"I sure hope there's a top involved!"

I started giggling, which then turned to full-on laughter—often the case with a continual flow of rum into my system—and couldn't stop.

"All right, clearly you are in no shape to make fashion decisions, so I will need to get myself over there and put you together, or maybe I'll buy you the dress I saw that'd be perfect for the ballet."

"What dress? I'm not going to the ballet."

"Maybe you should! And I have some free press passes coming my way so we can remedy that."

"You've got the life—ballet, fashion shows, fancy lit parties."

"Oh, sweetness, as your people would say, it's a poopload of work always being on. Frankly, I envy how you don't have to hustle and deal with all these soirées and shenanigans. But the good news is I do know how to make you even more fabulous than you already are."

And he did, or at least tried. Holding up a black blazer the next day at Loehmann's, he said it would go nicely with my purse. I told him an old folktale about a man who took a button to a tailor and asked him to make a shirt for it. Spencer laughed and said I came up with the strangest stories and that you'd think I was from some foreign land. Then he hung a gold-colored multichain necklace around my neck before giving me the nod of approval and handing over the blazer for me to try. I looked in the mirror. I liked that version of myself.

A couple of evenings later, I dressed in a pair of skinny black pants, a loose gray tank, and the fitted black blazer accessorized with the necklace to meet Peter at a hip bar and restaurant in downtown New Brunswick. After the pre-date with Spencer, I couldn't imagine the date being nearly as fun or that I would stay beyond a drink, but somehow Peter and I ended up talking for hours—he about how Melville drove his son to shoot himself and me about the recent flooding at Spring Lake Township and how it was affecting the storm sewers, my project at the time. That date turned into another and another, and soon we were seeing each other regularly. Shortly after, Peter landed an assistant professorship in the English department and began teaching freshman expository writing and literature courses, continuing his research on the American Renaissance, and working toward tenure.

The conversation was fun and new, and I was satisfied to finally have someone appropriate to focus some of my affection on. Vector-like, we moved at normal relationship speed with a direction—forward. Our path: even. And with Spencer around, not only did the evenness of Peter's and my relationship landscape not bother me, it was in fact necessary to keep my emotional cartwheels for Spencer in check. The threesome worked: Peter was the stabilizer and Spencer the catalyst. Since Spencer's death, however, we had been wading through a deepening pool of grief, with Peter and me both trying to pull us out but failing. Little light seemed to escape this bottomless hole. With just the two of us now, we lacked highs and lows. We didn't fight or play hard and spiraled down to everydayness, dining at one of several local restaurants each week and watching television the other days. Together, we were as inconspicuous as a pair of khakis.

"So about tonight: did you want to go out or just stay in and grab pizza?" Peter said, bringing me back to Friday night, date night.

"I'll call Sal's and place an order." I stood up from the couch and walked over to the phone. At times like these, with Spencer gone and everything else, everydayness was a kind of cure.

5. Missile

TOURAN

It's early morning and everyone is asleep. We're all in Grandma's backyard, my mom and dad, Grandma, my aunt, and three cousins. Sleeping in the mountains is different than at home in the big city. The air feels lighter and chillier, almost like just-vanished cold water. And the sky looks bluer. Maybe because there are fewer buildings here in Grandma's town than back home.

We got in late afternoon yesterday—it took about five and a half hours. It's one of my favorite drives, well, at least the last hour of it. Looking out the car window is like seeing one painting after another: large plots of land chopped into patchworks of vineyards, meadows of wild mint snaked by streams, and fields colored by orange-red poppies—all spread in the shadow of snow-capped mountains reaching tall into the clear sky.

Clouds shift forms every few minutes. I pull the heavy blanket over my shoulders, look up, and start to imagine shapes. That cloud looks like a crook—his nose is big and humpy, his chin sticks out too much, and he looks as if he's running too fast. Maybe trying to get away from someone chasing him. The other cloud looks like a basket with big pieces of fresh baked bread. Mmmmm, big fluffy rolls. I want some of those.

Something moves nearby. It's a gecko. The gray critter scurries up the coarse, yellowing wall of the yard. I follow it with my eyes until it gets to the top and disappears into the neighbor's garden. Nothing else is moving except the gentle, barely noticeable swing of Grandma's potted red geraniums in the breeze.

It's really quiet. I wonder whether if someone dropped a pin, I'd really hear it. My eyes are getting heavy again and I'm sleepy. I let them close, and just as I'm about to pass out, there's a really loud explosion, a concussion of air, car horns, and screams. Without thinking I duck under the covers, curl onto my side, and put my hands over my ringing ears. But it's as if the sound is in my head and eating away at my insides like acid. Then starts the raining, of debris—broken pieces of structures: windows, walls, furniture. The first thing I feel lands on the side of my waist with a sticking force. It's hefty and makes me gasp for air. The rest I don't feel as much. They're just making the blanket heavier and heavier, slowly pinning me down. Everyone in the yard and all the yards around us is screaming. In my lightless cocoon, that's all I hear, the continuous muffled cry of an entire town.

"Lily, Lily, are you okay?" I hear Dad from the other side of the yard. "Listen to me. Stay under the covers until I tell you to get out. You hear me? Just stay put. Don't move."

"Daddy. Daddy. Daddy." I open my eyes but everything under the thick magenta covers is dark. My cousins and I used to put two chairs close to each other and make a pretend house roof with this very same blanket. We loved being under it, which always smelled sweet like bubble gum because of Grandma's detergent. The familiar smell makes me feel like staying here forever. I don't want to find out what's going on, or how it smells, out there. I wipe the tears off my face and roll into a tight ball. Now I can make out my cousins screaming and crying and calling for my Aunt Mona. I'm not making any sounds—it's as though my abilities to produce emotions have shut down—and just stay put.

"Okay, baby, come on." Dad carefully pushes the covers off of me. They have a layer of broken glass over them. Everything, everything that was clean and perfect just a few minutes ago is covered with gray dust and debris. I look around the yard. It looks colorless. The windows of my grandmother's two-story house are gone—just cutouts in a facade. The main door is ripped out and nowhere to be seen. Shards are everywhere: in the garden, on the cement ground, on the stairs. For a few seconds all is quiet. I look up at the sky. The pretty clouds are gone. Instead the sky is pouring parts of people's houses and clothes and probably other things I don't want to think about.

"It was a missile," Mom walks into the yard from inside the house, wearing a jacket over her long velvet nightgown. "Here, put these on before you stand up." She hands me my shoes.

But Dad whips me up into his arms anyway, and in a few minutes or seconds, I can't tell, our whole household is up and running toward the front door to flee and see what it's like out there, outside the walls, on the streets. Apparently, the whole town is doing the same. Everyone in my world's running. We join the runners.

I look down for a second and see something covered in soot lying near Dad's foot. Dad covers my eyes with his left hand. "Look up at me, baby. Don't look down."

I know it must be something bad, like a dead dog or cat or something. I listen and don't look down. I don't want to see whatever it is. But I can't stop smelling the burning. Burning houses, burning bodies, burning trees, burning furniture. I feel so sick. All the people and houses and trees spiral around my head, and I throw up.

6. Plum Tomato

NEW JERSEY

I woke up on my side with my shoulder in a pool of vomit on the bathroom floor. A phone was ringing—I don't know for how long.

"Where in the world are you?" Tina said over the receiver.

"I am not sure." My head was throbbing and the room seemed out of focus.

"Well, you've already missed an hour of work. You had an 8:00 AM phone meeting with Tom. Charlie was looking for you."

I looked at the clock—it was almost eight thirty. "Jesus. Okay, I'm coming." I made my way back to the bathroom, flushed the remnants of the previous evening's nightmare, and cleaned the tiles around the toilet. I had no idea how I'd gotten there or what had happened, and the fear and the uncertainty felt too great for me to grasp. But I refused to make it into something that wasn't there. It was, after all, just vomit. I must have gotten sick from food, or a virus. Or just sick.

I stood at the mirror, looked at myself, and ran a frigid hand over my face. It's just the light. It's the damn fluorescent light. But it wasn't. The light never before painted rings under my eyes, and the light had never made me look like the air was sucked out of my cheeks.

On the way to the office I blasted my car stereo and hummed along to Glenn Gould playing Bach's *French Suites* in a nervous, erratic style. This was our ritual, Glenn's and mine; we got to be intimate when I started studying for my professional engineering exam—an exam I needed if I wanted to sign off on sewer designs and receive a fatter paycheck. After Spencer introduced me to the works, I started playing the album over and over again every night after work as I tried to stop myself from falling asleep and drooling all over my study guides. I attributed my miraculous passing of the difficult, day-long exam to the sounds produced by that ivory-and-ebony keyboard, some half a century ago. To this day, partly as a ritual and partly because it was a new superstition, I listen to this arrangement of notes when my head needs a reboot.

"What is happening to me?" I asked Spencer—the empty passenger's seat.

The first month after his death, I met Spencer in a dream alleyway almost every night and woke up to reality angry every morning. In some dreams I knew what was about to happen and I would cross the street ahead of Spencer and the blue Ford Explorer would hit me instead. In others, I'd wake up and he'd be sleeping next to me. And then I'd wake up again, alone. It's only in the face of death that one realizes we are the feeblest and saddest creatures in this world.

On the drive over to the office, I started thinking I needed to speak to someone. *Would Peter understand? He would make a big deal of it and coddle me. Or, worse, brush it off.* Both of which I was sure I wasn't equipped to handle. *Maybe Tina?* Tina was a good bet, I convinced myself, mostly because I wanted to tell someone soon and Tina was a forty-minute ride away. She was also the most levelheaded person I knew and the next best thing to a best friend.

It was 9:37 by the time I got to the office parking lot. I left my purse in the car so it wouldn't be too obvious I was just making it in for the day. Of course, my coworkers were not going to let me get by so easy and shot silly comments as I walked past their desks.

"Nice of you to join us." Joe rolled his chair toward the opening of his cube as I walked by.

"How was brunch? That mimosa good?" Kevin said without lifting his head from the plans he was working on.

"You're early, no?" our environmental tech shouted.

Not wanting to encourage their childish behavior—one that I myself had engaged in many times when they were late—I made no eye contact with any of them, plopped myself on my chair as fast as I could, and immediately started looking busy. Burying my head in my plans, I drew a sewer line here, erased one there, designing a maze of subterranean passages, and wondered if somewhere down in the sewers there was another world with another woman sitting at a desk designing sewers waiting to talk to her friend and another one inside her world and on and on—an infinite number of women within each other's worlds all doing the same thing, living the same life. I did this for hours, drawing up sewers and imagining multitudes of lives.

"Lunch in ten?" Tina knocked on the cube wall.

"I got in so late. Won't look that good if I jump out now," I glanced at my watch—a few minutes after noon—and whispered.

"You got to eat. Besides, the big boss is out—playing golf with Danson."

I gave her a blank look.

"Doesn't matter, potential client. C'mon, you can work a bit later this eve."

"You are going to get me fired."

"That's what I'm here for." She cracked a smile. "Besides, I don't want to eat alone."

"Yeah, sure," I said with the same neutral-pH tone Peter uses. Eager for a pair of willing ears, I didn't need much convincing.

I ordered a beer once we were seated at Aggi's, a place down the road from our office that served a conglomerate of foods from Creole cuisine to sushi to Thai salads. Despite the fact that I was normally against inauthentic fusions, the food was pretty decent.

"Since when do you drink during a workday?" Tina asked me as if I were betraying her.

I shrugged. "Don't worry, I can design fecalways with a bit of alcohol in my system. You know, like waterways but . . ." Though I'd made a joke, I didn't smile. Instead my wavering voice gave away the shifting of my internal tectonic plates.

Tina rolled her steel blue eyes, unimpressed with my attempt.

"Actually, I only have admin work to do in the afternoon." We ordered our usual: I got the spicy chicken pasta and Tina the jambalaya. Recently, I had become more aware of the fragility of the world we were designing and made sure to do that work when I was at my sharpest, usually in the mornings.

"So what happened this morning?" she asked at last.

The question couldn't come soon enough. From the moment I'd decided to tell Tina, I wanted to pour out my thoughts. But then, when the query presented itself, and I started to put it all together in my head, the story seemed even more unbelievable than the experience. "I was tired," was the best I could do.

"Woman, you were almost two hours late for work. Missed a phone meeting with your most important client, and all you have to offer is you were tired?"

I said nothing.

"Things are better, no?" Her tone was gentler, as one's is when talking to a child or about death.

"Sure." No, they were worse. It actually doesn't get easier as time goes by. It gets harder. True, I'd stopped losing my breath every time my eyes landed on a Ford Explorer on the highway, stopped Googling Spencer's name to read and reread what went down that night, and had stopped crying in the middle of the workday. But those initial sensations were instead replaced with weird dreams, a background general annoyance with myself and Peter, and a ripped-open feeling under my ribcage. "The truth is I have these nightmares and I'm not sleeping through the night."

She gave me a sympathetic look and squeezed a lemon into her water glass and placed it on her napkin.

"It's complicated." I wanted to say more but how to start?

"Of course it is. It'll take time. When I called you this morning you said you didn't know where you were?"

I wondered if she really wanted to know the answer and if I really wanted to tell her the answer. "I was confused."

"Have you thought about maybe seeing someone? When my friend John lost his dad, he . . ." She rambled on, but I wasn't listening anymore. Everyone knew someone who had lost someone, and everyone had a recipe for how to deal with it. Even if they've never had the experience, they imagine the loss and then envision what they would do if they were in the situation. I'd heard it before from friends and family. I knew the drill. My mind left the conversation while my body sat dutifully in a gesture of gratitude for Tina's unsolicited, nonexpert advice. Always the nonexperts. Besides, I wasn't going to unload my memories on a shrink, just to pick over and dissect them until they were robbed of their luster, dulled and without power. Instead I clung to that power of remembering my first time meeting Spencer. Two weeks prior to my senior year of engineering school, a girlfriend and I were supposed to move into a dingy off-campus apartment when the deal fell through at the last minute. We had no choice but to put in for on-campus housing and each ended up in different buildings. Frustrated about living with people I didn't know for my last year of school, I had no interest in making new friends in the building. But then, on the third morning of the semester, I was sitting in the apartment's living room looking over my syllabus for Unit Processes and having instant coffee when there was a knock on the door.

"Hi!" said a trim, sandy-haired, young man when I opened the door. Though he wasn't much taller than me, his long limbs fooled the eye otherwise.

"Hello!" *Aren't you a sight for sore eyes*, I wanted to say but didn't.

"I'm Spencer," he said in a measured tempo, enunciating every syllable. "I live over there." He pointed to the open door across from our apartment.

"Your place looks nicer than ours," I said, looking over at the same drab school furniture arranged differently, with black-and-white photos hanging from clothespins on the wall behind a sofa outfitted with colorful decorative cushions and a nice throw. "I'm Emma."

"It's the same tired furniture. We just added accents." As if to say, what are you gonna do? "Nice to meet you, Emma."

"I'm sorry, you want to come in?"

"Sure. But, actually, I'm wondering if I can borrow some milk?" He was articulate, not the usual frat boy gorilla, and I immediately felt the force of his gravity. Unbeknownst to me, the neighbor whose name was Spencer wasn't interested in women and was to become my new best friend. After college, we went on to live together for two years before we both managed to get our own places. I, with a stable engineering job, had saved enough of a down payment for a two-bedroom, newly built first-floor condo, and Spencer, with his inconsistent, and at times in short supply, writing income, rented a small and run-down New Brunswick studio that, in true Spencer fashion, he turned into a magazine photo-shoot-worthy space with little but paint, accents, and yard-sale purchases.

"Hello? Are you here?" Tina was waving her fork in front of my eyes. This was becoming a thing, and I had a sudden urge to knock the damn utensil out of her hand. Instead I crunched my napkin in a tight fist under the table.

"Sure, maybe you're right." It was a safe thing to say.

"But here's what I still don't understand, these nightmares happen that often? 'Cause, honestly, and I say this only because I care, you seem out of it a lot of the time."

I nodded, my chin resting in the cup of my left hand, my elbow on the table—as if the table were the only thing holding me upright. "Here's the thing, Tina, even if I could articulate what's going on, which I'm not sure I can do, I wonder if you could even be helpful." I took a sip of beer and mindlessly moved my pasta around.

"What the hell is that supposed to mean?" She slammed her fork down on the table and almost looked like she might get up. "I'm just trying to help." Tina's face had taken on a reddish hue, and I felt molecules of heat coming off of it and poking my face like a flurry of microswords.

I couldn't tell if she was mad because she cared or because she was just angry that I wasn't trusting her with my secret. Despite all that I thought of her inability to relate to me, she was the only person I really had to talk to. I couldn't tell my parents, who were miles away and would just get worried and probably come stay with me, which would make things infinitely worse, and I had hardly kept in touch with other friends over the last several years while spending all my time with Spencer and Peter. I needed Tina more than the boundaries of our relationship would have normally allowed, and I didn't want to piss her off. I wondered, however, if this was just something companionable and pleasant she felt she had to do. "Of course you are, sorry. Didn't mean to be so flippant."

Tina eased up and picked up her fork again.

Do I tell her about how the other night I dreamed I was seeking shelter under a table and woke up going about my day as if nothing had occurred only to find all the dining room chairs pushed away from the table? That I had no recollection of how they were moved? Do I tell her about the gunpowder smell? And what do I say? I didn't even possess the language to explain any of it. But I wanted to give it words and to make it real. Maybe if it were real, someone might be able to explain it. Anyone actually. Maybe even Tina. I took a gulp of beer, hoping that as the bubbly liquid worked its way through my veins, it would put the inside machinery of my body into a lower gear. "Here's the thing, Tina: I just feel strange, like something is off. And I wonder if these nightmares aren't just normal nightmares. I can't explain it. I'm not even sure they are nightmares. They seem so real. And it's not one dream replayed over and over. It's like a story. It's sequential, kind of like a serial."

"A serial? Maybe you're subconsciously thinking about the same thing all the time and it keeps preoccupying you in your dreams."

I sighed.

"Don't do that," she said.

"What?"

"Look like I just shut you down. What are your nightmares about and when did they start? Was it when, when . . . ?" She was struggling to get it out. She wanted to say when Spencer was killed but didn't have the heart. No one ever did.

"No," and all of a sudden I found my inner container so full it started overflowing with words. "A few weeks ago, I went to sleep and had what I thought was just a nightmare. I dreamed I was a child in some war-stricken place, bombs and all that. Thought nothing of it, right? We all have crazy dreams, no big deal. But a few nights later, same scenario, but not the same dream. It was a continuation of the first one. Again, I thought no big deal. They say your dreams could pick up again at a later time. But it's become a regular thing now and each night it's the next episode, same little girl, same characters, same life, the continuity of which is a nightmare. It's all a little too real, you know? It's like I never sleep, I'm always awake, living someone's life: my own and then this girl's whose body and world I'm in. It's like the universe is trying to tell me something."

"What?" Tina threw her hands up in frustration.

"That's what I'd like to find out. Last night I went to bed and woke up this morning in the bathroom. The last thing I remember from the dream is throwing up. Before then, there was an earsplitting blast, broken bits of building everywhere, a gray blanket of dust over everything. And the smell, I don't think I can ever get that smell out of my insides—incinerated bodies and trees and who knows what. There was a hand out of a door, Tina, a hand, as if reaching for help but I know it wasn't connected to a body." My voice was getting thinner so I stopped with the descriptions. "When you called, I woke up with my shoulder in a puddle of puke."

"That's crazy," she said, genuinely intrigued. "In these nightmares, there's a young girl?" Her voice was now quieter, as if this was the most important piece of information.

I nodded and folded my napkin into as many little squares as I could before turning it back into a crumpled ball and holding it under the table. "I mean, I think it's me. I'm her. I dunno. It's all very confusing."

"And what reason do you have to think that they're a bigger deal than any old dream? I mean other than waking up in the bathroom today?" Her voice was louder and more certain, the way someone's is when they believe they just discovered a novel thought. "It's probably just you who's trying to tell you something, not the universe."

"Have your dreams ever continued for weeks?" I asked. "And have you smelled the same smells as in the dream?"

"I guess not. But I also haven't lost anyone that close to me. I mean you were with him practically every day." She had a valid point. "What does Peter think?"

"Peter doesn't know." I gave an apologetic look, admitting betrayal.

"You haven't told your boyfriend?" Tina looked at me disapprovingly. She liked Peter. He had the metrics she looked for in a guy, and though she never said it, we both knew that she believed I was no longer appreciating him as I should. Maybe she was right. Peter had all the necessary qualities to be a model partner—he just didn't exceed them, and I felt terrible for thinking that. "Doesn't he sleep over? Can't he just look at you and tell you're not sleeping?"

"Probably. He hasn't said anything, though. And as far as telling him, he is—how shall I put this—very linear. Linear thinker: A follows B follows C. He won't think much of it. That it's just heartache, that they're just nightmares, or maybe that I'm losing it. And maybe I am." I looked at Tina to gauge if she was also thinking this but couldn't quite read her. I had a feeling she was in Peter's camp on this. And who could blame them? The world is a level place until something rocks it, until something or someone that existed, that was part of this world, suddenly isn't and that world is no longer the same and it's then that we need a new vocabulary to define it.

"You're the linear engineer. Give the guy some credit. And maybe it's natural that you're experiencing some odd way of grieving. I mean, who can prepare?" She took a small silver pin out of her purse and secured her hair away from her face. I reminded myself to be appreciative of her being nonjudgmental. For the most part.

"So you don't think something other than nightmares is happening here?"

"Like what? No," she said definitively. "Things just took a wrong turn and now you're having a hard time coping."

"Wrong turn, wrong world, wrong everything," I said, emotions brewing inside. It took everything I had not to start screaming or crying or running out. I was still clutching that napkin like it was the only life preserver I had in a turbulent sea. *Wrong turn? Wrong turn?*

"How do you mean?"

"You know what Spencer used to say to me? He used to say 'in a better world I'd fuck you and we'd be together.' Maybe if the world was better, he wouldn't have been on that street that night, out clubbing and looking for a guy who would never love him as much as he deserved." *But the world hadn't been better, Tina. Not for Spencer and me. Especially not for my Spencer.*

"Jesus, Emma, you can't think like that. The world is what it is and there's no guarantee anything would have been different even if all those things were true. Even I can see that this is grief and I'm no counselor." She sounded kind, her typically crisp voice dipped in honey.

"This doesn't sound like some ordinary part of the grieving process—I already went through that," I said, rolling my shoulders out, trying to ease up my muscles. "I go to sleep and then I wake up in a different world. Spencer is not a part of that world or this one. It's all wrong."

"Just consider seeing someone? It's coming up on four months, you should really start thinking about how to move forward."

As if feelings check the calendar. It's not like we say to ourselves, "It's been this many days since my best friend died, so come tomorrow I'm going to be over it." It had been three months and two days, actually.

That evening, I stood over the stove, watching blue and yellow flames heat my water to a boil. Bubbles formed one after another and popped by the time they made their way to the water's surface. It was time to dump in the spaghetti. But I just stood there, captivated by the fizz machine. My earlier conversation with Tina had drained all of my energy. I had rehearsed the whole thing in the car that morning, and for days on and off before then. It was supposed to work out differently. I'd tell her about the suspicious happenings, the strange dreams, and she'd think of solutions. We'd figure it out and solve the whole thing like good engineers. But it didn't happen that way, and my body, having lost its boost of adrenaline, decided to melt into blubber.

Plopping myself on the spongy oversized couch, I stared straight ahead at the fireplace. It was sprinkled with burnt remainders of what used to be wood just a year ago. It's how things work, I guess. All things are just remnants of their previous versions. I placed a cushion on the armrest of the sofa and lay back. On the ceiling above the couch was a water stain shaped like a plum tomato. Spencer and I painted the ceiling three times after a leaking pipe from the upstairs neighbor created the overhead fruit art. I'd lie on the couch watching Spencer balance himself on the ladder we'd borrowed from a neighbor while trying to use the roller on the ceiling.

"Dark Angel, I don't know how you get me into these things." He waved the roller over my head in an attempt to get a few drops of paint on me. "My people aren't handy."

"Says the man who whipped that studio apartment into shape in two weeks. And you'll get paint on the couch." I protected my head with my hands.

"Maybe then we could get rid of it." Spencer never liked the shabby-chic look. He said the whole style should just be called shabby. If furniture wasn't clean and simple, he was most likely averse. Give the man mid-century furniture and he was happy, but never a puffy this or that.

"Seriously though, this is a Ben Sherman shirt and now I have a paint stain on it. The water gods have cursed this place. First, the Great Flood of 2005 and now this. DA, you're a magnet for disaster."

He was right. During my ownership of it, my condo had gone through several catastrophes. The most notable was the aforementioned flood. I'd come home after a long day at work on a freezing January evening to find the entire place submerged in a gazillion gallons of water. The water heater had burst right after I left for work. For eight hours, city water came gushing in through the burst pipe. Because it was so cold, any water that would have normally escaped through the door and window frames froze when it came into contact with the outside world, forming a seal that kept the water indoors. My own personal natatorium. When I'd walked in, I actually burst into laughter.

My bathroom rug was floating in the living room and documents that I thought were invaluable drifted around like blank water lilies. When the gravity of the situation finally hit me, the first person I called was Spencer.

"Spence, you've got to come over." I was cracking up. "You'll never believe what's happened." And with that I proceeded to tell him.

"Oh, sweet Poseidon, how do you get yourself in these quandaries?"

"Please come with buckets, ice picks, and whatever else is useful to get a pool emptied out in the middle of winter."

"Do you realize I'm with grade-A boy meat as we speak?" he whispered, clearly not wanting the boy meat to hear him. "But I'll be a good husband and will let my flaming night die down to a dull roar and come to my wife's rescue."

Forty-five minutes later Spencer, my lifesaver, opened the front door and walked in to rescue my world.

"Honey, I'm ho— . . . holy motha, this is a lot of water." His mouth went to a flat line. "I thought you were exaggerating, but my gawwwd." He took off his shoes outside the front door before entering the living room, rolled up his jeans and walked into the ankle-deep water and put them on the kitchen counter, did a quick scan of the room, and examined an electrical outlet by the door.

"You're lucky. Water hasn't reached the outlets, else you could've gotten electrocuted."

"First thing I did was shut it off from the fuse box," I said, pouring water from a bucket in my hand out the door.

"Also, you realize you've created an ice skating rink in the parking lot." He put a hand over mine to stop me from pouring.

"How the fuck does this shit happen to me?" With that I busted out laughing and so did he. So hard that tears were running down my face and my stomach was twisting in painful motions.

Peter, whom I started seeing after these events, later explained to us that we should have used primer to cover the ceiling stain. He offered several times, even after Spencer's death, to repaint the area for me, but I didn't want to erase the memory. Though we'd both lost a fixture, the degree to which Spencer was embedded in our lives differed greatly. And emotionally, I desperately wanted Peter to notice every reminder and every date that corresponded to an event—Spencer's birthday, the monthly anniversary of his death. But he couldn't, wouldn't, and often didn't. Each time something went amiss I hurt inside and detested him a little.

7. Back in the City

TOURAN

We've only been away for three days, but the blossoms that were on our cherry trees are now all on the ground like a lush pink carpet. Instead the branches are bursting with tiny pea-green leaves.

After the missile hit Grandma's town, we all fled to the village where she was born, twenty minutes farther up the mountains away from her house. On our way out, I saw the complex of buildings that were hit—mostly flattened with smoke rising up from mounds of wreckage and dust clouds floating around. Much of the town's walls seemed to have been chopped short or gone too, exposing remainders of furniture, fixtures, and wires. I threw up on the car ride too, making Dad stop the car a bunch of times. Mom said it was shock or something, a response to trauma. She took me to a small clinic in the village and a doctor gave me a thick, sweet, grape-flavored syrup to stop the puking. The medicine gave me a headache and made me really sleepy. That night, we stayed over at my mom's aunt's house, one I'd never met, and left to come back home the next day. Grandma went back to her house with two of my uncles to clean up the mess.

Now Dad's sitting at the big wooden table on our patio reading a book, nodding off every few minutes. Mom's sweeping the yard, cleaning up what's left of spring, filling large plastic bags with blossoms, and I'm lying on the short prickly grass on my belly trying for a third time to draw a bird. In each of my first two sketches, the thing looked off. The first one had a neck that was way too long, the second was more a duck if you ask me—which I guess is a bird but not what I had in mind—and this last one, while the best of the three, looks small but pretty darn fat somehow. At least it's clearly a bird. Fat birds are kinda cute, actually.

"Lily?" Mom yells.

I turn my head to look at her.

"Someone's at the door. Can you get it?"

The cool grass pokes up between my bare toes as I make my way to the stairs, which are no longer hot now that the sun is slipping away, and walk down to the front, lower part of the yard and open the door.

Mimi's standing on the other side: "Wanna play?"

"Let me ask."

Mom gives me the go-ahead and I throw on my shoes and am out the door. Mimi's wearing new jeans—tight, tapered, dark blue ones. I like them a lot but don't say anything to her. If I tell her how much I like them and then later get similar ones, she'll think I copied her. But if I don't say anything, I can get them and she'll never know that she had hers before mine.

"How was your grandma's house?" She forces her hands into her pants pockets, and we're slowly walking down the street together.

"A missile hit while we were there," I say, walking slightly slower, trying to sneak little looks over to her back pockets to see if I can see a label. If I had those jeans, I'd look as cute as her. Maybe. She's wearing this white short-sleeved T-shirt with frilly sleeves. I don't own any shirts with frilly sleeves, but my regular white T-shirt would still look good. Not as cute but pretty close. It's hard to be as cute too when you're a foot taller. Somehow, the short kids are always the adorable ones—at least to the adults.

"No way." Her overly large eyes widen and she stops walking and looks directly at me. She really looks like a cartoon girl now. "Were you super scared? Was it close?" she says, curious and bewildered.

"Yeah, it was pretty close. All the windows broke and fell on my head," I embellish a little. "But I wasn't scared. I mean a little but it was kind of like an adventure. I walked over to my cousins and pulled the covers over their heads so they wouldn't get hurt." I look down at the asphalt. I can't lie when looking at her face. The cuteness gets even to me.

"You actually walked around while stuff was coming down?"

"I don't know. Either during or after—it all happened so fast." I can tell she's impressed, so I stop while I'm ahead. "Then we ran away from there and stayed at another place close by and got back yesterday."

"Wow, a missile. That's never happened here. Only bombs. And I've never even seen a bomb. Did you see it as it came down? Is it, like, pointy and stuff, like on TV?"

"We didn't see the missile. Just heard it when it hit and then everything around us seemed to just collapse. And then everyone was acting insane— screaming and crying—'cause they were scared. It was like everything was fine and quiet one minute and chaotic and loud the next. Just like that." I snap my fingers for effect then stop for a second and feel like my lunch is making its way back up into my mouth.

"Crazy." Mimi doesn't seem to notice and keeps walking.

She is right. It was crazy. I mean, a freaking missile. Even *we* weren't used to that.

"Did you go to your aunts' place?" I ask, not wanting to relive the missile experience anymore.

"Yeah, we did. Got back this morning. Nothing happened up north. Definitely nothing like your story. I just played with my cousins mostly and then we went shopping." She starts walking again and I speed up next to her.

Aha, so the jeans were from a shopping trip with her cousins, who lived close to this large department store that had a lot of cool clothes. We have one like it here in the city too. Maybe I can convince Mom to take me. "Hey, you want to get our bikes and go get ice cream?"

"Yeah, let's." With the way I feel, I can't imagine scarfing down something treacly-sweet, but I take off running as if that's the only thing in the world I ever want.

8. Appointment

NEW JERSEY

A loud thump on the window woke me up. The alarm clock said 5:47. No reason to be awake yet. It was probably the wind. My lids drooped shut again, but then I heard it a second time. I got out of bed and walked over to the living room. A bird was flying into the windowpane of the balcony door. The bird hit the window again and then sat on the railing and looked at me. I had never seen one like it—a fat little thing with a gray body and a white underbelly and tail. Our dark eyes locked through the glass for a few seconds. Then it flew into the glass again, losing feathers on impact. It lurched around in a circle several times, heaving and wild-eyed, before throwing itself into the air. I flinched and went to reach for the doorknob, but it had already disappeared before I made it out.

Fully awake, I decided to begin the day by making coffee in the French press. Standing by the stove I thought of "Thirteen Ways of Looking at a Blackbird," a Wallace Stevens poem that Spencer had emailed me once and I'd loved so much that I'd memorized. I wasn't much into poetry before I met him. In fact, I didn't even know Wallace Stevens, but the poet was one of many Spencer exposed me to. That morning, like the needle of a gramophone stuck on a bar of music, my needle was stuck on only one part of the poem:

I know noble accents
And lucid, inescapable rhythms;
But I know, too,
That the blackbird is involved
In what I know.

When the blackbird flew out of sight,
It marked the edge
Of one of many circles.

I turned off the stove and poured water over the coffee grounds, pulled a cup from the cupboard, and waited for the thing to brew.

But I know, too,
That the blackbird is involved
In what I know.

I didn't want to think about the blackbird anymore, so I pressed the coffee, poured myself a cup, and headed out to the balcony in my nightgown, hoping that none of the neighbors were awake to see so much of my bare legs and chest. It looked to be a spectacular day, stray threads of white clouds afloat a crisp blue sky and the sun falling softly on the apple blossoms that had landed on the grass beyond my balcony like white polka dots on a green fabric. They were the last of the blooms. By now, every trace of blossom should have disappeared already, but with the slightly cooler than usual temperatures, spring continued springing. Empty terra-cotta pots were stacked in the corner of the balcony begging for something to live inside them.

Any other year, by then I would have started planting geraniums, petunias, verbenas, and million bells, in the hope of turning my cubicle-sized balcony into an oasis. Spencer and I always made a day of it. With classical music in the background when I had a say, and Moby when he did, we'd plant and water and garden. In a few weeks, there would've been morning glories climbing the railings, tomatoes budding, and flowers blooming. It was the gardener's equivalent of a tacky Christmas yard. That year, though, the balcony would be bare. Somehow, without Spencer, it all seemed wrong. I stared at the empty pots for a bit, then put my feet up on the railing, closed my eyes, and let the sun stream onto my eyelids, to let the light in. I don't know how long I did this but then I heard another thump and realized the strange bird or a relative of his was back to banging his head into the window.

"I feel your pain, birdie," I said in a low voice as a robin flew away and I stood up as if to see him off. "I want to bang my head too." My eyes were dry, but I knew that if I said anything more to the bird or to the air—since birdie was already gone—the pieces of myself I was so tightly holding together would dislodge and fall apart. So instead I headed to the bathroom and started brushing my teeth. I looked at the woman peering back. First strands of gray hair. Dark circles. All pronounced. I spit out the toothpaste and took off my nightgown, which now draped on me as if on a hanger. Maybe Tina was right. Maybe it was time I saw someone, someone who could explain death to me. Someone who could explain life to me. Someone who could explain these confusing sensations and dreams. Is there such a someone?

I grabbed a pair of black slacks but put them back in the closet and instead reached for my skinny blue jeans and smiled, mysteriously pleased.

When I got to the office, I pulled up the website for my insurance, went through a list of doctors my plan covered and spotted a couple of psychologists that seemed close to my house, and picked up the phone. The lady on the phone from the first place said they weren't taking new patients, but the second one worked out.

"Actually, we have a cancellation this evening for six thirty, would you like to come in?" the older sounding woman on the phone said to me. *Perfect.*

The receptionist's desk was decorated with pink and white streamers around a homemade banner devised of construction paper that said "Happy Mother's Day." It was made by a kid, like the art we made in grade school: turning pieces of colored paper into a series of loops to make a paper worm, pinning a cut sheet onto a stick to make a pinwheel, and folding and folding a round sheet and then carving it strategically to make paper chandeliers, all of which my parents would have to house and praise for months as masterpieces. The plump receptionist with the bun on her head took my forms and led me to Dr. Linda Thompson's office. Despite the colorful reception area, her office felt empty and gutted. The doctor got up from her desk to shake my hand. She was slim, with skin so pale you'd think she had never left the confines of the office. Her face was bony, her nose thin and pointy, her light hazel eyes large, and her cheekbones high. Every one of her features was placed on her body with care by a sophisticated sculptor. Her shoulder-length, copper-tinged hair hung down her sparsely freckled face. The ends of her barely-there eyebrows, the same hue of her hair, almost touched the multitude of small creases that were edging out from her eyes. She couldn't have been more than ten years older than me, if that—the sun, however, is kinder to us olive girls.

She sat and motioned me to do the same on a chair across from her desk.

"What brings you here today?" she said looking down at the folder with my paperwork. "Dreams?"

"Sort of." I began fidgeting. "I have these strange sensations."

"Tell me about them." Her voice was warm and curvy, inviting me to take the plunge.

"I guess they're dreams but they're very real." I ran through the past few nights in my head and tried to decide how to explain what these things really were.

"You don't seem sure these are dreams," she said, her face a mirror of my doubts.

You bet I don't, I wanted to say. But instead I said, "I suppose the best word to explain them would be dreams. Or nightmares. But they are strange, sort of like a television series with every episode followed by the next. Each one a continuation of another, and in some strange way I am both foreign to, and belong in, these dreams."

"Continuing dreams could happen."

"For almost a month?" I asked.

"Seems slightly long. But then again a good percentage of people have recurring dreams." She put her elbows on her desk and played around with the pen, slowly twirling it between her index finger and thumb. "Dreams are thoughts and feelings we experience when sleeping, during what we call the REM cycle. I can't say we understand dreams quite well, but they're often a reflection of our subconscious."

"So you think somewhere in my consciousness this stuff is happening and since I can't access it when awake, I dream it?" Maybe it was the engineering training, but I was an extrapolator by nature and drew fast conclusions. "Is this all a part of me or am I a part of something else? I wonder."

She made some notes in her notepad. "Tell me about them."

"These, these, um, dreams seem so real and it's always the same setting." I sat up straight and glanced down at the busy street through the window behind her desk. "Everybody has nightmares, right? You dream about something that upsets you, you get up, and it's over, right?"

Without any assurances that what I was telling her was normal, I was nervous to continue. But reasoned with myself that's why I was there, so I went on and opened the floodgates before I had a change of heart and told her about the recent episodes, the war, and the sensations from the dreams that were creeping into the daily life I was familiar with.

"Have you experienced war before?" she asked.

"No. I mean, of course not, I've lived here all my life. Unless you count the ill-conceived, televised, spectacular morass over there that I pay for with my taxes," I said about the invasion of Iraq.

"Is the concept of war something that occupies your mind in some way?"

"What do you mean?"

"Do you have a friend or an acquaintance in a war, or is your father a veteran? Is this something you identify with?"

"No." The only person I knew who was remotely associated with war was my father, who had opposed the Vietnam War and was exempted by attending graduate school, even though he never intended to finish. He is a pacifist through and through.

"Is this place a recognized location? Does it resemble New Jersey or somewhere you've been?"

I shook my head. "In fact, so much of it is so foreign to me—the scenery, the landscape, the people—but in a way I feel as though I've known it forever, as if I've been there before. It feels more familiar than my own childhood home. Strange, huh?"

"If you've never traveled to such a place or haven't had ideas of war occupy your thoughts, why do you think you are having these dreams?"

"That's why I'm here. I mean there's the news over the years. Congo. Afghanistan. Lebanon. Iraq. As my friend would say, it's a continual kaleidoscope of devastation. But nothing I've seen or read about looks like what I am experiencing in these dreams."

"Do you and your friend talk about this often?"

"Spencer died." It was the first time I said it like that. No stammering, hesitation, or searching for the perfect choice of words. There, dead. Done.

"Well, this changes things. What happened?"

"He, Spencer, my friend, was hit by a car a few months ago."

She said nothing and just used her light eyes to ask for more details.

"That's it, nothing more. Dead on the scene." My tone was as cold as her office decor. My delivery had no affectation. Somehow, I thought pronouncing horrid news in a detached manner meant I was removed from it myself.

"I'm sure it's been hard."

With a nod, emotions ran down my body like a powerful waterfall washing away the starch in my backbone. I went into a stupor.

We were both quiet for a while. Eyes on the floor, I looked at the void beyond.

Finally, Dr. Thompson said: "Did these nightmares begin soon after Spencer's death?"

"No, less than a month ago. Two or so months after his death."

She scribbled notes while my eyes wandered around her office. It was stark. The wall to my right was covered with certificates and degrees. I was glad to see that she had gone to Harvard Medical School, but it seemed even Harvard couldn't explain this to me. The wall to my left was completely blank with the exception of a black-and-white figure drawing hanging a little off center. I was surprised that there was no couch. Aren't therapists all supposed to have couches?

"Often when people experience posttraumatic stress disorder, which is an emotional and possibly physical response to trauma, they can have many reactions, one of which could be recurring nightmares," she said. "Can we talk about his death?"

"There's really no more to tell. He died. It sucks. My life has sucked since."

"How?"

"I mean, I'm living, working, going out, doing what I should, but underneath it all, there's this unending empty space. He was the closest person to me. I have to keep myself occupied, otherwise I'll keep replaying what happened over and over in my head."

"Were you in a romantic relationship with this person?"

"Oh, no. He was my best friend. I have a boyfriend, Peter. His name is Peter. My boyfriend, Peter." I kept saying *Peter*, as if by saying it, I further validated my relationship.

She slowly nodded and finally said: "You just said Spencer was the closest person to you. Was he closer to you than Peter?"

I thought about this. I'd never really broken it down like that before, but when she said it, it sounded so obvious. "We weren't romantic, Spencer and I, so we weren't close physically or intimately. But I guess our relationship was tight in other ways. Is that bad?"

"Not unless you think it's bad. We don't determine whom we love and how much we love each person." She gave me a reassuring look to ease my newly discovered guilt.

"It's not that I love him more." I intentionally referred to my feelings about Spencer in the present tense. Though he was dead, my love wasn't. "It's that I love each of them differently. Also, I knew Spencer way before Peter, so it's kind of expected to have been closer to him, right?" I knew it wasn't. I was making excuses for the relationship Peter and I were holding onto so tightly but that was melting like an ice cube in our warm, well-intentioned grasp.

Spencer had a multiyear head start on Peter. How does anyone compete with that? The two of us were already in a very established relationship when

Peter came into my life. The first time they met, I was more nervous than I had been on my first date with Peter, or anyone for that matter. Peter and I had already been seeing each other for more than a month and it seemed like a good thing, a solid something. Despite Spencer's urgings, I had delayed the meetup, convinced they wouldn't like each other—or more like I was convinced Spencer wouldn't like Peter: would think that his name was trite, his research boring, or some other something. But I knew I had to give in, and finally did. I'd already set the table and had the salmon filet in the oven when Peter arrived, clearly impressed.

"Look at all this." He admired and examined the table. "I love a good beet salad." He walked to his bag on the floor and pulled out a bottle of wine and handed it to me.

"You remembered." I admired the Alsatian Riesling sweating in my hand. "Should we open it?"

"Maybe wait for your friend?" He said the right thing.

"Of course."

Spencer arrived with his own spectrum of red, rosé, and white bottles, a splurge for him I'm sure. But with members of his magazine and literary circles he worked hard to impress, and I suspect he treated Peter as such until he could get comfortable, until he realized that Peter was more like me and not part of some socially elite crust. I wondered if the trio of wines would make Peter feel inadequate but instead he said: "I guess we're not going anywhere tonight!" To which the three of us laughed and cheered by clinking glasses filled with Riesling, my sips bigger than what my frame could accommodate.

"This is delicious," Spencer said, clearly impressed.

"Lucky pick," said Peter, who winked at me.

Lightheaded, I felt as though my living room contained the entire universe and that in that moment we were the captured essence of every happiness.

By the time we sat down to the slightly burnt salmon, we'd moved on to Spencer's white.

"So I know what you do, but what *else* do you do?" Spencer asked Peter. "For fun, I mean."

"For fun, I don't know, what does anyone do for fun?" Peter looked at the fish on his plate with enthusiasm and put a small piece of it in his mouth. "This, Emma, is out of this world," he said generously, then continued: " I guess I like camping and hiking. Oh, and I coach youth soccer."

I was sure team sports was foreign territory for my best friend. But to my surprise, Spencer, his eyes glazed over from too much wine, said: "You don't say? I love soccer, well, football."

"You do?" I said a bit too loudly, my eyebrows reaching for the ceiling.

"For your information, yes. In fact, I watch the World Cup religiously."

"How do I not know this?"

"I don't know that I was in town during the last one. You'll see, in what is it, two years from now, for one month my availability will revolve around the FIFA schedule."

"We should watch together," Peter said, confident in the future of our relationships.

"I'll drink to that." Spencer raised his glass to meet Peter's above the table.

Dr. Thompson's question snapped me out of a recollection I could have happily lingered on: "Let me ask you something, it seems that you were very fond of your best friend. Why weren't the two of you together?"

"Spencer was gay. But if he weren't, there is little doubt in my mind, and most likely his, that we'd be together. Maybe he'd even be alive today."

"Why is that?"

Because he would have been at home with me on the sofa, satisfied and in love and under my quilt. "I feel as though when one small thing changes in the world, the sequence of events then changes and the whole system moves differently. You know what the observer effect is?"

Her cold face cracked some semblance of a smile.

"So you know that the act of observation alters the outcome of an event."

She gave me a blank look, waiting for me to reach some kind of conclusion. So I continued.

"If I'd been with Spencer that night, even if he crossed that street, just my mere presence, my being the observer in some sense, might have changed how things were set in motion, and he could have lived. Or if we were together, everything would be different."

"That's interesting. But a tall order, don't you think? A lot of 'what-ifs.' I mean, conversely, things could have gone even more wrong, if this theory of yours holds. Correct?"

"Maybe," I said, not really understanding what she meant about things having gone more wrong. How could things go more wrong? In my book they were as wrong as they got. "But it could've gone better too. He could be breathing air now. Instead he is rotting away in a wooden box." It was so graphic what I said, how I said it. But that's how I thought of him. My poor Spencer.

"So you feel guilty somehow?"

I said nothing.

"That's a lot to expect from yourself," she continued.

"I am not expecting anything, I am just saying, who knows? Maybe if I even went with him, something would have changed. He wanted me to go that night. He asked me. But I was tired and chose to stay home, and he died." My words came out paced and measured. I felt as though she didn't understand me. A single tear rolled down the hill of my right cheek and I dropped my head. When the tear disappeared I looked up again.

"Emma, sometimes we don't have the ability to properly process grief. So we backtrack to the time when the tragic incident occurred and try to find a logic to our course of action that would have avoided the event. It's a common feeling, but most people are able to work through it and come to terms with the fact that they have no individual responsibility for the tragedy."

"I would rather talk about my dreams."

"Talk about whatever you like," she said crisply, professionally accommodating.

Silence took over the room again. I had to switch thoughts away from Spencer—not an easy task. Finally, I said, "There's something odd about these nightmares, which makes me wonder if that's what they are. The last few times, when I woke up I was either somewhere other than in bed, or I found something amiss or changed. For example, this one time I dreamed the girl's grandmother's favorite dish, this beautiful white porcelain salad plate with small maroon flowers, was broken after a missile hit nearby, and when I woke up the next day one of my dishes in the sink from the previous night had a large crack in it. I'm seeing physical effects of the nightmare here in this world."

"This world?" she said.

"I think of them as different worlds now."

"Is it possible that maybe the dish cracked when you or someone else put it in the sink or that it was already cracked and you only just saw it?"

I sighed. "Look, I know there are all kinds of logical explanations, and, like you, I want one of them to be true. In fact, I pray that one of them is true. But something about these doesn't seem logical." Her office became claustrophobic. I felt my lungs shrink and grasped for breaths, large and small, however much I could take in. I'd always turned to the predictable world of authority for order and sense. But authority and order were now letting me down. The night that Spencer died, the driver got away and I put all my faith into the justice system, which, surprisingly, came through and, finally, after weeks of following up, they arrested the person responsible for the hit. But then, sitting in Harvard's office, I felt as though order and predictability could only go so far in making sense of the world, and it seemed we'd gone that far.

"You've also never lost a best friend."

"How many times can you lose a best friend anyway?"

"Emma, we're almost out of time, but I want you to do something. Keep a journal of these dreams with as much detail as possible. It'll help you and us to figure out what's going on with you."

Disoriented, I nodded. The idea of following standard procedure was the only route I knew to make sense of things, so I would pursue it but wondered if I was wasting both my time and Harvard's.

9. Rationing

TOURAN

Mom and Dad are whispering. Pushing my hair behind my ears, I try my hardest to listen but can't make out any words. I put the pencil in the math notebook, place it on the bed, and quietly walk to my bedroom door and press my ear against it. I can make out some words but not enough: "quota," and "lines" come through clearly.

In cartoons, when people eavesdrop, they use a cup to better hear through walls. On my white bookcase there is a glass of water from a few nights ago. I tiptoe back and grab it, making as little noise as possible. The water has a dusty film on the surface. Yuck. I dump it in the planter. By the time Mom finds out I watered the fake geranium, I'll be in school. Or maybe it will dry up. Whatever. I'm holding the glass to the door and my ear is pressed to the bottom of it. Nope, not better. If anything, it sounds worse. More muffled. I'm probably doing it all wrong. Maybe I should put the bottom of the glass against the wall and put my ear to the rim. Lucky for me, they start talking louder and the glass is unnecessary. Now, I'm hearing the word "ration" a lot.

"No, not every week. Every month we get two bottles of milk, three or four sticks of butter, and a small amount of rice and meat," Mom's saying.

"Even petrol will be rationed. We'll have to store whatever we are able to in canisters. We get ration coupons . . ."

"What other options do we have?" Dad says.

"Black market. But the prices are already sky-high. We can supplement when we really have to, but I don't see how else we can afford it. Yesterday I heard from the neighbor that the price of butter's already tripled. And it hasn't even begun. This is just in anticipation."

"Stupid war. And at the end, just a bunch of dead people." Dad's talking in a normal voice now.

"Shhh, I don't want her to hear."

"She'll hear soon enough. Kids talk about everything in school."

I go back and sit on the bed, open the notebook, and start working on transforming fractions to decimals, something I'm very good at. But can't stop thinking about the broken-open homes in Grandma's town, ripped from their roots by some strong force. And how do they go back up again? Brick by brick, by hand. It will be a long time before they can build it all back up and put that town together again. I feel a tightening behind my eyes and switch over to what Mom and Dad were saying and what it means. Are we not going to have food anymore? Or less of it? I can give up butter, but the other stuff we usually have for lunch and dinner will be tough for me not to eat. But I should do it. Otherwise, how will my parents be able to afford it all? We're not super rich or even a little rich like Mimi's family. We're normal.

The war's been very strange. When I used to think of war, before it came to our city, I imagined tanks on the roads, people hiding behind bags of sand, shooting at each other, dust being raised on the streets, and Red Cross nurses with cute little white hats carrying bloody people into tents. Just like the movies. But it hasn't been like that. Everything seems normal. I still go to school. Our street is still covered by asphalt and there are no tanks or men crawling on the ground with guns. I've never even seen a tank or a gun in real life. Our war only seems to happen at night, when it's dark and bombers can't be seen. Maybe men do crawl around with guns at night, but if they do, they do a real good job of hiding everything when the sun comes up.

I finish my homework and head over to the kitchen when Mom calls for me. Her chicken looks so yummy. What's worse is that she's made fried potatoes with it. My favorite. It all smells like restaurant food and I can't wait to have some. But I know I can't eat it. The rationing. I have to remember the rationing.

"No, no. I don't want so much, Mommy. I'm not hungry," I say as Mom puts a big piece of breast and a mountain of steaming fries on my plate.

"You must be hungry. You didn't even have a snack when you got home from school." She hands me the plate.

She's right. I'm hungry. But if I drink enough water, I won't want the chicken or the fries.

"I don't want all this." I put a bunch of fries back in the main dish.

"You don't want fried potatoes? What did you do with my daughter, the one who eats all the fries?" Mom smiles. She's in an unusually good mood for someone who has to make a little food last a long time. She puts a small piece of chicken and some salad on her plate. It's hard to tell if she's doing this for the rationing or not, because she always eats so little. Everyone her age is forever on a diet. But Dad opens a beer and sits at the table. He takes a chicken leg, some breast, and a heap of potatoes. He doesn't seem to care much about the rationing.

I'm trying to decide if I should have some bread, definitely not with butter, and then the electricity is cut. Mom quickly lights the candle on the kitchen table with the ever-accessible box of matches, and the sound of the siren fills the neighborhood.

"Let's go." Dad extends his hand, wraps it around mine, and we start heading out of the house, into the yard, and down to the basement. Before we're out, I turn around and look at the round kitchen table. Three empty chairs are pushed away, and the food, which just minutes ago I wondered about eating, now looks colorless and cold under the bluish light of the moon sneaking in through the windows.

Down in the basement, the ground rumbles and shakes in the dark. The antiaircraft fire seems to last a long time tonight. I'm not looking out the window and am sitting on Mom's lap. Eventually I fall asleep against her arm and dream of clean gray corridors that lead from quiet rooms to more quiet rooms.

10. One Love

NEW JERSEY

In the hallway, I stood in a towel, watching the kitchen clock's minute hand move one tick at a time, getting closer to ten. My body was no longer dripping and my hair only slightly damp. I couldn't decide where to go. I had been pondering that since I stepped out of the shower. The phone started ringing. I looked at the island, where it rested on its charger, but didn't make a move. Instead I turned around, walked to the bedroom, and sat on the bed and stared at the wall, ignoring the persistent caller.

Taoists believed that similar to life, death is a facet of reality, a shift from being to nonbeing, and that without one the other has no meaning. This explanation had once made theoretical sense to me. Turns out that abstract understanding is useless. In the first month or so after Spencer died, my brain obsessed over the horrific seconds between impact and death, the pain of an almost five-thousand-pound mass knocking him onto the pavement, the thoughts that occupied him just before he had none at all. And the void, the void his nonbeing left in my being. It was as if Spencer's death was a sudden cliff from which I just kept falling.

Now my thoughts alternated between losing him and the dreams.

Everything else I thought about or did was mechanical, to simply continue living.

The phone rang again. I retucked the towel under my armpit and this time rushed out of the bedroom. Whoever it was, they needed to talk to me. The caller ID showed Peter's cell number.

"Hey there, I've been trying to call you for a while," I imagined him in the kitchen, holding the cordless with one hand while wiping the stove or the counters with the other—weekend cleaning.

"Sorry, I was in the shower. Is everything okay?" I glanced at the counter and noticed a blinking light on the answering machine.

"I just wanted to make sure *you* are okay."

"Why? I'm fine. You only just left this morning." I walked into the kitchen and poured myself a cold cup of coffee left over from our morning together.

"You know, last night?" he said in his kindest voice.

"What do you mean? What happened last night?" *Did we have a fight I was unaware of?*

"I woke up in the middle of the night and you weren't in bed. But the bathroom light was on with the door closed."

"Oh." I had no recollection, and he hadn't mentioned anything that morning before he left. "What time?"

"You don't remember?" When I didn't answer, he finally said, "I don't know—early morning. Maybe two or three."

I put my cup down on the counter and sat on the tiles of the kitchen, holding the phone up between my neck and shoulder and hugging my ice-cold ankles with unsteady hands. Maybe I was sleepwalking like Harvard said.

"Emma?" Peter said.

"Did you check on me?" I finally mustered, at once afraid of what he might or might not have discovered, grabbing a piece of the towel and squeezing it like a stress ball.

"No. I thought you were using the bathroom. But it seemed like you were in there a long time. I was only half-awake and fell back asleep."

I eased up a bit. "I have to go. I'm meeting Tina at the mall."

"Angel, are you okay?"

"Yeah. I do have to go, though." Letting the towel go, I hit the off button and put the receiver next to me, then picked it up and slammed it on the floor. The battery cover fell off, and I left the whole mess there. I threw on some clothes, walked out to the balcony, and sat at the small, white plastic table. Something red was popping its head from the wooden flower box that Spencer had fastened to the railing. It was a geranium bud, just bursting open into the world. We had planted it last summer, and with all that had happened I'd forgotten to bring it in for the winter. The thing should have died.

Even with me sitting there, the little bud was the only living thing on my balcony. I reached over and squeezed one of the leaves between my fingers, took a long whiff, and closed my eyes. It was last summer all over again, when the days were long and sunny. Spencer and I had come up with the idea of pretending we were on some tropical island when we sat out on the balcony. He would make fresh piña coladas in the blender, we'd put on a Bob Marley CD, and instead of sitting on chairs we'd perch ourselves on the concrete slab of the balcony. At that level, the morning glories we had planted obstructed our view of condo building number 10 across the grass, and we'd imagine that beyond the twisted vines was a sea. A clear, turquoise, never-ending expanse of water spraying the air with salt. Instead of the sounds of cars driving by on the highway behind the building, we heard gentle waves rolling over white Caribbean sand and Marley singing "One Love."

"C'mon, Emmabelle, sing it with me," Spencer would say, swaying his upper body from side to side, starting with his neck and ending at his hips, piping the lines I never seemed to know properly. Eyes closed, he'd utter the words in sync with Bob while I, half-buzzed, would chime in during the chorus swinging my arms to that happy reggae upstroke. 1& 2& 3& 4&.

The continuous sound of cars driving on Route 18 melded together to create a hum interrupted only by a loud lawn mower that was circling the development, perfuming the outside with green. I stared at the blue siding of building number 10 and beyond everything in my line of sight and sat like that until I got up in a hurry to go meet Tina.

She was already waiting for me at the entrance to Nordstrom. Leaning against the outside wall of the store, she had one leg planted on the ground and one bent, her foot pushing against the wall. Even with her body not fully erect, Tina was taller than most. She was wearing a short-sleeved white shirt with her top three buttons undone, revealing the slight hollow between her small breasts, accentuated by a long, thin gold pendant necklace, and had one hand in the pocket of her wide-legged jeans. I don't think she saw me walking toward her from the parking lot. Her head was down, and even if she did see me, she didn't indicate as much. Her eyes were hidden behind dark wayfarer sunglasses with light blue frames.

"Must be very important," I said over the nearby highway noise that permeated the parking lot air.

Tina looked up: "What?" She stepped off the wall.

"Whatever you're thinking of." I gave her a hug.

"The new job that's coming our way next week." She opened the first set of doors into the store and I followed.

I shrugged my shoulders, no idea what she was speaking of.

"Eatontown. You need to get your head out of the clouds."

"What are we doing in Eatontown?" I looked at the rows of leather bags hanging to my right.

"Upgrading their water system."

"Sounds amazing." I was being only half-sarcastic. We rarely got water jobs. In fact, during my time at the company, only once had a water job come through. So in our microcosm, this was as rare as a supermoon in combination with a lunar eclipse.

"Yeah, too bad I won't get it." Her eyes did that thing where they rotated up and then to the side. I knew the roll well—coupled with her almost brisk tone, I had a feeling she was taking a jab at me. It was either on purpose or slipped out. "What do you think?" She picked up a pair of silver sneakers.

"Love 'em," I said, happy to not walk into the path of resentment where the conversation could've easily gone. Even the sneakers she picked up to change the subject were cute. My eyes would have never stopped on them over the mounds of shoes scattered on tables. She had a style and it worked for her.

She put them down. "Let's go find us clothes." This was the second time Tina and I had gone shopping together and the third time we'd hung out on a weekend. It was her way of being there for me after losing Spencer, like a dutiful coworker friend. I welcomed the distraction.

I looked at the sneakers one last time, knowing it wouldn't be right for me to grab them or show even a hint of interest, especially if Tina was ready to turn everything into a turf war.

An hour passed, then another and another until we were immersed in a consumer paradise of apparel and accessories. I followed Tina's lead from store to store. For brief moments, when she'd disappear behind a rack of dresses or a row of folded shirts, I'd expect Spencer to walk out from around a corner, to hang around my neck a necklace he'd picked for me. But then Tina would appear, snapping everything back to the reality that she was my only friend now, one I wasn't even sure I liked.

After a good few hours of flipping through racks of shirts and skirts, dresses and shoes, I plopped myself on the sofa back home with my feet on the coffee table and the TV running in the background and took out my purchases for the day—three tops and a skirt—to admire and to reassess my decision to buy them. The skirt, a black A-line number, wasn't really my style, but I saw Tina eyeing it from across the aisle and I grabbed it before she did. But on that sofa, laying it on my thighs, I wasn't sure why I did such a thing. It was childish. I should return it, I thought, but decided it best to let it go. It was a skirt, not a Nobel Prize.

The sun was just beginning to set, and my sheer white curtains swayed to the rhythm of the evening. Taking in the rich, sweet scent of the lilacs coming in through the open windows from the edges of the walkway outside, I held the white eyelet blouse to myself and tried to look down to see if I still liked it in the natural light of my own home. Typically Spencer would be the voice of reason when it came to keeping or ditching new clothes. I tried to think about what he would say. "That's too girly, it's got no edge," or maybe he'd say, "You look fresh. Very spring. Delish." Yeah. That's what I wanted to hear. I looked delish in these new clothes. I was hoping the purchases would cheer me up, but deep down I cared little about them and tossed the bag and the garments on the floor next to the sofa. Instead I started flipping channels without paying attention to anything, going all the way up the channel lineup and then working my way back down, as if just the act of flipping was itself the end goal. I skipped over channel 13, as I'd done once before, but this time I went right back to it, because for the fraction of a second that the picture appeared and disappeared I was sure I'd seen Spencer.

He looked to be in his early thirties with curly dark hair, talking about time travel with a screenshot of people walking backward behind him. I turned up the volume and sat up to listen more carefully.

"The idea of time travel and parallel universes has mesmerized people for centuries," he said. "Now, newer ideas about how the universe is built puts forward the possibility that there could be more dimensions than the three dimensions of space and the one dimension of time." It was his eyes. Something about that exact shade of emerald reminded me of Spencer. They too were small beaming ovals, with edges that curled up a hair and corners that creased with every word. There weren't too many eyes that smiled like that.

The next shot was of a gray-haired woman, a cosmologist from Harvard. *Is every freaking person from Harvard?* "In fiction, one can travel faster than the speed of light in order to change the past." Images of the 1970s Superman movie took over with the late Christopher Reeve flying around the globe and everything going in reverse. I couldn't take my eyes off the screen and leaned closer to the TV. The little hamster started jogging in my head, and slowly wheels began turning.

"But, mathematically, breaking the light barrier doesn't work," she continued as they showed equations on a blackboard.

The younger man, this time identified in a graphic as Kerr Jacobs, a physics professor from New York University, returned. "One way of traveling to another time period or to a parallel universe is through a wormhole—it's a shortcut, a tunnel, if you will, between different regions of space-time. But here's the thing: if you somehow manage to go into a parallel universe and save John Lennon, you saved someone else's Lennon; your Beatles front man still died. These people are essentially identical to the people of your universe, but they are in fact different."

The show went on for another twenty-some minutes. I was captivated— by him and his words, his theory. When it was over I shut off the TV and, as if fueled by some force, walked to the bathroom door. Darkness was setting in, but I hadn't yet turned on the lights, and the hallway was bathed in a leaden gloom. Before I realized anything was unusual, before that day when the condo was taken over by that horrid burning smell, I had thrice woken up in the bathroom. But thought little of it. Then there was the morning I woke up in a puddle of vomit last week. And then last night. Again last night. The bathroom. My breathing became heavy and loud. I was rushing to get as much oxygen as I could from the air, and it seemed it was all running out. I should've known. The bathroom was suspect all along. A wormhole?

I grabbed the doorknob but didn't turn it. My body was wood and my heart beat in my temples. It took all the courage I had: I took a deep breath and in one quick move opened the door. With the click of a switch, light spread through the underwhelming room. Nothing extraordinary: tub, toilet, a tube of toothpaste with the cap off sitting on the sink counter, a pink hairbrush with a few dark strands still hanging on. For an instant, relief set in, and I felt elasticity return to each relaxing muscle as I realized how I'd given into such irrationality and was about to walk out, but an instant later a feeling of mistrust of all that was porcelain came over me.

I'm losing my fucking mind, I thought. But instead of turning around and leaving, I took another step in and stood by the toilet, lifted the cover carefully, and slowly moved my hand over it. I am not sure what I was expecting to happen. Maybe that my hand would be sucked in by the wormhole that was the toilet.

Then my eyes caught sight of the sink and another wave of crazy rippled in. Right hand trembling, I held it over the bowl and lowered it to the drain. Nothing. I looked around and moved to the tub and did the same. Not sucked into any kind of hole, I sat at the edge of the tub, put my feet inside, and leaned a shoulder into the wall. Soap scum had crept into the spaces between the tiles, forming pink and black stains. I went to open the window for ventilation so I could spray bleach for a good cleaning, when I thought maybe, just maybe, it's the window. Looking up from my seated position, I squinted at it distrustfully.

It is the window. My window is a goddamn black hole, or a wormhole, some kind of bad hole anyway.

That's where I went the night before. I had walked to the bathroom, closed the door, and gotten sucked into the window.

The longer I sat there, the more of a life the window took on. I was becoming so anxious that I could taste the Ruby Tuesday burger I had with Tina earlier. I started to imagine all kinds of people living inside the window, or is it outside the window? Wars, dinner parties, births and deaths. Maybe it leads to other places too. Maybe someone was standing by a window in another world, imagining my world. I got up and reached over to the caddy hanging from the showerhead, grabbed the soap, took a step back from the tub and threw it at the window, pretty sure it would get swallowed. But nothing. The bar just hit the glass and fell right into the tub, leaving behind a light blue smudge on the tiles as it slid down. Sanity was slithering away from me like a slippery fish. A wormhole, really? Even if there were a wormhole, why would it be in the bathroom, why not the living room, dining room, or elsewhere? Little made sense anymore.

After spraying bleach all over, I closed the door behind me and grabbed the phone and sat on the sofa. Minutes passed, maybe an hour. The very last of the day had given way to complete darkness. The neighbors' lights had come on, but my living room was illuminated only by the dim blue light of the muted television.

Soon after we'd met, Spencer and I had gone to the American Museum of Natural History. The Rose Center for Earth and Space had recently been completed and opened, with a new planetarium that showed the exact position of the stars as seen from Earth. I'd never been to a planetarium but knew enough about astronomy to get excited and wanted to show Spencer the wonders of the universe. Though at times he complained, he enjoyed dipping his toes in the predictable worlds of science and math through me. We walked around a spiral that wrapped around the inverted bowl of the theater, tracing the birth of the universe. Spencer and I started at the Big Bang and journeyed on to the present. If I were to be born again, I'd maybe want to be a physicist, I told him. To which he replied, "Sweet Jesus and Mary, only you would go from one nerdy profession to another." Then he reminded me how I'd previously said I had wanted to be a violinist. And I reminded him that was after we'd seen Anne-Sophie Mutter play at the State Theatre New Jersey. "I like that you're flexible," he said, pulling me closer to him as we walked into the dark theater to watch the fake stars. After the show, he asked me if I wanted to go downtown and meet a new boy he'd just met. I asked if it was serious, and he said he was only serious with me. I'd meet Derek another time, I responded.

I shut off the TV and picked up the phone, examining the buttons, wondering which combinations of numbers to press. Parents? I could see Mom's small chin making tiny sideway movements once she realized she couldn't piece together her daughter's words into coherent ideas. And Dad saying nothing, the kitchen receiver to his ear, the call ending with a declaration of their intent to take the next flight out of Miami.

Tina at least had a science background, so it was plausible she would entertain this idea, and even if she didn't, what was there really to lose? I tapped my fingers on the receiver for a while but finally gave in.

"You already missing me?" she said.

"Actually, I was just watching TV and saw an interesting show on PBS," I said.

"There's an oxymoron."

"You're an engineer—you should appreciate this kind of stuff," I said. "You ever think about alternate universes?"

"Not recently," she chuckled.

"Seriously. Those dreams I told you about? The continuing ones? What if they aren't what they seem? What if I were being transported to another region of space-time, a different universe, if you will?" I tried to will the caterpillars in my stomach not to transform into butterflies and whirl out of me.

"Hold on," she said with a compassion that was atypical of her. Maybe she feared that I was really crazy, that grief was holding the reins. "You think you're traveling between universes now because you saw it on a TV show?"

"It was a documentary—a science documentary. It could be a possibility, no?"

"Everything is possible, but is it probable?" she said.

"Time is the fourth dimension." I was saying what she already knew.

"I feel like I am back in college physics again."

"If you can somehow cut through space-time, you can end up in another universe, and there are as many universes out there as there are outcomes for every single decision or event. The professor on the show just said . . ."

"You sure you weren't watching *Back to the Future*? Like I said, everything is a possibility," she sighed. "It isn't real. It's probably some theory they're throwing around, like we could go to Mars but we really can't."

"We *can* go to Mars if we can survive in space and have the right life support system and build a little Earth where everything recycles and . . . never mind. This isn't the same."

"Seriously, Emma, just for a second think about what you're proposing," she said, the way a person does when they want to use their words to shake another person into reason. Tina was a sharp engineer, she too was all about reason—just like I had been.

"I know. I know." I knew. I really did.

"You know what I think, Emma? I think you love it."

"Love what?"

"I think you actually are thrilled. Your life is, rightfully, painful right now. Maybe this thing keeps happening because you want it to."

"You think I want this?" I said softly, as both a statement and a question. "To live in two different space-times and be the only person who can slip back and forth?" I felt a brewing rage but managed to keep it inside.

"I didn't mean it badly, just that maybe, whatever this is, maybe it's not all horrible."

I didn't quite understand what she was saying but didn't want to ask.

"Hey, listen, if you figure out how to time travel or multitravel or whatever you call it, can you go ahead and get me next week's winning Mega Millions numbers?" she said, trying to end on a joke.

"Goodbye," I said with a voice that quickly dwindled into silence.

"I'm just teasing. See you tomorrow. Get some sleep," she said, almost like a worried sister. Maybe she was a good friend after all.

I'd forgotten about the bleach. Vapors seeped out from under the bathroom door, and the strong odor was taking over the rest of the condo. I put down the phone, walked into the bathroom, and turned on the showerhead, moving it around to wash the chemical off the tiles and tried to cleanse myself of my earlier thoughts. But I couldn't. Back on the couch, ideas of parallel universes began simmering again. I knew it was science fiction. Despite the fact that I always loved science and fiction, I never got into that genre. So there was no compartment in my head to hold ideas like traveling to multiverses.

I picked up the phone and dialed Spencer's number but hung up before the familiar recording came on—*The number you have dialed is no longer in service*—and stood at the window, engulfing the darkness of the night with my eyes and letting the information settle in. Exhaustion came over me like a sudden and forceful wave. It had been many weeks since I'd slept like I'd used to. Days and nights blended into one another, and time looped in a circle in which I was stuck going round and round and round. It had to make sense, this idea that the scientists were presenting as a mathematical possibility. It had to. Else, what choice of answers did I have?

I thought about pulling out my college physics text. Instead I sat at my desk and started searching on my computer for the program I'd just seen. It only took a few clicks to find the title, *Tunneling Through Space-Time,* and jot down the names of the scientists. I browsed through the text and watched the trailers, then looked up some of the math on the internet but couldn't make much of it. Engineering students stop at single-variable calculus and linear algebra, but physicists go on to take vector calculus and real and complex analysis and even more math in grad school, courses whose names didn't even mean anything to me. I didn't possess the tools to decipher the original studies used for the show. But I knew I couldn't trust just the television program, where concepts are commercialized for the masses, and needed a reputable source that could translate these complex ideas for a layperson like me. Someone who could simply tell me whether or not I was really traveling to an alternate universe, to another version of myself.

Was she me? Did something in her universe change and therefore create her and her world, not me and my world? I perked up at this idea, at the potential of living another life, a young life, one full of possibilities.

I browsed the internet for Kerr Jacobs, the green-eyed professor at NYU, Spencer's look-alike, and scrolled through his images—mostly I focused on his eyes, brilliantly green. The more I stared at them, the more convinced I became I needed to speak to him. But how? I started composing a brief email about seeing his work on television and my interest in learning more about multiverses and if he had some time to meet. I'd be grateful, I wrote. That night, I thought, I would sleep well.

11. The New War

TOURAN

I just finished my homework and am lying on the couch reading a book. Dad's putting blue tape on our large windows and sliding glass doors in the shape of the letter X. This, he says, stops glass from shattering everywhere and flying around if a bomb hits near our house. I'm not sure how this will work. I don't believe tape can hold so much glass together. But all the neighbors have done it, so maybe the adults know something.

I told Dad I wished my room had no windows. He said not to worry and that he'd make them extra secure by adding the letters of my name on there with tape. I only have three windows, so he got only the L, I, and L underneath each X. He says Lily is a powerful force that'll keep all the bad stuff away. I know better than to believe that, but somehow those windows seem more secure.

Mom's walking around the house with a shoe, looking angry. Her face is determined and her eyes focused. You can tell she has a goal. She's started her own war. Ever since the bombing started, our city's been taken over by roaches. They're everywhere: on the street, in houses, and, worst of all, in the basements where we hide out most nights. They're big and brown and, as if that isn't bad enough, many of them have wings. Flying roaches.

Every night before I go to sleep I wish for my family to be safe during the bombing and for roaches not to crawl onto my body while I'm sleeping. Mom has decided it's time to kill them all, one by one, with her own shoe if she has to. I think they're winning though; the news says since the war began, there are many, many more roaches than people in the city. It seems a war zone is a bad place for humans and a good home for gross critters.

"Have you brushed your hair, baby?" Mom says to me, holding the shoe up over my head. She looks like she's about to squash me. "And change your shirt to something nicer."

"Why?" It's my favorite blue T-shirt because the color of it reminds me of our pool and everyone knows I love our pool, so I wear it as often as I can.

"You've worn it two days in a row, and if you need another reason there's a stain on it. We have company coming in a few minutes. Put that book away and get ready. Your friend Nima is coming." She's stepped away from me now and has her eyes on something in the corner of the room.

"Fine." I give in and head off to my bedroom. My friend, huh? Nima's not really my friend. Our parents just think so because we're almost the same age, but I'd rather play with my real friends like Mimi. Nima and I only play with each other when there is no one else to play with. But whatever, I won't argue with smash-things-with-a-shoe Mom.

I pull open my drawer and poke around for a clean shirt and take out a short-sleeved white tee and change into it. I then stand in front of the mirror, brush my hair, part it to the side, and pull it off of my face with a gold bobby pin. I put on shoes too because I know that if I don't, Mom will make me come back for them, especially given that the roaches are on the move. Hoping I can get all of it done in one shot so I can get back to my book, where these three kids and their dog are on an adventure after their boat washes up on an uninhabited island, but before I have a chance to sit down, the doorbell rings. I can never get back to the darn island it seems.

Dad goes out to the yard and walks back in with Nima and his parents. His mom is wearing a floral dress and pink shiny heels. I really want ones just like them one day when I'm older. She's really pretty and has long hair too that goes down her back. I want all of that—the dress, the hair, the cotton candy–colored lipstick. Nima's walking a few steps behind his parents, as if he doesn't want to be here. And who can blame him? He probably wants to read *his* book or whatever it is he was doing. Instead they probably forced him to come like they're forcing me to wear a clean shirt and hang with him. I scan him up and down and look at his slim jeans and short-sleeved gray T-shirt. He always looks cool. I never do. My jeans are never as fitted as I want them to be. I asked Mom to take me to the same department store Mimi went to with her cousins so I can buy jeans like hers, but when I showed them to her Mom said they look stupid and wouldn't let me get ones that tight. Instead I gotta wear these loose beige corduroys.

"Lily, you've grown at least three centimeters since we last saw you!" Nima's mom says as she gives me a kiss on the cheek.

I smile, proud of my vertical achievement, as if I had something to do with it.

"She'll be a tall one for sure," Mom says. "You kids go on and play, we'll call you for dinner." She puts her hand on Nima's shoulder and guides him toward me.

I lead the way out of the living room.

We walk into my room and I wish I had put away my toys before he came in. My favorite doll's on the bed, the one my mom's friend I call *aunt* brought me from abroad. It has long, dark hair and huge eyes. There is also a large stuffed rabbit sitting on my nightstand. Nima's done playing with silly toys. He's a year and a half older than me. His room has posters of different singers, and he even has a guitar hanging on his wall. I don't want him to think I am still a kid. He scans the room with his eyes and comments on the nice light that's bouncing off the walls. It's always that way in late afternoon in my room. Luckily, his eyes go straight from the walls to the bookshelf and he walks toward it. I follow behind, grabbing the doll by the hair and tossing her into a wooden crate in the corner.

"Are you reading anything now?" he asks.

"A story of these kids stranded on a desert island, lots of adventure. Their boat breaks and they're building another one from wood they're gathering to get back home. But I kind of like them being stuck on the island together. What're you reading?"

"A book on cameras, how they work and stuff." He sits on the edge of the bed and looks slightly bored. He looks kind of cute, though, with his curly brown hair. It's the first time I notice that. Usually, I just spend our time together wishing I could get back to whatever it was I was doing before we had to hang out.

"You like photos?" I sit next to him, both of us facing the open door.

"Yeah, black-and-white ones mostly. It's fun." He lies across my bed and stares at my ceiling, my bare white ceiling that I've wanted to put stickers of glowing planets and stars on but never did and now wish I had.

"I'd like to learn to take good photos." I lie back too and stare up like him, our legs dangling off the side. "The ones I take usually come out crooked or fuzzy or both."

"All you have to do is follow a few rules and then just keep doing it over and over and you'll learn as you go along. Wish I could go out and take photos during raids, but those guys won't let me." He means his parents. "I know it's weird but there's something beautiful about the raids—or at least how the sky lights up before everything goes down."

It's kind of cool he finds beauty in something everyone else runs from.

"So when is your school over for the year?" he asks.

"In like three weeks."

"Same," he says.

"You doing anything fun for summer vacation?"

"Parentals said something about getting out of town. They say the bombing is just going to get worse and the city might get hit so they want to get away for a few months. They said you guys might be coming too," he says.

"What?" I sit up, feeling embarrassed. Turns out I'm the only person who doesn't know anything about this getaway. Once I'm over the shock of finding this out, I get a little excited thinking about going to an unknown place with Nima. It'll be like our own desert island. When we get back to the living room, the grown-ups are talking about just that.

"I'll ask a friend of mine," Dad's saying. "He knows someone who has a walnut orchard less than two hours from here in the mountains. The property is huge but the living quarters are tiny. And if he hasn't yet rented it out, we could take it. I think it'll be reasonable too. It's in a small village, not much demand."

Nima's dad shakes his head. "These days, everything's in demand. Any which way people can get out of town, they will. People are pitching tents on the side of the road."

"A friend of mine managed to get something that sounds really nice, three bedrooms," Mom says.

"The neighbor's chicken lays goose eggs," snaps Nima's dad. "Everything sounds nice from afar."

"I'll call first thing. Hopefully, it's available and we'll at least catch a break for a few months," Dad says, trying to keep the tone positive.

"Hopefully," Nima's dad says. "You never know where they'll hit next."

"Well, anything is better than being in the city," his wife chimes in.

"I doubt this village is on anyone's radar," Dad says. "And being nestled within mountains makes it hard for these warplanes to get to."

"Maybe we should just move there for good," Nima's dad jokes.

Mom motions everyone to the kitchen. "Enough war talk. We could do this all day. Let's go have some dinner. You guys are staying, right? I made some beef and herbed lima bean rice."

Beef and rice? What's Mom thinking? With all the rationing, we are now feeding other people? I want to take everyone's plate and fill each one with a small portion and almost reach out to do so but hold myself back. Mom doesn't seem to care and starts serving the guests like there's a drove of cows and a field of rice out in the yard. I think I'm going to eat normal tonight too. Obviously, we're still doing okay. Maybe the beef and rice are leftovers from before the rationing. Or does that even matter?

12. Waiting for Kerr

NEW JERSEY

It was 2:48 AM on a Saturday when I got the call. At first, the ringing seemed like it was in my dream, a telephone magically appearing as I was walking through a metal tunnel to board a plane at Newark Airport. So I ignored it, riding along on the REM cycle. The ringing then became louder and louder until I opened my eyes and peered at the alarm clock to ground myself in a sense of time and realized it was coming from the living room.

"Hello?"

There wasn't much happening on the other side, mostly silence and a couple of almost muted sniffles.

"Hello?" I repeated with a crackly voice, ready to hang up.

"Emma?" said a man who seemed to struggle to reach me from the bottom of the deepest well.

"Yeah."

"It's Derek, Spencer's . . ." He didn't finish the sentence but I knew who he was. Spencer's on and off Australian guy. Not quite a boyfriend, but he was a fixture of sorts in Spencer's life. I also knew something wasn't right, so I didn't dare ask and waited for Derek to continue.

"Emma," he said breaking the string of silence and random sobs, "Spencer." Then he went mute, saying nothing for a while. "He was hit by a car," Derek's voice trailed off, the sound waves getting smaller as he finished the sentence. I didn't hear much else. A collapse of the ribcage, the air trapped inside. I didn't wait for him to say more and hung up the phone and sat on the floor, feeling as though I was suspended in a vacuum. The phone rang again and again, then every few minutes several more times. I didn't move. Derek gave up trying and stillness took over the night again.

·

The two weeks that followed my email could have been called *Waiting for Kerr*. It was as if I was stuck in a Samuel Beckett play. It was just dismal. By a click of the send button, I'd been transformed into a teenage girl waiting for a boy to call, except I was an adult waiting for a physicist to help explain worlds to me. Simple stuff. Or maybe it was his small green Spencer eyes. Each time I looked at Kerr Jacob's website headshot, his face became more familiar. His eyes stared directly at me. Sometimes, if I looked at the photo long enough, I'd think those eyes belonged to Spencer and that through Kerr he was looking at me, crossing space-time boundaries and making some sort of cosmic contact. That's when I'd get up from my desk and run outside, afraid that if I stayed focused on the screen too long, I'd make myself a tinfoil hat and head to the bathroom looking for a wormhole again.

Before I'd met Peter, Spencer and I, fueled by the dramatics common to twenty-year-olds, made a pact one day that if we both didn't find suitable life partners, he and I would have a child together.

"Think of how beautiful our child would be with your brilliant eyes and my dark hair," I'd said. It was during those moments that'd I'd let myself believe that a relationship with Spencer would work out and that somehow we were close to being a unit.

"You're just trying to live out your own unrealized fantasy of having green eyes, dear heart." He kissed my right eye. "I love your dark ones." He half closed his lids and gave me a fierce look to imitate a powerful gaze.

"Maybe I am. But where would I find better genes to make a gorgeous baby?" I said, knowing I'd be appealing to Spencer's vanity. Despite being handsome on pretty much every scale, and maybe because of it, Spencer put a lot of stock into his appearance and was quick to find fault with his physical attributes. I made sure to always alleviate his insecurities.

"I am not a piece of toast, so why are you buttering me up, Emmabelle?" He sounded pleased.

We filled those missing hollow spaces in each other—he was one of those rare charms who could shine a special light onto anyone and repeatedly chose me, the one I could call when I felt slighted at the office, or had a unicorn of an idea in the middle of the night. And I was his champion when he thought the world seemed unkind. He was my gateway to worlds I didn't know—parties, art shows, and readings—and I was the friend around whom he didn't have to dress up or pull out his palette of fancy vocabulary to impress. And together we carved out a path to make crossing this thorn forest of a life easier and more interesting. Now that he was gone I was left to do it alone—a daunting task.

I checked my email as often as I could—first thing I did when I got home, last when I left the house, and a few times in between. But no word from Kerr. The eons between weekends turned into eternity. I did my best to follow through on my own research in case he never got back to me and to occupy my time and to keep believing that the reason I'd contacted him was because of physics and multiverses and not because he was increasingly becoming a simulacrum of someone I was desperately looking to contact.

I spent hours after work poring through myriad books on parallel universes, starting from the popular science scripts and continuing to the technically written journal articles that I found at the various Rutgers University libraries and online. Some of it I understood, most of it I didn't. A number of theories, many of them in popular texts, said that travel to parallel worlds was possible, and many technical ones said it wasn't. I could follow a little bit of the theory and math but still not enough to make an educated assumption.

Every once in a while, I'd cyberstalk my researcher to see if I could find something on him, like if he was on sabbatical and couldn't get back to me, or on his past or personal life, but nothing interesting came up. Maybe it was the combination of the grieving, the nightmares, my fading relationship with Peter, and the familiarity of Kerr's face, which seemed to increase by each passing day, but I'd put a lot of stock into a man I didn't know, and kept waiting.

The benefit of my waiting was an alleviation I did not expect, a reprieve from the mundaneness. I had the feeling of being a curious student again, someone with goals. I learned quite a bit about the science behind some of what the researchers talked about on the show, background that I needed to speak to anyone who was going to try and explain anything related to wormholes and space-time and multiverses to me. Physics had become my pastime.

Time, I learned, is a dimension like length, width, and height. When I walk from the couch to the bathroom, I'm moving in a direction through space, making headway in all the spatial dimensions. But it turns out that I'm also traveling forward in the fourth dimension, time.

Together, time and space create a four-dimensional fabric, space-time. And there are ways that two regions of space-time could be linked, say by means of two connecting black holes, a wormhole. Through those, one can end up in a different time in their own universe or even some other universe. I didn't really understand the details of what this stuff meant, but what I knew or thought I knew at the time was that I was ending up somewhere else, and there was some evidence to support the hypothesis that I hadn't completely lost my mind.

Per Dr. Thompson's recommendation, I'd also started keeping a journal of my nightly episodes, carrying it everywhere with me and writing down as much detail as I remembered. That way, we could track my progress or lack thereof every couple of weeks when we met and take stock. The vignettes were vivid with details that involved colors, sounds, and smells, textures that were now becoming as familiar as a home. At times, the scenes frightened me, but at times they comforted me. Each was a well-thought-out movie scene and I, a participant and its only viewer. One day while at the library it occurred to me to leave the physics section and go through past news articles on wars to see if I could make any connections. I sat on one of the tall stools and started searching the library's databases on one of the computers. I knew that the details of my episodes—the clothes, music, and decor—matched the eighties or nineties, so I searched for wars in those decades. There were so many: the invasion of Granada, the Falklands War, the Iran–Iraq War, the Soviet war in Afghanistan, and the list went on. And the death tolls went on. So many of the descriptions matched my episodes that I couldn't decide if the war Lily was in matched any of those. I looked for clues, cities that resembled my dreamland—with a backdrop of mountains, with tall sycamore trees and concrete, flat-roofed buildings—but that only knocked out a few choices and left me still with too many possibilities. And did it matter? I looked through pictures of dead soldiers, perished children, skeleton cities, and rubble, so much rubble. The outcome of war was all the same, no matter where it happened and to whom it happened. She could have belonged to any of these countries or to a war in a parallel world that never even existed in my world, the world of perfect little concept houses I designed sewers for every day.

In the evening when I lay in bed I thought of showing up at Kerr's office at NYU. When everything was without color and my mind was not fully sharp, the option seemed viable. I'd just walk in and talk to him. But when the sun cleared my head the next day, I'd realize how absurd it would be to do that and put it out of my mind. The temptation of seeing his face and connecting my gaze to his, however, kept popping up for several nights, and it was easy to convince myself one way or another depending on my mood. If I saw him, maybe he would have a message for me. It would be like seeing Spencer, a physical reminder of the features and gestures I might have forgotten. The thought excited and eased me at once. Fully aware of this newly developed obsessive tendency and the strong potential to realize and later regret it, I made another appointment to see Dr. Thompson.

"I have contacted a physicist about my episodes," I told her at the appointment. I felt slightly more comfortable speaking with her this time.

"A physicist?" she said, sounding caught off guard.

"I have a theory, and it's just a theory, and it's a little farfetched—" my voice quaked and fractured, "that, that the episodes might be connected to some aspect of physics. That maybe I can explain them with a parallel universe." My words were disjointed and weak, breaking apart from the sentences and shamefully hiding in some corner of her room. It was as though I'd been spending my time in a wormhole of my own—obsessive, strange, credulous.

"I'm sorry did you say 'parallel universe'?" Her eyes grew in size and shot me a worried look before her face took on a hardening professional and clinical mask that hid what she was really thinking: *Is this paranoid schizophrenia? Do I need to evaluate her for delusional disorder?*

My forehead became an oven and my brain felt too large for my skull under the pressure. It was a bad idea to share this with her. It was a bad idea, period. And yet I worked to justify it: "I didn't come up with it. I heard it from scientists and followed through a bit and found some, albeit all theoretical, evidence to support that this could happen. I'm not saying it is happening, but it could." I was rambling and could hear myself starting to sound defensive, my pitch higher than usual. "It just seems that, mathematically, the possibility is not out. In fact it is quite possible." This time, the words came out as more reasonable and in control. Or so I thought. Something about the word "mathematics" makes everything sound more legit.

"So, if I'm understanding you correctly, you are suggesting that you might be traveling to an alternate universe?" she finally said, her voice reiterating absurdity.

"I'm not ruling it out. It's another explanation in addition to nightmares, and me being crazy. Right? That gives it a 33.33 percent chance." I managed an upward mouth motion, the start of a smile, though I didn't quite get there. I hadn't mentioned the fourth possibility, that Kerr could be a version of Spencer and that these possibilities now each had a 25 percent chance, which meant that as a whole Kerr somehow made up a 50 percent possibility of some explanation, whatever that was. Under her desk an intrusion of large brown cockroaches circled her heels. I nearly let out a scream and looked up to warn her but when I raised my hand and started to point at them, they'd turned to vapor.

Unaware, she processed what I'd told her and, sounding like her therapist self, said, "If you give all those possibilities the same weight, then yes, but do they deserve the same amount of consideration?"

"To me, it almost can carry more weight than the other two, since I don't believe these are regular nightmares. I actually miss regular dreaming, in fact I'm not even resting anymore, and I'm hoping I've not lost my head." My gaze glided around the room looking for the vanished critters.

"Do you see or hear things others don't when you're awake?"

I stopped looking around the room and focused on her again. "I think you're misunderstanding the situation. This is a leap from the norm, I know. But one thing I've learned during this experience is that I need to keep adjusting how I view things to make sense of them. I'm not the same Emma of a year ago and neither are my circumstances, and Spencer's not here. So why should how I solve problems stay the same?"

"That's a good observation," she said. "But you need to stay within the realm of what's realistic."

"What part of my story is realistic anyway?" *I am telling you I am becoming another being and ending up in a war-stricken place and you're talking about realism?*

"Let's not rule out the pressures of grieving," she said following the Occam's razor line of thinking. "Is there any evidence in your dreams that you're in a different time period?"

"I don't know. It could be ten, twenty, or thirty years ago. But I wouldn't say with certainty that I am time traveling, just poking a hole through space-time into another region. I contacted a researcher—this, this physicist to learn more and see what I can find out about the theories on the topic."

"Sounds like you're doing your research," she said. "I think this is a good step for you, to systematically try to understand what you are proposing. It'll help you sort it out in your head."

"The thing is, he hasn't written me back and I feel as if he is the key to all of this."

"Is there anyone else you can contact? Why him specifically?" I knew she was humoring me at this point, but she had a good question here—one whose answer I was not ready to fully admit to myself and definitely not to Dr. T. "Well, he seems to be the top researcher in this particular field and the closest in terms of distance."

"Perhaps he has colleagues that might prove helpful?"

"He probably does. I just have to find out who they are." I didn't want to tell her that I already had a list of people who were as qualified, who knew just as much, maybe more, who might have already answered me but didn't have the same Spencer eyes.

"If you are truly exploring theories, such as parallel universes, why not explore reincarnation? And many other possibilities that fall in the realm of the metaphysical? Why fixate on this one particular idea?" It was clear she wasn't on board with me. At least Tina indulged me a little. Harvard, however, was not having it.

"So do you think I should call him?" *Now I was getting to the real question. The reason I'd come here. Should I do it? Yes, say I should and I'll call him.*

"That really depends on you. But as I'm sure you know, you have to be prepared for the fact that there will be no guarantee he has an answer for you."

I nodded in agreement but knew that the minute Kerr and I met it would all be sorted out. That we would speak some secret language no one else had access to, just like Spencer and me.

"I'm thinking I should," I said after a long silence.

"Again, that's up to you. But if it were me, I would reconsider the possibility of a parallel universe and try and focus on the root cause of your distress. There are some wonderful sleep studies we could run to see what's happening with your body while you sleep. I highly recommend . . ."

I stopped listening. All I wanted to do was make a run for it. It made all the sense in the world, at least in her world, that I was in a state of mourning, irrational and tired, but in my heart of hearts, I believed there to be an infinite number of universes out there for every single outcome of every single event, and somehow, through a time loop, a tunnel, or a wormhole, if you will, I was periodically ending up in one of them. And somehow Spencer and Kerr were a part of it. And did it matter if any of it was true in a way that was explainable within the rules and realms we've set for ourselves? I decided not. If I experienced it, then on some level it was real.

13. Birthday Roses

TOURAN

Dad and I spent the morning putting up orange and green streamers in the living room. He'd stand on a chair at the corner of the room, tacking his end to the ceiling, while I'd park myself on the carpet, twisting and twisting each streamer to make it look all wavy. We also made some crazy-looking paper chandeliers with white and pink paper—I learned how to make those at school. Now, most of the living room ceiling is decorated with some kind of paper, making it look more like the floor of an art class than a ceiling.

There's a chocolate cake in the fridge, and on the living room coffee table are trays of mini bologna, egg, and sausage sandwiches that Mom made for everyone. Fifteen of my friends are here. Most are from my class, but I also invited some of the neighbor kids like Mimi and also family friends like Nima. I didn't think my parents would throw me a party this year with the rationing and bombing, but nothing seems different from the previous birthdays. So far, at least.

"You want to change the music? I brought you a tape," Mimi says.

I swallow the bologna bite in my mouth and take the tape from her. "Sure, what's on here?"

"It's a mix my cousin made."

"Cool." I know her cousin. She's a couple of years older than us and has music we don't.

I walk over to the stereo on the floor and switch out the tape that's playing for the mix. Repeating drum beats and rhythmic electric guitars fill the living room. It's making the floor vibrate. The outside air brings in the smell of our garden roses and honeysuckle through the large living room windows. Some of my friends start dancing to the music.

Nima comes up to me: "Hey, I brought you something." He hands me a book about photography.

"Is this what you were reading?" I say, examining the heavy gift. "Thanks."

"Yeah, but I'm now reading another book on how to make cameras." He leans back and puts a foot against the wall.

"Making your own? Sounds hard."

"Well, they're easy cameras."

I say, "Maybe I can learn too."

"We can try to make one when you come over to our house."

I smile, happy at the thought of going over to Nima's house and working on a cool project. My girlfriends are looking at me from the other side of the room, smiling. They all have little crushes on Nima, with his curly hair and cool kicks. I feel triumphant at having his attention on me in front of all my friends, especially Mimi.

Everyone's head turns to the kitchen door. Mom carries the cake. She's wearing a blue sleeveless dress with heeled strappy sandals. Her honey-colored eyes look like they're dancing to the music, and she's all smiles—one big red smile.

The cake looks super delicious: twelve candles on a thick layer of dark chocolate icing. My friends' hungry eyes are following my mom as she places it on the coffee table. Dad cuts off the music and everyone starts singing the birthday song while I think about what to wish for: maybe a new bike—the green one I saw in the store window last month—or good grades, maybe that polka-dot skirt that Mom said was too expensive. The song ends and it's time for me to blow out the candles. Eyes closed, I let out a big puff and wish with all my might for the raids to stop. Forever.

Mom's already cutting the cake when I open my eyes and everyone's shoving gifts my way to open. Dad's taking photos each time I rip apart colorful wrapping paper. Books, pink sneakers, another book, a necklace, and a bunch of toys. The other kids probably wish they were me, getting all these gifts and all this attention. Mom hands me my piece of cake—the best one because it has the biggest flower on it. A chocolate rose.

I stick my fork through the hard chocolate into the gooey filling, when everything goes dark and a siren takes over the atmosphere.

The kids, used to these kinds of interruptions, look over at my mom for instructions without saying anything or panicking. Mom's face on the other hand, goes pale, almost gray. Her hands tremble and she lets out a small shriek before leaning over to Dad, who's standing behind me, and whispers that should a bomb drop on our house tonight she'd never forgive herself. She means that all of us kids are in one place, other people's kids.

"Don't worry," he whispers back. "It'll be okay."

"But during a birthday? For the love of God."

"Huh," he almost chuckles. "War doesn't know birthdays from ordinary days. It's a paintbrush of ruin, whirling around and staining everything in sight. I'll take care of this." With that, Dad walks to the kitchen and returns with a lit candle, taking some of the darkness away.

"Hey, guys, let's all head down to the basement," he announces.

In a matter of minutes or maybe seconds—time moves differently during raids—Mom and Dad gather everyone and lead us out of the house, into the yard, to the opening of the basement. Though everyone seems hurried, everything feels slow—hazy movements of kids through a dark molasses. It's beautiful, the neatly manicured roses of the yard lit by a young moon, its light filtering through and around the edges of thick clouds. I think of going back, of taking the piece of cake with the rose, of placing on it one of the candles tossed onto that small plate with the other blown-out ones, and lighting it again, carrying it through the blue-hued garden, and blowing it out once more under a sky dotted with airplanes. But before I have a chance, I'm funneled into the hole of the basement. The sky begins turning red and gold, and I'm unable to change course.

14. Meeting

NEW JERSEY | NEW YORK

With a coin I scratched off the covering layer of one of the Win for Life game cards I'd bought on the way to work. This is what I did on mornings when I really didn't want to go in. I'd stop at the convenience store a few blocks from the office and buy myself a cup of coffee with a few scratch-off cards. A thousand dollars a week for life was enough. Enough to keep me away from the sewers, a job I no longer needed now that I couldn't have the future I'd planned for, one that included Spencer in it.

I looked at the numbers peeking out from under the layer of metallic silver coating to see if they were a match for the winning numbers. No dice. Of course. I never won. When I was applying to Rutgers, I was so excited to be part of their engineering program—I'd always been good at math and the sciences, and the idea of building things for a living fit. My parents seemed pleased too. It was a sound and stable choice, my father, an insurance agent, said. It made them happy that I too could lead a life in which I wouldn't suffer financially, in which I too could own a house, raise a child or two, and follow in the footsteps of the suburbanites in our lives. I was content, because I thought I could achieve all my parents had *and* make a difference in people's lives. In my head, I imagined bringing clean water to those who needed it, designing sewer systems for remote rural areas—maybe even a village on a different continent. But then at a career fair I handed out several resumes, got a few calls from local firms—that were not doing anything close to what I'd dreamed of, and whose only villages were rows of similar-looking housing units in treeless developments on the rare bits of land left in the area that came complete with granite countertops and stainless steel appliances in the kitchen. I was asked to come in for some interviews and received an offer for a position, which I took, and seven years later, there I was, still deep inside a job that I had once liked but had come to feel neutral about, though with no motivation to get out. Only now, without Spencer, it was becoming increasingly intolerable—a tiny rock in my shoe that I kept stepping on.

It had been sixteen days since I'd sent my email, but Kerr hadn't emailed or called. I'd done my best to try not to think about him, occupying myself with cleaning and organizing and cooking. But then I'd find a skirt I'd bought with Spencer or discover an old note he'd left me in my pile of desk papers, and my mind would lose its anchor, first drifting to my best friend and then to his imitation, the physicist, before giving in to a strong urge to look up Kerr and stare at his photo. And each time I'd find something new that would be familiar, like the way his right canine was a hint shorter than his left canine— it was almost unnoticeable unless you stared at his smile for a bit too long as I had many times. I would have never noticed it with Spencer either if he hadn't mentioned it. Leave it to him to notice the slightest bit of something in himself that was less than perfect.

I dodged the idea of a sleep study and instead focused on other homework from my therapist. Every morning when I awoke from sleep and got back from being the little girl in the other world, I wrote down anything that I remembered, the entire sequence of events. Then, I'd review my notes for accuracy and look for clues, patterns, for signs, signs to another dimension, to another world. Dr. Thompson's idea of this exercise, I suspect, was to have me find evidence of my own irrationality and get on a path leading to something more sound. But the path always took me back to Spencer, then Kerr.

I finally gave in and called his office while my internal unsettled particles danced, collided, and exploded of their own accord. A woman, maybe his assistant or a graduate student, answered in a warm voice and said he had been away till the end of last week and was for the most part working from home the rest of the summer. "He only comes in one day a week. Email him," she said, "it's the best way to get in touch." I explained that I already had. "Try again, your first email might have fallen through the cracks. He was very busy at the end of the semester. He's good at answering."

"Can I make an appointment for a day he's coming in?" I asked. I went on to explain how I was interested in becoming a graduate student and had a research project in mind aligned with his expertise and would really like to meet him. My story, made up on the spot, sounded convincing, so much so that I began to believe it myself. *I was going to grad school.* Maybe that was the answer to my stagnant life, to my post–Win for Life dreams.

She checked his book and gave me an appointment for the only day he was coming in the following week. Wednesday morning. I put in a request to take a personal day and spent the rest of the days thinking about what I was going to say, what I was going wear, and how I was going to manage getting myself into the city. Since Spencer's death I hadn't set foot in Manhattan, much less gone into the vicinity of the Village, where he'd had his accident. Besides, New York was always Spencer's city. I went there with him, for him, and most often via him.

When I was a kid, my parents took me to see the Empire State Building, the dinosaurs at the American Museum of Natural History, and the like. We always took the NJ Transit trains into the city and the escalators up to Seventh Avenue outside Penn Station, where we waited for a yellow taxi. I would get dizzy looking up at the tall buildings that surrounded New York's dwellers and would marvel at the strong wind that seemed to blow through each street, lifting bits of garbage into small and short-lived airborne whirlpools. We hardly ever walked the streets, maybe several short blocks, but instead jumped onto some mode of transportation. That's how I knew to visit New York. I was always an observer, never a part of it.

With Spencer, the experience was organic. We walked for hours, often aimlessly, mixed into the sea of people making their daily waves. We didn't change the city with our presence. We were part of the fiber, woven into the landscape of the streets. Never disrupting its ebb and flow. Always going with the urban grain. We had become the observed, the ones people like my parents and my former self would look at as the whole that was the city. And then that city we so trusted and became a part of betrayed us and destroyed him and went on hustling and bustling with no one taking note of its missing member.

Each time I thought about New York, my body acted as if it were injected with Novocaine, and my eyes would feel like hollow, deep holes overflowing with emptiness. Yet when the morning of the meeting arrived, after throwing up the little coffee I had in my stomach, I was determined. I changed my clothes several times. Although I'd already decided on an outfit earlier in the week, on the day of, jeans and a T-shirt hardly seemed like the right choice for an encounter with a big-name scientist, for the look-alike of Spencer, who always said I should play up my waist-long, thick hair, and large eyes. I finally decided on a black linen shirtdress that had a loose belt attached. It was put-together and pretty but hardly appeared as if I was trying too hard. A something-I-just-threw-on kind of look. I paired it with red flat sandals, took one look at the growing pile of clothes on the bed and then at myself in the mirror. After spraying a little bit of perfume on my hair—a little trick I'd learned from Spencer to spread your scent each time you moved your head—I left the musky confines of my home.

Kerr's office was in a brick brownstone on the northern side of Washington Square Park, one of many lined up against one another. It was a charming building with a short wrought iron fence, adorned with filigree ornamentation typical of the nineteenth-century Italian Renaissance period, establishing the front perimeter. I swung the gate open and walked under the shadow cast by the large tree in the small garden out front and headed up the stairs to the main door.

On the second floor, all the walls and ceilings were painted white—giving the entire house a certain uniformity—accented with butterscotch doorframes complementing the oak parquet floors. A warm light coming in through the tall windows gleamed off the mirror above an old dusty fireplace in the waiting room. The place reminded me of a time back in high school when I thought being an engineer meant designing such rooms or at least components of beautiful spaces. I sat down on a sofa after letting the young woman at the desk know who I was and tried to imagine the house's potential previous inhabitants—families with little girls and boys running around. It was my way of not allowing my mind to spiral out of control and collapse into a singularity, an obsessive conviction that my theory was the only possible explanation. On the table in front of me sat a stack of small paper plates and a partially eaten rectangular cake with the words *Happy Birthday, Lisa* mostly intact. From the nearly empty waiting area, it was evident that Lisa and her colleagues were back to their lab or offices.

Warmth descended from his office. Kerr stood up from his chair and greeted me when I walked in. My knees loosened so much that I had to hold on to the back of the chair facing his desk. It was his slightly crooked smile. How the left side of his lips crept up a little more than the right side, which made his left eye slightly smaller at even the hint of a grin. That was one of the things I joked about and loved on Spencer's face—perfect in every way but slightly imperfect with that specific expression. And here it was, the same asymmetrical unfurled lip on a different face.

He was taller than he appeared on the show, towering over me by nearly half a foot, and seemed quite fit, the rare breed of scientist who cared about his appearance. He wore a light gray chambray button-down shirt and dark jeans. His dark, curly brown hair, cut short, had a slightly messy look to it, but in a neat way, careful carelessness, something Spencer had told me Italians call sprezzatura. Kerr's face, angular and well proportioned, gave him an over-all charming appearance. I took a deep breath to keep myself upright and extended my hand, and he shook it. He smiled a small, polite, professional, and oddly familiar smile, perfected over time on students and colleagues, and motioned for me to sit down on one of the chairs across his desk.

"So, I'm told you're interested in pursuing a graduate degree in physics." He looked directly into my eyes. All I wanted to do was stare into them, but instead I found other things to look at around the room, like the large black desk telephone, angled to face him, the stack of papers, a picture of an older attractive couple, likely his parents, and the branches of an American elm out-side the window behind him.

"I've been interested in research involving multiverses." I took a breath of courage. "And when I saw you on a show about it, I thought to contact you." I quickly glanced into his eyes just to see if the Spencer eye-smile was still there, the one I saw on the show. As if staring into the sun, I quickly looked away again, heart pounding. I wasn't thrilled about starting the meeting with a slight distortion of truth but didn't have the nerve to begin with the entire truth or even half of it. Gnawing at my lower lip, I was likely eating away at my coral lipstick.

"That's right." He didn't sound convinced and gave me an I-don't-know-what-you're-talking-about look. Did he mean *that's right*, he got my email and just remembered he never answered it, or *that's right*, he remembered that the show recently aired? I kept quiet to see if he'd continue.

And he did: "What is your background, Emmabelle?"

I froze. "I'm sorry," I said and then went silent and for seconds we stayed in a big vacuum of words before I could continue: "I'm sorry, can you repeat what you just said?"

"Your background, Emma?" he repeated.

"Right. I'm a civil engineer and have been working in that field for about, oh, seven years now." The words were marching out of my mouth in a rush, faster than usual.

"And you're interested in making a career change?" He looked at me tentatively. This time, I tried to focus on the books on the shelf to his right, hoping to divert my gaze and attention from the thing that scared and excited me most.

"I've always had an interest in physics but hadn't considered it seriously until I saw the show and thought I want to learn more about this kind of research." Fact and fiction were muddled beyond my ability to sort them out.

A look at his uneven and familiar smile. I remembered the canine and quickly took a mental measure of his. Right one was shorter in person too. My heart pumped blood and oxygen as fast as it could manage, supplementing all the air I was losing through my short, shallow breaths. I ran my fingers through my hair and the smell of orange blossoms permeated the space around me.

Kerr put his elbows on the desk, inching his light olive face closer. "What you saw on the show was a popularization of a theory, a small aspect of bigger research projects."

I said nothing. I didn't care about the show.

"I guess what I'm trying to say is that the idea of alternate universes is not really a part of my research but an aspect that the producers thought would make learning certain facets of the science more palatable to a general audience," he continued. "But, unfortunately, it's not in itself a topic that anyone here is actually working on."

I wanted to say nothing, to just go along with the conversation because maybe if we went on talking about it, I could just keep hanging out here and being around this man: "But you spoke on the topic as if it were, I mean everyone on the show did. So why did they choose you to be on?"

"As far as I know, none of the researchers on the show is specifically focused on the subject. Those are some theoretical ideas that we're all aware of, but it's not at the core of what any of us are working on."

"Dr. Jacobs . . ."

"Please, call me Kerr."

"Kerr, so what you're saying is that it's not possible for an object or a living thing, a person, to travel to an alternate universe?"

"Well, there are theories, equations, math, that support it . . ." He kept talking. He was being generous, going on about a show he didn't seem to regard all that highly to some stranger showing up to be all fangirl. Though his words were different than Spencer's, his generosity wasn't, and it put me at ease.

"So it is possible?" I could feel the fire in my cheeks, quite flushed I was sure. "For a person or object?"

"To actually travel to an alternate universe?" he leaned back and his chair did too, tilted his head, and squinted his eyes. "In theory, yes. But there are a lot of what-ifs that have to come together for it to work, so I'm afraid not," he said politely, giving me once more that time-tested professional smile, which made me happy in ways he could not understand. "I would encourage you to explore other topics within modern physics to see if they interest you." It sounded like the final word. He was saying it's over. That I had to go.

I leaned back in my chair and zoned out. My hopes of reaching something at the end of *that* rabbit hole had been discarded and flushed down into the sewers the rest of my life was falling into. I tilted my head back and stared at the ceiling. White. Simple. I thought of my ceiling and then of Spencer. My ceiling, not so simple.

Sensing my dismay, Kerr softened his tone even more. "May I ask you something?" This time his smile was different, more personal.

I nodded, pleased he wanted to keep talking, to keep this going.

"You seem very interested in this particular aspect of physics, but your background is in engineering, so it begs the question why? Why is it that you want to change your career and why to this?"

I pushed my hair out of my face. He waited. "I just thought it might be a possibility," I said, wanting to tell him more, his familiarity putting me at ease. "And Einstein's field equations indicate these bridges between space-time exist, that we can take shortcuts to another time or place." I tried to make my case and for a moment forgot who was sitting across from me, and spoke as if I were merely convincing Spencer to have Mexican instead of sushi.

He smiled and I thought I had won him over. "I like your enthusiasm, Emma. The thing is wormholes, which are only theoretical at this point, are highly unstable, meaning they will collapse before anything can make it through and, while everything is a possibility, there's a lot up for debate," he said. "What I'm saying is it just isn't practically possible. But if this is something that you're very interested in studying, and if you or I come across a funding source for the research, we can talk about it further. I can also let you know if I can think of anyone working on it. But as I said, I doubt . . ." He went on, but I could no longer focus on his words, everything he said swirled into a large *no* to me, an end to this relationship, and I was feeling dizzy. Somewhere, though, in the midst of it all, I still had a small bit of hope.

As soon as he stopped speaking and I realized we'd come to the end of the conversation, I stood up and thanked him in a small voice, the volume of which was lowered by rejection.

"I have your email, right?" He came around from behind the desk and walked me over to the office door.

"Yes. Here's my card anyway. It has my number on it also." I shook his hand, gripping it for too long, and for the seconds that our skin made contact and my sensory receptors picked up his warmth, I felt at ease again.

"Good meeting you. And you know where I'm at," he said kindly.

I walked out of his office and went to the park outside, walking all the way to the south side, and planted myself on a bench and burst into tears. Spencer was dead all over again and, while I thought I had him just moments ago in this strange experience, I didn't expect it to end so soon and to feel so disjointed from the living world again. After I drowned my eyes for a good ten or so minutes, I sat there watching the leaves on the trees pulsate and the happy people absorbing vitamin D by the glistening fountain. I was jealous of their joy, their feet soaking in the dirty water, their hands holding books, lovers, and ice cream cones. I desperately wanted what they had, their cheerfulness. I just didn't know how to get there.

When I walked through the door of my home, I hit the play button on my answering machine and listened to the entirety of the message. It was the last message Spencer had left me. It was the sweetest one too. When I heard it months ago, I knew I had to keep it. Instinctively, I must have known it would be his last.

My not-wife, how I adore your voice. On my way to city. Last chance. Will miss you. Husband loves you much.

At times, I believed I killed him by not deleting that message. Had I pressed that red button on my answering machine when I first heard his voice, I would have left room for a final message at another time, some future moment, when his voice would've been gravelly and we were frail and wrinkle-faced.

But at some deeper level I accepted the finality of that message. I gave in to his death.

I'd heard once that only the dead don't speak. But for me it was the only voice I wanted to hear. I hit play again: *My not-wife, how I adore your voice. On my way to city. Last chance. Will miss you. Husband loves you much.*

15. Summerhouse

TOURAN

The morning sky is so blue and clean, it's hard to imagine it was dirtied with planes and antiaircraft fire just a couple of nights ago. Everyone is either on their way out or has already left. Our street is nearly empty and the gentle and lazy summer wind knocking on doors of vacant houses is the only sound in our city of nearly eight million, whose air waves are normally filled with horns and chatter and door closings. I'll miss Mimi and my other friends, but they're not staying either. This summer's not like the others, not for anyone. Our car is packed with food and sheets and pillows and everything else we need to spend the summer away from our house. I'm carrying to the car a small bag I packed for myself, in addition to the one Mom put together for me. I wanted my games, books, a deck of cards, and things to keep busy with. Who knows what this place will be like? There's probably no stores around and no toys at the house. I have a small chess set in there too. Figured Nima and I could play when we get bored and maybe I'll finally be able to learn for real. Maybe, I'll be a chess player when I grow up and be super famous. I think about this for a bit and decide I don't like it that much to do it my whole life. Maybe I'll be a swimmer—now that's something I could do every day.

I put the bag in Dad's SUV and stand with my back to it and face the empty concrete pool, painted almost exactly the same shade as the sky. This is the first year Mom and Dad haven't filled it for the summer and the air in the yard doesn't have that chlorine smell that I love so much. It's my favorite thing to do, swim in this pool. Floating on my back, weightless, staring at a clear sky is like flying. When I'm in the water, I feel like I'm not fixed to one place, that I belong to all of the world. Can't believe we won't get to use it this year. But Mom and Dad say that even the pool doesn't make it worth it to stay in the city. I'm not so sure I agree.

"You all set?" Dad asks as he walks down the stairs from the patio to the car. He's carrying a big sack of rice.

I take my eyes off the blue hole and make the tiniest nod. "You think there's a pool there for me to swim in?"

"There are streams and rivers so clear you can see every rock under the water and maybe even a few fish if you're lucky. It's really something. You won't even miss the pool. I promise." He closes the trunk and comes over to me.

"But I can't swim in the streams, can I?" I look up at him. I feel small and my question makes me feel even smaller.

He lifts me by the armpits and sits me on the hood of the car. We're almost face-to-face, and I can see all the gray hair framing the little creases and folds around his eyes. "Listen, you're going to have a great time, and you'll get to play in the streams. Look at it as an adventure. Besides, your friend Nima'll be there too. You'll get to explore together." Though I'm not happy about this retreat from the real world, I like that at least Nima will be there with me.

Dad smiles, gives me a kiss on the forehead, and puts me down, then goes around the car to bring a plastic bag back to me. "And look what I brought for us." He pulls out a hammock. "You always wanted to use this thing."

"Can I sleep in it at night too?" I'm feeling thrilled. I've wanted to sleep in the hammock since I discovered it one night on a basement shelf during a raid.

"Of course."

"I'm about to lock up the house," Mom's yelling from the patio. "All set?"

And off we go, away from our home for a whole summer. I watch our house get smaller as we head down the short street and silently say goodbye to it and to the pool and to my neighbors. At least I'll get to have adventures with Nima. The sun, coming through the car window, is welcoming on my face, and I'm bubbling over with excitement, thinking of the days to come in a place filled with people and sounds and warmth. Summer seems exciting again. Maybe Nima and I really will become good friends.

We're barely out of the city, but I'm already sprawled out on the back seat and half-asleep, blocking the light with my hand over my head. I dream about swimming in clear rivers and sleeping in the hammock between tall trees on a riverbank, suspended above glistening water and sparkling silver fish under a bright sun. I try to imagine my room at the summerhouse, if it'll have stars I can stare at on the ceiling, or a large window looking out onto a river, if the last girl in it left some of her toys, maybe a storybook or a doll. I dream of playing hide-and-seek with Nima, of sneaking into his room at night to talk when everyone is asleep, of sleeping and reading and sunshine. I'm dreaming of summer like it used to be, before the basement trips, when the only thing we cared about was crisping our skins by the pool and sleeping through the night and waking up to do it again and again until the days started getting shorter and the temperature dipped.

I don't know how long I've been asleep, but when I open my eyes my first question is how much longer till we get there.

Mom turns to the back seat and puts a hand on my arm. She's wearing large brown sunglasses. "Not long, baby. Sit up and look out the window. You're missing the scenery."

We're in a valley, and stretching on both sides of the car are fields of red poppies and white wildflowers growing all the way up to the foot of the mountains.

"But how long till we actually get there?"

"Well," Dad says, "the place is only seventy-seven kilometers from our house and we left about forty-five to fifty minutes ago, so I'm guessing only about fifteen to twenty minutes. But it all depends on the road. It's getting kind of bumpy and we have to go a lot slower."

Our tires turn up rocks the size of golf balls. The pots and pans are clanking in the trunk. I turn around and look out the back window. There's a cloud of dust trailing the car. There are no other cars behind.

"How come there're no houses here?" I ask, worried we're the only people in this dusty landscape.

"You just can't see them from here. There aren't as many as in the city and they're probably behind the mountain or on a different road. You'll see, once we get to the village—there'll be plenty of houses," Dad says.

Everyone is quiet in the car for the next few minutes, probably wondering what in the world we got ourselves into. We pass a small pond. In it, you can see a reflection of the snow-capped summit to the right of the car. It makes me want to jump in and take a dip. As we drive through the narrow opening between the mountains ahead, a large green field opens up and trees and houses start popping up. Most of the homes have clay walls, and some have slanted roofs. Houses in the city are made with bricks and have roofs you can walk on. Dad pulls out a sheet of paper, hands it to Mom, and asks her to figure out where we need to go next. A few turns later and we're pulling into a smaller tree-lined dirt road heading uphill onto a wooded property. The car stops and I look up at a small clay house peering above a short wall. I've never stayed in a house made of clay before, one that looks like it would start to crumble at a touch. Mom takes out a key from an envelope, and I follow her out of the car. Dad gets out and starts checking something under the hood.

"I guess Nima and his parents haven't arrived yet," she says as she unlocks the old wooden door to the yard. At the end of the yard is a house. There's nothing out front except a raggedy old metal faucet and a small walkway to a side yard. Everything is clay-colored—the ground, the outside of the house, the walls, all the same shade of earthy gray. Mom's red shirt is the only bit of color in this drab world.

"This is it?" I say as soon as I walk into the L-shaped room and then run out to the wooden balcony. "Where's my room? Where's the bathroom and the kitchen?"

"Outside in the side yard." Mom is behind me.

"In the yard?" I say and walk out to find them. I head to the walkway that leads to a narrow corridor with a ceiling. There's an old small white stove, a fridge, and a small room, which I guess is the bathroom. There's no door to the bathroom. Just a toilet. Next to it, in another closet-sized room, is a showerhead with bits of red rust. It too is completely exposed.

"Mom! Mom!" I yell. "There's no door to the bathroom. I don't wanna stay here. I wanna go home." I can't control the tears rolling down my face and realize that something is really wrong with our life that we have to do this, to live here.

"Lily. It's no big deal. We can get a curtain or something."

"I don't wanna stay here. Please let's go home. Please, please." I can't stop and feel as though I'm getting younger and sillier by the minute. I want to crouch and put my head between my knees, to get smaller and disappear or at least pretend to disappear, just like I do in the basement back at home. First it's the raids, then it's this house, which might as well be like those bombed houses, bombed back to the Stone Ages. Why can't we just go back to our lives before the war, when all I did was ride my bike with Mimi around the neighborhood looking for imaginary thieves and swim in the pool while Mom made us spaghetti?

"Lily," she squats down in front of me and wipes my face with her hand. "Sweetness, listen to me. This place may not be like home, but it's much safer for us to stay here during the summer vacation. We're very lucky to have even found this. It's not all bad. Come to the balcony with me. I want to show you something." She takes my hand in hers and leads me back into the house and to the large balcony lined with flower boxes, from which yellow, pink, and purple petunias cascade down the railing. The leaves on the tall trees are swinging in a dry mountain breeze, and light is dappled below on the sloped ground. Everything is calm, and looking at it makes it seem like all is well with the world. Or at least okay.

"Now look at that. You see the stream through the walnut trees?" She is down on her knees and pointing straight ahead with one hand, while holding me with the other.

Sloping down from the house is a narrow path surrounded by walnut trees leading to a clear stream snaking its way through the downward incline of the land. On the other side are what seem to be fruit trees. "You think maybe I can sleep on the balcony tonight?" I remember the hammock.

"I don't see why not, as long as you use a mosquito net," she says. "Now go wash your face." She kisses me on the cheek and stands up. "I'm going to go help Daddy bring in our stuff."

16. Rules and Lines

NEW JERSEY

I decided to squeeze in a quick swim after a day at the office before my date night with Peter and quickly changed out of my work clothes into a sporty blue Nike two-piece. It was 6:24 PM and the pool closed at seven on weekdays. The act of swimming gave me a freedom I never experienced on dry land. For the few minutes I managed to spend in the water, I wasn't an engineer, a grieving friend, a girlfriend, or an irrational being. I was encapsulated by the fluidity of water—a supportive substance that would also allow me to move in ways that I couldn't outside of it, a rare combination. I walked across the lawn, through the walkway that went past the empty tennis courts. Spencer and I once tried to play. Neither of us really knew how and we thought it'd be easy, given we were both reasonably fit. Armed with Peter's rackets and outfits that we thought looked tennis-like—Spencer sporting a white terry cloth headband and me with a short pleated white skirt, not meant for a sport—we headed to the court. It took all of fifteen minutes for us to be panting from running so much after missed balls to realize that perhaps this sport wasn't as easy as Serena and Venus made it look.

At the fence I put my face against the wiring and looked in. The vacant green court was a perfect rectangle with neatly drawn white lines defining each player's position. Spencer and I didn't stick within the lines. At one point I was in the court next to ours, chasing the ball, and at another point we were both on one side as I dribbled the ball right to his region of the court, before eventually sitting on a bench outside the fence, drinking water from the bottles we'd brought with us. I tried to recall every detail—the smell of almost sweat on my skin, the hue of exertion on Spencer's forehead, the harshness of the midday light—grasping at every sensation as if it were some magical fruit on a memory tree about to disappear. As soon as I'd picked all I could, I took my face out of the fence and headed to the pool, where I dropped my coverup and towel on a lounge chair and nodded to the teenage lifeguard sitting in his station. He greeted me back with a smile. The place was near empty. Other than a mom drying off her two young children, everyone had already left. I stood at the edge of the deep end and dove in, feeling the cold water brush first against my fingers and arms, then my face, neck, and shoulders, followed by the rest of my body. After just one lap, the chill had turned into warmth, and I was just putting one arm and its opposite leg up and then the other leg and arm and repeating this motion until I hit one end of the pool and had to turn. In that trance nothing outside the water could touch me—neither loss, nor love, nor fear. It's a beautiful thing, this unawareness, the buoyancy.

I met Peter for dinner at a small Italian restaurant in New Brunswick. I'd thrown on a spaghetti strap, A-line, short, black-and-brown printed dress from the pile of clothes I'd created a couple of days prior for my meeting with Kerr. Spencer had named the dress "old faithful," because I had owned it since my senior year of college and wore it when I didn't want to think about my outfit. It was comfortable, didn't require a bra, and looked decent enough—it was reliable and, well, faithful, a staple for outings with Peter, who rarely seemed to care what I wore. Before I left the condo, I looked at my bare legs, which appeared longer in the wooden mirror leaning against the wall than in reality, and for several suspended moments thought I was about to meet Kerr. If I met him again, it'd go better, I thought. It had to. And though I cringed at what he might have thought of me after our meeting, I could only think of seeing him. Again. Once more even.

The restaurant lights were dimmed. A pinprick of disappointment set in upon seeing Peter. He studied the large leather-bound menu, looking like the subject of a Rembrandt portrait, illuminated only on one side of his perfect and angular nose by the small candle on our table. My menu was untouched from the time the waiter had placed it in front of me. I was predictable. I knew I wanted the pasta alla norma, a classic Italian dish, a classic Emma dish. Just like I went to work every morning, laid out sewer lines with the same constraints, I ordered the same dish at the same restaurant with the same person. Sameness was what I did best. It was the zone in which I lived. I'd come to despise it but didn't have the courage to be different from what I was, to escape it.

The episodes, I suspected, for better or for worse, would be, or already were, changing that. Maybe. At least they had me navel-gazing, thinking about something beyond my grasp, beyond my everydayness, beyond the mechanical world I lived in, and, although that scared me, it also thrilled me—not knowing, unpredictability, and an uncertain future. Maybe Tina was onto something. Maybe I wanted this. Whatever *this* was.

"Okay, it's decided, I'm getting the seafood Alfredo," Peter said, shut the menu a bit too loudly, and placed it to his right on the table.

"After all that and you're getting the same thing you always do? Let me guess, you're going to put cheese on it too." I took a piece of warm bread from the basket on the table and dipped it in the olive oil sitting at the bottom of a small white porcelain bowl.

"Sure, but you're getting the same dish you always get," he winked.

"Yes, but I didn't spend a gazillion minutes studying the menu." I put the bread in my mouth. "At least I recognize that I'm boring and unadventurous."

"But I work hard at it!" Peter chuckled and I followed his lead. "Anyhoo. I got you a present." He bent down and grabbed a dark green Barnes & Noble bag from his messenger bag and handed it to me over the table.

"What's this about? Am I missing an anniversary or something?" I was surprised. Other than the occasional flowers, I hadn't received a gift from Peter in a while, not counting my birthday.

"I don't need an occasion to treat my girl."

I smiled and felt the weight of the package in my hands.

"Are you going to open it or what?"

"Of course." I put the bag on my lap, reached into it, and grabbed a store-gift-wrapped package. "Books, eh?"

"I've noticed you've taken an interest in physics and thought you might like to add a couple more to your collection." He leaned forward over the table, his triumphant smile now fully on display, thanks to the candle.

I ripped open the paper. The top book was *Electromagnetism, an Introduction*. Underneath it was another entitled *Waves and Vibrations*. I smiled a little smile in a gesture of appreciation despite the very missed mark of subject matters, which were far from parallel universes or the particular area of physics I had been studying. I reached over and gave him a kiss. I knew I should be grateful.

"Have you read these? If you have, I have the receipt."

"I actually haven't." I looked into his eyes, working hard to impart gratitude with my gaze.

"Perfect!"

"You're very sweet." It was true, he was sweet. I, on the other hand, felt not so kind as my mind, as if too unruly to harness under my appreciation for

Peter, kept drifting to Kerr, who undoubtedly would not make such a mistake, though the comparison was as unfair as it got. I put the books in their bag and placed it on the floor next to my chair and tried to be in the present, with my boyfriend: "I really appreciate this, Peter," I said. "How was your day?"

"Same old. Dave emailed me, he wants to go camping in the Delaware Water Gap next weekend with the boys and I thought to check with you. I can finally use the knife you got me . . ."

I didn't hear most of what Peter was saying. As much as I tried, I couldn't keep my thoughts in check, which, uncontainable as they were, kept dashing back to Kerr and our meeting. I traced the Braille of his smile with my mind, the one that was perfectly Spencer's. But there was something else, something I hadn't even noticed until I thought about it then, until I had some time to absorb the meeting. It was the way he articulated his words, pronouncing every single sound in a syllable and hanging onto it for a split second longer than most. I continued to examine his every move and tried to decipher what each gesture and intonation might have implied. He said he would let me know if he thought of someone else working on the topic. He left the door open for us to meet again. He wanted me to call him by his first name, to move into a less formal zone. He called me Emmabelle, or didn't. There was something there. There had to be.

The food came and we both started eating. Peter continued talking. Every few minutes, I'd snap back, catch a word, and nod to stay attentive. But through most of dinner my attention alternated between the steam rising from the mountain of eggplant, cheese, and sauce, the wine, and Kerr.

"You haven't said much. How has your day been?" Peter finally said three-quarters of the way into our meals.

"I was listening to you," I took a sip of Merlot to push down a bite.

"You won't be disappointed if I go camping and we don't spend the weekend together?"

"Of course not, go enjoy."

"My place or yours?" Peter said on our way out of the restaurant.

"Mine." I never much liked staying at Peter's, still sort of a bachelor pad with little more than the bare necessities: a couch, television, bed, bookshelf, computer, bike in the dining room—all neatly placed. Hardly any pictures on the walls or plants on the naked surfaces. The only sign of life in that place was Peter himself. I also didn't have more than the basic provisions there, deodorant, toothbrush, and a nightgown. My makeup bag and clothes I always carried back and forth between the two apartments, never committing myself to staying long.

"I'll follow your car then."

Peter closed my car door and I turned the switch, waiting for him to pull behind me. On the ride over, I'd occasionally glance in the rearview mirror, following his car's trail behind mine, at times imagining it was Kerr who was coming home with me. For those seconds I'd experience a thrill I hadn't known since before Spencer's death.

It was almost 11:00 PM when we got home.

"Whoa! What blew up here? That's quite a pile you got there." Peter pointed to the clothes now on the bedroom floor, the peppering of shoes around the bed, and the pile of papers on the comforter. "Were all these outfit changes for me?"

"No, I was looking for something the other day, and as you can see it got out of control." I didn't want to lie and hadn't yet gotten around to mentioning Kerr to Peter. But there was nothing to mention, really, so I left it at that.

"Well, I hope you found whatever you were looking for." He sat at the edge of the bed and removed his shirt and pants and lay back on the bed in his boxers.

"Not yet."

I lay next to Peter. It was deep enough into the night that everything sounded and felt gentle. Peter's hand grabbed my waist. He then pulled me closer and kissed my neck. Though our bodies were making contact in multiple places, darkness was seeping between us and softly pushing us apart. I placed a hand on Peter's back and pulled myself closer but immediately felt my grip loosen, losing to the bleakness of the force. I rolled over onto my back, widening the gap between us.

"Tell me something." It occurred to me then that because I hadn't shared the episodes, a significant event, with Peter, by hiding this innermost incident of my life, central to everything in that time period, *I* was the force, the one pushing myself away from him. "Do you ever wonder if there's another world out there?"

He turned to the side to face me. I could feel his gaze poring over my face but kept mine on the dark ceiling. "Of course. In fact, I think we should travel more. We seem to never go anywhere and it's partially my fault."

"I don't mean other countries or cities. I mean other worlds," I made an arc in the air with my right hand in the dark, gesturing to something upward as if the worlds were somewhere above. I paused for a few seconds waiting for a reaction, but Peter said nothing, and so I continued. "Parallel worlds. Worlds like ours, similar to ours, but different." My voice shifted and broke, as if struck by an inner earthquake. I sat up and continued. "Even worlds just like ours where another Peter is making different decisions than you, each with a different outcome. Maybe even a young Peter or a not-Peter. You but as someone else, in a different setup. Different people, different world. You know, little bubbles of space-time with entire worlds inside them." The more I tried to clarify, the more the fragments of my voice dissolved into incoherence. It was happening again. Just like the time I tried first with Tina and then with Kerr, my words extinguished the other world. It was as if all of what made up my other life existed only if I never spoke of it.

"I guess I don't," he said gently. "No, I don't think there are other worlds out there." He sounded more assured of his convictions this time, as if that extra second between the sentences he uttered made him realize what I was really talking about. "Maybe alien ones on another planet or something of the sort but not the way you mean. What on earth made you think of such a thing, anyway?" He sounded curious.

"I don't know. Reading physics books about alternate universes. But the possibility of it, you don't think that there might be a chance, a slight, slight chance?" I was pressing it, desperate. Desperate for someone to believe me. Believe this thing. The darkness in the room was so all-encompassing and heavy that it was pinning me down. Utterly frustrated, I pushed against everyone else's bland world as if they were keeping me away from expanding mine. The idea of staying within the confines of the domain I had always known was becoming suffocating. I got out of bed and walked to the kitchen—hard, stomping my feet with every step, making deliberately loud sounds to annoy him, to make my feet hurt, to let out an anger I couldn't even understand. My muscles, stiff and numb at once, flailed as though they weren't my own.

Peter came after me. "Hey, what's going on?"

I kept walking to the kitchen—my feet pounding. I turned the faucet and filled a cup with water under the soft light of the lawn lamp coming through the window.

"Emma?"

I didn't want to answer him. So instead I sat at the bistro table and put my head down on its glass, silently letting tears stain the surface. I cried because Peter didn't understand me, Tina didn't understand me, Dr. Thompson didn't understand me, Kerr didn't understand me. But really I cried because I missed Spencer, because I was mad at him for pretending we were husband and wife and then leaving me. For fracturing our perfect threesome. I cried because I realized the world has no loyalty to anyone.

"I don't know how what I said was wrong." He stood by me and stroked my hair. Then knelt down and with his hand lifted my wet face off the table. "To me, it's all here and now. This is reality—you and me here—and it's wonderful and that's the only world I know."

I wanted to say: *But isn't reality based on perception? Isn't something real when you observe it? And if night after night I was observing another world, wasn't it then real?* Instead I said "I know. I'm sorry. You didn't do anything wrong." I placed my face back on the table and stared at the floor through the wet glass and knew that in Peter's world of black and white, of rules and lines, this kind of logic or lack thereof wouldn't go far. That night, I fell asleep in his arms, our bodies cocooned in the night, and woke up to other possibilities.

17. The Almond in the Apricot

TOURAN

"You goddamn sons of bitches, you better run, 'cause if I catch you again stealing from my orchard, I'll flog you with my stick." The elderly man's yelling at us from the top of a steep slope and waving a cane in the air.

We're quite a ways downhill from him but continue running toward the stream, both scared of getting caught and also just enjoying the rush of being chased. The ground is a little slick from the morning rain, and rocks tumble down when our feet dislodge them. They pierce the flowing water below and disturb the resting birds—the only other things that stir the otherwise-still afternoon.

We stop at the stream and I stumble, my legs shaky from the run, but Nima's arms immediately wrap around and catch me before I fall in. He lets me go and we bust into giggles.

"That was so close," I say catching my breath for a second.

"But fun."

"And worth it." I take out an apricot from my pocket and extend my hand to proudly show him my loot.

"How many you've got?"

I start to empty my pockets. "Only two. I thought I had more. Maybe they fell out."

"Well, fear not, look here." Nima takes three out from his front pockets and one from each back pocket.

"Five. Whoa! You did good."

We take off our shoes, stuff our socks inside, and leave them under a tree on the bank. He puts three of his apricots down on the ground next to our shoes and sticks the other two back in his pockets. I bring both of mine with me.

I step into the water. It's super clear and frigid. The small blister on the little toe of my right foot feels so much better. Nima rolls up his pants and follows me in. We each bend down and wash our fruit. Much of the stream water comes from several mountain springs, and other than the occasional feet that pass through or some animal swimming or drinking from it, it's super clean. The strong afternoon sun beats down on our soaking feet, making them look like they're floating. The water cools the sun-warmed apricots. We walk back to the water's edge, sit on the dirt with our feet submerged, and eat our harvest.

"These taste so much better than the ones in our orchard," he says of the few trees in front of our little rental.

I take a bite into an apricot and the flesh bursts in my mouth, an exploding sugary sun, its juice running down my fingers like little rays. "They're so sweet."

"Maybe they just taste better because we stole 'em." He licks the liquid trailing down his wrist.

"No, they're definitely sweeter." I take a pit out of my mouth and aim it toward a tree on the other side of the water.

"Don't throw that away." He grabs my hand and pulls it down.

"It's a pit."

"There's an almond in there if you break it."

"No there isn't," I say.

"Yes there is."

"Almonds come from almond trees, not apricot trees."

He takes the pit from me and washes it in the stream. Then he puts it on a large rock and looks around until he finds another rock and uses it to crush and break the pit. Inside's a cream-colored, tear-shaped nut, much like an almond.

"Here, eat it." He extends his hand to me, holding up the nut like a trophy. "Try it."

I shake my head. "Nuh-uh."

"Go on."

I take it from him and, examining its smooth flesh carefully, I hold it to the sun. "How do you know it's not poisonous?"

"'Cause I've eaten them before. And I asked. It's only poisonous if you eat way too much, like everything is anyway. It's an almond."

"It is not an almond. I have seen almond trees," I say. "There are actually a couple of almond trees around here. I can show you. This isn't an almond."

"Trust me, just eat it."

I put the nut on my tongue, move it around, and then crush it between my teeth. The sweet and milky flavor of an almond fills my mouth. "Holy cow! This tastes just like an almond. I don't believe it."

"Told you." He lies back on the ground, smiling proudly.

"I'm a believer!" I also lie back and start to stare at the sky through the empty spaces around the tree branches. Their leaves sway to the lazy afternoon's rhythm. The aftertaste of the almond, this seed that lives inside another fruit, is still in my mouth. I move around the leftover bits of it with my tongue and wonder what I'd find if I could crush the bits with a tiny hammer, a seed to another seed and then another. Is that how this all works? There's only one small cloud up in the sky. Otherwise, everything is an aquamarine blue. Just like a cartoon. A light mass of air brushes over my face, carrying with it the smell of jasmine from the bushes on the other side of the stream. I keep twirling my foot in the water. Nima is staring up too; his light brown curls spread on the dirt. I raise my foot up quickly and suddenly splash him.

"Hey!" He's startled but smiling. Then he does the same and gets me back.

I get up and stand in the stream facing him, cup my hands together, and start throwing water on him. He gets up to chase me and I start running around in the water, doing my best to get away. We're screaming and laughing at the same time. We're both super soaked, and I sit on the smooth stones at the bottom of the stream 'cause it doesn't matter anymore. He sits next to me. The water, slowly rushing by, reaches a little higher than our waists.

"Well, now, our moms are going to be really happy when we go back dripping wet," I say.

"You started it," he says, allowing an eddy current to move his hand around.

"It was just too easy. You were so oblivious," I say. I can't tell if it's from the running around or the excitement of playing in water with my new favorite person, but I'm happy and feel like the sun is concentrated on my cheeks.

Nima keeps looking at my face and not saying anything. His eyes look like gooey honey in the sunlight.

"What? Why are you looking at me like that?"

"I'm just wondering if you wanna kiss?" He looks down at his hand.

"You mean *kiss* kiss? On the mouth?" I say.

"Yeah, why not?"

I know he has kissed girls before. He's thirteen and a half years old and my friends told me that he hung out with this girl named Panny and even bought her a leather bracelet. I'm younger and never seriously thought about kissing a boy. I mean, I have, but not about it actually happening. But I'm up for it. I mean definitely with Nima. He's the cutest boy I know.

"Okay, but only if you don't tell anybody," I say. By "anybody" I really mean my mom 'cause I think she'd kill me if she found out.

"I won't, and stop worrying about your mom," he says as if reading my mind.

I move myself closer to him and stick my face into his, close my eyes, and press my lips together. He leans forward and I feel his lips touching mine. My mouth opens slightly and his lips fall into that just barely open space and send the fastest flutters I've ever known down my mouth into the rest of my body. It's so strong that I immediately close my mouth and keep it locked tight. And as quickly as our lips touch, we both pull back. I take my right hand out of the water and wipe my mouth, making it wet.

"Next time you should leave your mouth a little open." His eyes look bigger than usual.

"Why?" I say.

"Because kissing with your mouth closed is like kissing your aunt."

"I'll think about it." I stand up and start to wring my shorts. "I'm going to sit out in the sun to dry off. They won't let us in like this." I walk out of the water. He follows.

18. Office Mechanics

NEW JERSEY

What had been left of the coffee had turned into a thick sludge at the bottom of the pot. After quickly rinsing the pot, I turned the filter basket upside down in the garbage, put in a fresh filter, and emptied two coffee packages into it, looking around like a criminal when adding the second package. I liked my coffee strong. I hit the on button and waited till the hot water started dripping into the carafe.

Empty mug in hand, I walked to the mailroom to check my box and to kill time. Orderly brown wooden mail cubes lined two walls of the small room. I let my eyes run from the top to the bottom of the column where my box was placed, looking through others'. It was all about compartments, limits and bounds of where our cars, our offices, our mail, and ourselves fit into the world. There was nothing of importance in my mail cube—a couple of water and sewer pump catalogues. I slowly flipped through each one before throwing them all in the large blue recycling bin with the catalogues others had tossed. The aroma of the dark roast brew circulated in the room.

Peter is the one who got me hooked on strong coffee—sort of. A few months into seeing each other, he'd arranged for us to go on a trip up to the picturesque town of Rhinebeck in the Hudson Valley, where a hot air balloon festival was being held. We were on the road before 4:00 AM, trying to make the 6:30 AM balloon launches. No later than twenty minutes in, I passed out in the passenger seat. When I woke up, in the parking lot of the Duchess County Fairgrounds, the sun was slipping up behind Peter's head, who'd opened the car door on my side and handed me a warm cup.

"Stopped at this famous coffee stand and got you some wake-up juice."

I took a sip and got out of the car to stretch my legs: "Whoa, woken up I am. This is strong," I said, jolted into consciousness. "But, mmm, so good."

Peter winked: "Like I said, famous! Now drink up so you're ready for the views."

"Oh, I'm ready." I pulled out my digital camera from my bag and sat on the grass next to the car with my legs out in front of me.

"Don't sit, we're going up." He extended a hand to me.

"Up where?" As soon as I said it, I realized what he meant. "You're kidding."

"Surprise!" He said, pleased.

I took his hand and followed, nauseous at the thought of being suspended in the air inside a wicker basket powered by nothing but fire and air. But the exhilaration of being next to Peter, of holding on to him, was infinitely stronger. Desire has a way of tricking one into being more adventurous. It didn't take long before my nerves were replaced with awe and serenity. Bright, colorful, tear-shaped aircraft scattered the sky against a backdrop of greenery and the Hudson River as we gently floated toward the emerging sun.

Maybe it had nothing to do with the coffee itself and more with the feeling I associated with that day, but ever since, I doubled up on the beans.

I poured myself a cup of office coffee when Tina rounded the corner: "Morning."

"Hey there, what's happening?" I stepped away, making room for her to move into the beverage nook.

"I had the worst date last night," she began with no introduction, as if she couldn't contain the story any longer. "It was actually funny. Sitcom material, you know." She was especially chipper. "The guy's some kind of improv actor and he started rapping at the restaurant."

"No. He wasn't rapping."

"Oh, he actually stood up next to our table and started busting out some Eminem song. With moves and everything."

I burst out laughing. "What did you do?"

"What was I supposed to do? I just sat there, looking at the tablecloth, getting shorter by the minute and hoping that no one I knew was eating there."

"I take it that was the last date?"

"Oh, yes. It was a setup by a friend of mine who thought we'd have a lot in common." She filled her cup.

"And you don't? I said.

"Blaghhhhh," she said after she took a sip of the coffee, "you made this, didn't you? Tastes like dirt."

"Sorry." I shrugged an apology. "Add some hot water." I pointed to the water dispenser.

"What did you do last night?" she asked.

"Nothing special. Went out to dinner with Peter," I said feeling slightly superior to the woman who was forever dating and finding fault with each potential partner—though I had to give it to her, this one did not seem like a winner.

"Oh my god," she sighed. "You're so lucky to have him. I'd give anything to find someone normal."

"The neighbor's chicken lays goose eggs," I replied.

"Huh?"

"It means the grass is greener on the other side," I said, unaware of the chill that ran through me until a moment later, when I realized I was hosting the ghost of another world, with word choices not quite my own but somehow mine. Foreign but familiar. Then I felt a small and unexpected pleasure from this, spotting unexpected color in the language of a bland workplace.

"You come up with some strange expressions," she said. "By the way, anything come out of your time traveling escapades?"

I didn't answer her, worried she might pinpoint the source of the expression, that she might ridicule me, that she and her drab world might soil my distant and colorful one.

"Sorry, bad joke. It's my way of lovingly asking if you still have the nightmares," she said gently, almost sounding concerned.

"No. They went away."

Tina couldn't help me, so why bother anymore?

"Told you they were nothing to worry about."

I gave her a slight nod. "You were right."

"Okay, back to work." She began to walk away but stopped and turned around. "Oh, and you know that initial assessment Mayfield Township report you were to put together for this afternoon?"

"Yeah?" I said, surprised she knew anything about my Mayfield schedule.

"They don't need it till the end of the week." She smiled.

"How do you know?" I asked.

"Overheard Charlie." A smile built on her face. Her pupils were dilated and her brows lowered—it was both a friendly and a wicked expression.

"Awesome, don't have to rush to get it done now," I said. "Thanks!"

"You got it." She gave me a Hollywood wink and walked away.

I followed her to the cube area and continued to my own box. Plopping myself on the office chair, I moved the computer mouse to wake it up from its e-slumber and maximized my mail program on the screen. I moved slow, knowing I no longer had a deadline that afternoon. Moving slow suited me. I was foggy. Losing sleep was starting to wear on me. Maybe I could get home early and get some rest. I yawned a big yawn and clicked "refresh" to see if there was any new mail. Mail from Kerr, perhaps. Nothing, so I turned my chair to face the other desk and started looking at a new property I was working on. It wasn't due back to the client for a couple of days, but since I had a bit of time, I decided to switch gears from Mayfield and work on it. It was a subdivision with thirty-five new homes and hopeful owners that were probably expecting their flushes to work. I couldn't let them down. The Einstein of sewers started calculations. I pulled the scale out of the desk drawer and started to sketch out the lines, carefully calculating where each manhole would go and how steep and what size the in-between pipes needed to be for the goods to flow without a hitch.

Minuscule particles of dust floated in the space between my eyes and the pale blue paper of the plans. I ran my fingers over the main sewer line on the smooth paper and followed it until it joined the city line on the street. It was all just lines drawn with a pencil and a three-sided scale, but those two-dimensional sketches became a real thing, a world that worked.

The day came and went. And by 4:50 PM. I was nearly finished with the initial sketches of my project and about to shut down my desktop when Charlie came by and stood over the cube wall. I looked up. "Hi there," I said.

Charlie always took a fatherly tone when he spoke to me. This time, he approached me like a boss. "I just got a call from Tom at Mayfield saying he didn't get your initial assessment report."

"Right, I thought that got pushed back," I said, confused.

"How so? Last we left it is you were to email them the initial plan and paperwork by midafternoon today."

"Right, well . . ." I started to say *Tina overheard you,* but then came the tumble of realization that Tina was wrong, that it would look so bad if I mentioned I'd overheard something secondhand and didn't bother checking on it first with Charlie, and I thought better of it. Instead I sat there, looking and feeling stupid. Defeated. And in a diminished voice said, "I think there was a misunderstanding on my part, I'll put it together this evening and will have it to you by the morning."

"It has to go to Tom," he said. "But, actually, print it out and I'll take a hard copy with me when I meet with them."

"Right. Of course. And I'm sorry, won't happen again," I said calmly, and as professionally as I could muster. Inside, though, I was full of rage, a slew of emotions tensing and releasing in waves. I was angry at Tina but more so at myself.

He walked away and I immediately started working. If there was any chance of getting this thing done by morning I had to get going. I'd have to talk to Tina the next day—besides, I couldn't even look at her then. So much for getting home and getting some rest.

By the time I finished it was just before 10:00 PM. Except for mine, all the cubicle lights in our department were turned off, and other than the sound of the cleaning crew that came through every night to empty out the garbage, mop the floors, and clean the bathrooms, it was quiet. I couldn't imagine the forty-five-minute drive home and wanted to put my head down and go to sleep right there on the plans and folders but reluctantly packed up and picked up my purse. I had just hit the light switch under the shelf of my cubby when I saw Gus, one of the cleaning crew guys, carrying a large basket of apricots into Tina's cube. I rubbed my eyes in disbelief. It was dark and late, so I didn't trust my eyes or my brain. I stretched my neck, making myself taller, straining to see her desk over the hardly lit and otherwise-still air. But all I could see was a mostly dark space. Gus was emptying out her trash can into the large one he wheeled around. I tried to locate the basket, the bright orange-yellow pile of fruit, but I couldn't see it. I searched with my eyes, scanning as fast as I could, but then he looked up and saw me and I looked away, pretending I was looking for my keys and had just found them.

"Ah, here they are," I said for unneeded effect. "Good night, Gus."

He waved back.

That night, Kerr sent me an email, one I didn't see until the next morning because I was too tired and distraught to turn on my computer.

Emma,

I know how anxious you are to get more info on new research re multiverses and I came across something that might interest you. A colleague of mine recently came out with a paper that has connected the extra dimensions of M-theory to hidden universes, if you will. I just read some of his recent work and believe there may be some implications of the research that match your interests. You might like to speak with him to see if he's taking on grad students. In any case, I can forward you his info or if you'd like to chat with me about it, I'm available this week.

Warmly,

Kerr

19. Castling

TOURAN

Everything seems sleepy. Flies circle in the soupy, still air. I'm lying down on the balcony, reading a storybook about a young reporter and some friends on a journey to find a treasure buried in the sea. The page is bleached with sunlight. We had a lunch of rice and some local fish from the river. It was white, and as long as a fish is white and not too fishy, I'll eat it. My parents are out for a walk, and Nima's mom and dad are washing dishes out in the yard by the faucet. Nima's inside, flipping through a magazine. I steal quick glances over at him every few minutes after reading some pages. Each time, I look at a different part of him—the loose ringlets of his hair, his caramel candy eyes or skinny fingers. I adjust my pillow to prop my head up and look out through the wooden railing. As if sprinkled with gemstones, the stream is sparkling in the afternoon light through the trees and makes me want to walk over and go cool down in it. But too heavy from lunch, I lie back and stare up at the sky through the treetops, wondering what Mimi is doing right now. I haven't seen her in more than a month and can't wait to tell her all about my adventures with Nima.

"Hey." Nima's feet are right next to my head.

I look up at him, squinting to keep the bright sun out of my eyes. "I didn't hear you get up."

"I'm sneaky. Wanna do something?"

"Like what?" I say.

"I dunno, play a game or go to the stream." He smiles. Maybe this is code to go back to the water and kiss again. "Or we can stay around here since it's really hot." Maybe it isn't code.

"Either way, I'm always up for the stream," I say in case it's code. "But I also brought a chess set, if you'd rather stay."

"Where is it?" he says as though he's up for anything.

"Hold on." Getting up seems hard, as if I have to push through heavy air. I go to my game bag in the corner of the room and pull out a wooden box. Back on the balcony, I rest my pillow on the warm railing.

"What color do you wanna be?" he asks, opening the box and taking out the pieces.

"Black."

"You know white usually wins."

"Nuh-uh."

"Yep. Everyone knows that. It's like athletes that wear red—they usually win."

"Then why bother playing if you're black? And why don't all athletes wear red?" I say.

He doesn't respond.

"See?"

Nima shrugs. "Well, that wouldn't make sense. Anyway, I don't know if it's true but I've heard it." He probably heard all this from his psychiatrist uncle. He would know this kind of stuff—all he does is read and talk about why people do things and how it affects them. Nima places all the pieces on the board. I haven't played very much and still forget where the pieces go exactly. So I wait for him to arrange his side and follow his lead. No need for Nima to know. It's bad enough I didn't know about the color thing.

"You sure you don't want to be white?" he asks.

"Okay, I'll be white. Should we flip a coin to see who goes first?" I say.

"No. You go first." He turns the board so the white pieces are on my side.

"Why? 'Cause I'm a girl?"

"No, cause you're white. White always starts first. That's why it has an advantage."

"Oh. I knew that." I didn't. Since I have no strategy or experience, other than playing with my dad a few times, I move one of my pawns forward—the one all the way to the right of the board. It's the only move I can think of making. Nima also moves a pawn, except his is the one in front of the king. Doesn't seem like he thought much about it. I move my pawn forward again, the same one. His hand wavers over the board for a second and then moves his bishop. It doesn't take long before half my pieces are dead and his bishops and knights are checking me every few moves. Frustrated, I have no idea how to play anymore. The only time I played with anyone other than Dad was with Mimi, and she plays more like me, so it was more fun.

I'm zoning out when I notice that Nima moves his king two spaces toward a rook and then lifts the rook over the king and places it next to it.

"Hey, that's cheating. You can't move two pieces at one time," I protest.

"This is a special move. You can only do this once."

"No, you can't. My dad never told me about this." I'm no longer leaning on the pillow and am sitting up, alert. *Cheater. He just wants to make me look stupid so he can tell his friends back home what a dodo I am. No way I'm falling for that.* The space under my arms feels hot.

"Yes, you can. Look, it's called castling and it's so you can protect the king like this." He's moving his fingers over the board to show me how it's done.

"I don't believe it," I say, feeling my eyebrows do all kinds of twisty moves. "Is my dad back yet?" I yell toward Nima's parents in the yard.

"No, sweetie, they'll be back soon. Do you need something?" Nima's mom responds.

"No, thanks," I say, frustrated. I don't want anyone but my dad to answer this one.

"Seriously, I'm not cheating," Nima says. "You never believe anything I say. Remember the almond?"

I don't say anything and fold my arms.

"Did I lie about the almond?" He reaches over and touches my arm, lowering his head underneath mine to catch my eyes. He sounds sincere.

I shake my head: "So you can change the places of two pieces just like that?"

"Yep, just like that. It's a way to protect your king. Believe me, you'll thank me next time you play."

"Okay, I believe you." I unfold my arms and realize I trust him more than ever now, knowing he just taught me something that will help keep my most important piece out of harm's way. "Changing places to be safe."

"That's right."

"You can be white if you want next time." A smile widens on my face.

"Deal!" He looks happy.

20. Chess Games

NEW JERSEY

Only a handful of folks were at work. I put my stuff down on the desk, went and picked up the newly printed contour maps for Mayfield Township from my mailbox, and walked over to Tina's cube. It was just before 7:00 AM. And her desk light was off. She wouldn't be in the office for at least another thirty minutes. The folks who were in were busy with work. I casually peeked around her desk, then crouched down and looked under it, and finally opened the large file drawer, which I knew was where she placed her purse. Empty. I got down on all fours and started scanning the area under her desk.

"What. Are. You. Doing?" She said standing above me.

"I, I, my pencil, I lost my pencil." I stood up and walked out to let her in. Mistrust hung heavy between us.

"It's behind your ear." She pointed to my head and went straight to her chair.

"Huh," I faked a plastic chuckle and reached behind my right ear. "What do you know?" I hoped my voice wouldn't betray me.

She said nothing, nothing about the open drawer, about the fact that there were hundreds of No. 2 pencils in our supply closet and that no one in their right mind would waste their time crawling around looking for the one they'd dropped in someone else's cube. And I said nothing, nothing about her being uncharacteristically early, about the basket of apricots I swore I'd seen the night before, and about her misleading me on my report. I had every intention of confronting her when I went to sleep the previous night and when I'd woken up that morning but then wondered what good it would do. Either it was an honest mistake or it was a lie. Either she was a friend or she wasn't. No matter, it was best I waited and saw what happened. Better if she didn't know I was onto her if she were deceiving me.

"Well, I better get back to it," I pointed to the rolled maps I had resting on her cube wall.

She put her purse inside the drawer, closed it, and turned her chair around to face the desk without looking at me, and I walked away carrying the weight of yet another secret.

I couldn't concentrate on the contour maps. My eyes were heavy and my bones were rubber from lack of sleep. I sensed myself drifting, ghostlike. I thought of chess. I'd only ever played it a couple of times as a kid and knew hardly anything about the game. I turned my chair away from my work, faced the computer, and searched for "castling."

What do you know? The damn move existed. A trickle of energy pumped me into a severe upright position, as if I had just found proof of something substantial. A special move, the only one in the game where two pieces shift at once—switching places and ending up suddenly beside each other, protecting the most vulnerable piece, the one in potential danger. The current of energy turned to a cold blow.

Peter had suggested chess one evening when he was watching a documentary about lion cubs on television and Spencer and I wanted to play something to kill the after-dinner lull.

"Okay, I found Trivial Pursuit, which means you have to play too, Peter," Spencer said as he pulled a box off the top shelf of the living room closet.

"No thanks," Peter responded without turning around, almost dismissively.

"Please, please, play with us," I asked, my hands clasped in a pleading gesture, like I had many times in the past when it was just the two of us.

"You guys play," he said, placing the burden of this and anything else he didn't want to do with me onto Spencer.

"Wait, this is from 1984. Forget that," Spencer said upon closer examination of the dark blue cardboard box in his hand.

"Why?" I protested, sitting on the sofa with my feet on Peter's lap.

"Because the history category will be more like ancient history, mi amor," Spencer said. "Why do you even have this?"

"Because it's an awesome game. Right, Peter?" Peter and I had played it once with friends when we first started dating.

Peter, more absorbed in the show about African lions than the two fools bickering about a silly game, didn't hear me. Or pretended not to.

"And what in the world is Pente?" Spencer pulled out a tube and examined it as if it were some mysterious artifact.

"Oh, I love Pente," I said, having forgotten about that game. "You have to align five stones on the board—wait—and then . . ." I was struggling to remember exactly how it worked.

"If it's so complicated that you can't even explain it, I'm out." Spencer put the tube back on the top shelf.

"Wait, you didn't even give me a chance." I walked to the kitchen to top my drink with more gin. "It's originally Greek I think, or wait, no, Japanese," I mumbled to myself.

"How about chess?" Peter said, snapping back into the Americas during a commercial break and reaching under the coffee table to get a hold of the nice stone set he'd bought me. It was sitting below the various coffee-table books I had on gardening and world beaches and exotic pools. The game was and had for some time been decoration, and I had unsuccessfully tried on several occasions to remedy that situation with Peter, who was a very skilled player.

Spencer and I secretly rolled our eyes at each other from across the room, both too lazy to have to think that much during a game, ever. And likely because we knew we'd be as dismal at it as we were at tennis.

"Don't think I didn't see that," Peter scoffed. "I'm just surprised that of all people you two won't play chess. You'd actually like it."

"How about this?" Spencer pulled out a Connect Four set with two happy children, likely from the same era as the Trivial Pursuit edition, dropping chips into a bright yellow grid.

This time Peter rolled his eyes, intentionally in full view of the two of us. But we paid him no attention.

I took the dusty box from Spencer and wiped it with a damp paper towel. "I didn't even think I owned this anymore."

"You probably shouldn't!" Peter smiled, pleased with his joke.

"I so loved this game." I held it to my chest, remembering the click-clack of the plastic chips hitting one another as my childhood friend Becca and I sat poolside, snacking on my mom's homemade chocolate chip cookies and juice.

Spencer brought the box over and set up the game at the bistro table. "Play first round and winner plays Peter?" He sat in ready position, cupping a large glass of gin and tonic with his left hand, the small flat mole on his ring finger in view.

"I'll sit this one out," Peter said with his back to us on the couch, happy to return to the Kenyan savanna on the screen and relieved of the responsibility of entertaining his girlfriend.

"Hey!" Tina knocked on the wall of my cube, disrupting my foray into game night and bringing me back to the present and the office and speaking as if nothing had happened. As if this day of all days called for a regular *hey*. She was carrying a yellow manila folder between her arm and side.

"Are those mine?" I followed her lead.

"Shirley said they just came in for you, data for the north part of Mayfield Township."

"Oh, yeah, we're starting inspections there soon." As soon as I said it, I regretted it. Why was I revealing anything to this person who potentially lied to me?

"Well, here you go." She placed the folder on my desk and took a step to walk away but turned right back after seeing my screen.

"You play?"

"Huh?" I looked at the screen and realized what she was referring to. "Chess? Not really. You?"

She nodded. "With my father, mostly when I was younger but a little bit now and then too when I go home for a visit. I'm not half bad."

"I feel like I want to properly learn." Why was I telling her anything? Chess or otherwise. I kept forgetting about the previous day.

"That's nice." She almost smiled and took a step into my cubicle. "We can play sometime if you want."

"Maybe." I didn't know what to make of the offer.

"I'll destroy you."

She left me wordless, managing to shoot back only a look in response.

"In chess, silly." She was laughing.

Maybe it was her laughter that was just a bit too quiet, or the way the lines around her mouth deepened when it widened, or her declaration to defeat me. Whatever it was, it finally kindled the anger that had been just under the surface since the previous evening: "This might all be fun and games to you, but it's my career you're messing with."

Tina's smile faded instantly, and a look of genuine surprise took over her face. "It's just a game," she said, referring to chess.

"Can I interrupt?" Charlie stopped by the cube, standing outside it and resting his elbows on the wall, his sleeves rolled up. Tina and I fell silent. "I got your report, thanks for getting it to me last night, but I think you need to look through it again. It seems you forgot to include the southwestern part of the city in the infiltration and inflow section."

"I did?" It was unlike me, this kind of mistake. I was a meticulous engineer, thorough, exact. But this had turned into a rush job. I was tired, and now errors. And a big one—missing a whole section of town.

"I've made marks where you need to make the additions. I'll need the new version by midmorning to have it when I meet with them later." His eyes were beadier than usual, a look of concern for both the report and me.

"Okay," I said, knowing everything would have to go off without a hitch for me to be able to get it to him in time.

"You know, if you want, I'm happy to help," Tina said after tucking her white button-down more into her tailored pants and standing up even taller. Her eyes glowing like a child given reign of a toyshop. Up until that moment I'd forgotten she was still standing there, and just like that she wedged herself into my conversation with Charlie and into my project, or tried to.

"I got it, thanks," I said, coiled like a spring ready to unleash. I wanted to push her out of the dialogue, out of Charlie and me. In fact, I wanted to literally push her out of my cube. It took all the power I had left in me to not aim a muscle at her. Instead I kept myself composed and sat up a little taller to combat how diminutive and messy I was feeling next to her, my hair in a wet and disorderly bun, dressed in an unironed and untucked blouse with jeans and slip-on sneakers.

"I'm just saying, I've studied Mayfield a bit and am familiar," she said confidently.

Oh, are you? Studying? Since when?

"Well, it's not a bad idea, given the time constraints. Thank you, Tina, for coming through. I love this kind of teamwork," Charlie said, smiling first at Tina, clearly pleased, and then at me, encouraging the partnership.

"Really—thanks, all, but I'll get it done."

"Well, I'll leave you two to decide." Charlie tapped his pen on the top of the wall and walked away, leaving me and Tina in our tiny gray cube of a world.

21. Photogenics

TOURAN

It's been gray all morning, and raindrops have been racing down the sky for the last couple of hours. The swollen stream looks more like a ferocious river. Everything outside is muddy. The trees droop under their burden of water and the air is thick. Dad's reading, Nima's father is napping, and our moms are talking and drinking black tea. Nima's listening to music on his headphones and I'm drawing. I already have a house and some apricot trees and a boy and girl drawn up and am putting in a sun and a blue sky. I start to color my sky from white to blue and wonder how nice it would be to lie on the ground, hold the pencil in my hand, and color the gray sky away. I'd take an eraser and get rid of the clouds and draw in a big sun with rays reaching right to the ground, into the stream and onto my face.

Nima nudges me. "Hey, whatchya doing?"

"I'm making a drawing of us. Here we are by the apricot trees. I should put in a little stream too, and that man chasing us!"

"Is my hair really that curly?" He smiles, seemingly happy to see the drawing.

"That's how I think of it." It's like he doesn't care about doing his hair but somehow still manages to look cool. Not sure I captured that in the drawing.

"Pretty neat. I like it."

"Do you ever think how amazing it would be to be able to color the world?" I ask.

"Huh?"

"You know, like a coloring book, just paint it how you want it." I close my sketchbook and put the pencils back in their case.

"You're strange." He sits next to me.

"Think of it! You could get rid of everything you don't like. And think of the colors. You could color things how you want. Your sun could be pink, your sky yellow! You could make everything look like a cartoon."

"And how's that a good thing?" He opens my sketchbook and looks over at my drawing more carefully and says, "Hey, this is really good. You're a good artist." It's as if he is seeing it for the first time.

I shrug, acting as if I don't care but instead want to do a cartwheel and give him a hug after hearing the compliment. "You can have it if you like. It's us, after all," I say as coolly as I can, even though I just want to rip it out and shove it in his face.

"I'll pin it above my desk at home."

"I'll pull the page out for you when I'm done." This time I can't stop from half smiling. "Wish we could go outside."

"Yeah, me too," he says.

We sit there quietly, watching the rain. Thinking about our next move until he finally says, "I know what to do. Wanna take photos of the rain?"

"You got a camera?" I'm excited that we have a plan.

"No, but we can make one." His eyes sparkle like Mom's amber ring.

"Make a camera? They do that in factories. You need machines and stuff."

"No you don't. The first camera wasn't made in a factory. Haven't you ever heard of a pinhole camera? It was in that book I gave you."

I shake my head, but after the whole almond and castling thing, I'm thinking maybe I should just go along with him. "I haven't read the book yet but I brought it with me."

"Let's go see if we can find stuff to make one."

I get up and follow him. We grab a couple of plastic bags from Mom's shopping trip earlier and hold them overhead while we go through the yard to get to the kitchen. Rain is splashing dirt around, and my feet and ankles are already muddy and gross.

"What are we looking for?" I say once we're under the safety of the kitchen roof.

"A box or a tin can or something we can use for the body." He is rummaging through the cabinets and I start doing the same. "Basically we need a black cube or container."

"Okay," I say. There isn't much in there—some cups and saucers, a few dishes, spices, a large burlap sack of rice, and a few plastic bags of beans.

"Then we make a tiny hole in it that turns the light from one place upside down in another." Nima's talking faster than normal, happy to explain it all to me.

I don't really understand what that sentence even means, but I don't want to spoil his excitement. I open the drawers next to the sink and find a plastic flatware organizer with knives and forks and spoons neatly tucked in, and I know this must be my mom's handiwork. She lays everything out the same at home too. I'm about to close it when I notice an envelope peering from underneath the white organizer. It's unmarked and not sealed. I open it and see pictures, first of Nima's parents with a man I don't know and then photos of the man alone. Then another one of him and a woman.

Nima has found a box of sugar cubes he's emptying into a glass tumbler. "We can use this."

"Hey, look at this," I say. "Who are these photos of?"

He gets closer and looks over at what I'm holding in my hand. "That's my dad's best friend. I called him uncle."

"Called?"

"He was killed in a raid a few months ago."

I look at the photo again and then at the others in the stack. He's on a snowy mountain in one, holding his skis up like a trophy, standing next to a tree in a different one, and has his arms around Nima's dad in another. I go through them all, different poses, clothes, and scenery. He looks so alive I can't believe he's dead. I don't even really understand what dead means. I've never really known anyone killed in a raid. Except for people in the news or ones I've heard of through friends and friends of friends. Guess I'd never seen a picture of anyone who died. Someone so close to someone I know.

"You must miss him." I hand over the stack to Nima.

"I do but it's okay."

I lean in and give him a tight hug, hoping to transfer something good into his body through contact. Though I'm not sure which one of us needs that hug more.

"No, it's not. You must be so sad."

"I'm fine." He puts his arm around my shoulder as if to console me. "It's my dad who gets sad sometimes. I guess that's why he brought the photos." He puts the envelope back in the drawer and we stand like that, watching water come down for a bit until Nima finally breaks the silence: "Okay, let's go back and see if we can find other stuff around the place." He puts the box, a pair of scissors, and an empty soda can into a plastic bag and starts moving quickly through the mess pouring from the sky.

"What more do you need?" I say loudly over the sound of the rain, running behind him back into the yard.

"Tape, glue, black paper . . ."

"We don't have all that."

"There's some stuff in the living room cupboard. We can put what we have together and when my parents go to town tomorrow we can have them pick up what we're missing."

We sit in the room and start cutting things up. I still don't believe this is all really possible but am willing to see if it'll work and hope that it does.

"You know that tree on our side of the stream?"

"The big one whose branches sprawl over the water and create that weird ginormous shadow?" I say, knowing exactly what he's talking about. We both love that tree.

"We should take photos of it when we finish this thing." He's gluing cardboard together.

I can imagine it in my head already, in that spot we always sit, our feet in the water, where we ate the almonds, the tree to our right, its crazy roots reaching into the water like thirsty tentacles.

"Maybe you can climb the branch and I'll get you and the shadow and the stream all in one shot."

I can see the shot—the tree, the light, and the shadows—as if I'd seen it a million times already.

22. Belonging

NEW JERSEY

Dry tears had glued my eyes shut. I woke up clutching a picture of Spencer and me that had been sitting on the nightstand. We'd gone to a Cuban festival in New York. His tanned face mashed against mine, Spencer with his long arm held the camera in front of us and caught the moment on film. In the background, folks are waving flags behind the barricade across the street, creating blue, white, and red blurs, much like in Monet's painting associated with Bastille Day. We looked young, my face still retaining the plump remnants of childhood and Spencer's hair a moussed-up messy bob, before he went and chopped it off. I was very excited about the festival and had initially put forth the idea to Peter.

"I don't really want to go," he'd said. "You should go with Spencer."

"We can just stop by the festival for a few minutes." I was standing over the bed, folding my Saturday laundry. "After, we can go to the public library. They have a Melville exhibit with his manuscripts and letters," I said, trying to bribe him.

"No, thanks," he replied dismissively. "You and Spencer will have a better time together at the festival anyway. You're both into that stuff," he'd said, on his way to the kitchen.

"What stuff is that, anyway? Shredded beef and rice or pressed sandwiches?" I yelled out of the room, but Peter didn't respond.

The picture unlocked the memories of that day and evoked all the feelings of being there, in the midst of that large crowd, timba music, and food carts pumping cumin-scented smoke into the air, crammed between tall gray skyscrapers.

A great feeling of melancholy came over me as I woke more, not so much because I missed Spencer, but from some other feeling of missing, a strange combination of nostalgia and homesickness, much like the one I felt when I thought of my childhood and past—those days of swimming at the pool with my friends Becca and Ashley. The three of us were inseparable. Wearing our colorful swimsuits, we'd forever line up to jump off the diving board. Then lie back on our towels until we could no longer take the crackling of our skin from the sun and then swim until our muscles were too weak against the resistance of the water. After a long day at the pool, we'd head into the house and my mom would make us spaghetti with meatballs. Our skins still radiating the heat we'd absorbed all day and eyes burning from keeping them open in the chlorinated water, we'd sit at the table on the patio and devour it as if that were the only meal we'd ever eat. Then we'd head to my room and sit on the bed, whispering about our crushes, the cities we'd travel to, the people we wanted to become, and the men who would love us.

Though my old neighborhood of Old Bridge was just a twenty-minute drive away, it was a place that no longer existed: my parents had long since moved down south, and Becca, Ashley, and I had become different people, living our own versions of adulthood—Becca a mom of three in Colorado and Ashley working as a lawyer in Seattle after having suffered multiple nervous breakdowns. That world no longer was, this new one existed, and now I felt as though I belonged in another—a different kind of nostalgia.

I pushed the covers off, put my feet on the floor, and placed the photo on my lap and looked back at Spencer's cheerful face. After we'd taken that photo, Spencer put his lips on mine and took another one. It was an innocent kiss, our lips closed, pushed together tight and just long enough for him to hold and click the shutter, but its reverberations unnerved me. Still, I hadn't allowed myself to admit what it was I'd felt, because I knew it would be the end of us. Whatever the two of us, or three of us, were.

I'd lost track of time and realized I was already late for work—again. I stopped at the answering machine and played Spencer's message: *Emmabelle, I miss you. Why didn't you come with me to the city? Husband loves you much.* My mouth was agape long enough that it was becoming dry. This was not Spencer's last message. It was his voice. My Spencer's voice but not the message, not the one he left me the night he died. This was new. My hand over the button turned to concrete. Was this another message? Did I hear this right? Where did the old message go? I finally managed to hit play again with a hand I could hardly keep still: *My not-wife, how I adore your voice. On my way to city. Last chance. Will miss you. Husband loves you much.*

It *was* just me. My shoulders relaxed. I hit the button again and again and listened again and again, until I verified over many attempts that it was all the same last message. I was tired. How I wished. How I wished. The clock's ticking seemed loud, as if telling me to get going. I picked up my things and ran out.

Charlie was in his office and lifted his eyes from his desk and shot a glance toward me through the glass door as if to take note of my lateness when I walked by—another tick in my record of failure. Tina's beanpole frame was looming in my cubicle. She was placing a bound document on my desk.

"What's going on?" I said as soon as I got to my workspace.

"Oh, it's the Mayfield report. I made some improvements to it."

"I thought I made it clear yesterday that I'd take care of it, and I did," I said.

"I know you did. But after you left, I heard the meeting got pushed back so I took a look on the server just to make sure it all looked okay, and I thought there was some room for improvement and thought you could . . ." She seemed proud of herself.

"Oh, did you? You just happened to take a look? Seriously, you think I'm that stupid?" I cut her off and slammed my bag on the desk, because if I hadn't slammed it somewhere, I probably would have smacked her with it. A couple of people looked up but went back to pretending to mind their own business.

"What's wrong, Emma?" she said at the lowest possible decibel. "You are acting so weird."

"What's wrong is that I specifically said I was fine, that I didn't need help, and you went ahead behind my back and worked on *my* report?" I was yelling and whispering at the same time, knowing every person in the vicinity would take notice of the turbulence in my cubicle, especially Charlie, yet somehow hoping they wouldn't.

"I'm sorry, I didn't realize it was such a big deal. You just look so tired and distraught, and Charlie seemed to have been picking up on the mistakes in the report. I just wanted to help. I don't want your job to be in jeopardy," Tina said, her tone so gentle and caring I started to think that maybe I was wrong, that she really was trying to help me. I started to doubt my convictions about her and felt slightly embarrassed, and I sensed some of the anger escape through my pores.

"I didn't think you would be so upset. Just let me know if you ever need help." She put a hand on my shoulder, with a sincerity I couldn't help but recognize as such, and then walked away. Though my stomach was still choppy, I felt a certain shame for accusing her and sat down at my desk, with my shoulders rounded forward and my lids iron. Tina was right, I *was* very tired. I glanced at the report. All the numbers and formulas jumbled, like pieces of a large puzzle that I was incapable of deciphering, and the more I looked at the pages, the more they scrambled. On those foldout pages where the sewer maps went, I couldn't even figure out if the arrows were going the direction of the slope. All I wanted to do was to put my head on the pages and let myself go into a deep slumber. That, I knew, wasn't an option. Instead I sat there staring at the page, looking for something, anything, out of place, out of the ordinary, but was unable of finding it if it existed.

"Ready?" Charlie was standing at my cube with his jacket on, carrying a briefcase.

"Yes, here it is and, again, sorry I missed the mark before." I stood up and handed him the report.

He nodded, put the report in his briefcase, and walked away.

When I turned to sit, I noticed Tina speaking to Joe in the hallway. They were whispering. Joe was one of the engineers I'd picked to be on rotation for my Mayfield outdoor crew. The two of them hardly ever talked to each other. In fact, Tina didn't much like him, thought him a bit crude, rough around the edges, which he was: he spent most of the days working outside, typically with other men, telling inappropriate jokes, peeing in manholes, and saying things like, "All you women want is to find a guy who'll buy you expensive gifts." He was what one might call sexist in that harmless way we all put up with but at times despise, but I knew how to deal with him. He was a good engineer and we got along with each other just enough—that's all I cared about. Now he was with Tina, who had always made sure to avoid him, chatting so intently. I stole as many glances as I could without them noticing but couldn't understand what they might be up to. The small feeling of trust in Tina I had felt just a few minutes before was already disappearing.

23. Suspended in Time

TOURAN

"Do you need help?" Nima asks.

"No, I'm almost there." I pull myself up with my arms and position myself on one of the lower tree branches. My limbs are sore.

"You should go closer to the end of it." Nima is standing on the stream bank, holding the camera we made together.

"I'll fall." The shallow stream below doesn't look kind to a falling kid.

"You won't, and if you do, you'll fall into the water," he says. "The photo would be a lot cooler if you were on the tip of the branch."

"If the camera even works." You wouldn't think that thing is even a camera—it's a box held together with tape.

"It does."

"I won't believe it until I see a photo."

"You never believe anything 'til you see evidence. Have I lied to you yet?"

He's got me there—he's never lied to me. Ever. I trust him almost as much as my parents. I shimmy myself toward the edge of the thick branch, gently sandpapering my bare thighs. The branch is bending close to where it joins the trunk, so I stop. My heart's quick beating makes me nervous and excited.

"Why'd you stop?" he says, looking at me as if to say *come on.*

"It's bending."

"That's what branches do, but it's sturdy and you don't weigh much."

I keep moving toward the tip. I know the boy would run in and catch me if I fell. He's becoming my best friend. We spend every day together. It makes me sad, realizing how much shorter the days are starting to get and that summer is moving toward fall super fast.

"Okay, good. Just stay there. Now, pretend you're diving in."

"Like stand up?"

"No, silly, I don't want you to fall! Just sit on the edge and put your hands forward like Superman. I'll only get your front half and it will look like you're flying."

I start to let go with my hands when a sudden wind knocks me off balance, and I thrust my entire upper half onto the branch and wrap my limbs around it and let off a short but loud scream.

"What happened?" Nima drops the camera and runs into the water. He's standing directly underneath me and holding my legs.

"The wind made me lose my balance." I'm shaky.

"Okay, come down. I'll help you." He's holding both arms up, gesturing for me to jump into them.

"No, I'm okay. I want to do this." I sit up again.

"Are you sure? I don't want you to fall."

I nod and he goes back to the camera, places it over a boulder, and angles it up. "Okay, you have to hold real still with this camera, or else it'll be blurry."

I look down at the rocks catching the sunlight under the clear water, hold out my arms, and pose, trying hard not to move a muscle. He peels off the tape from the pinhole and counts to ten. And puts the tape back on.

"Okay. You can relax now; I need to reload it for the next shot. We'll have this moment suspended in time."

"More like me suspended from a tree," I chuckle.

24. Dinner with Kerr

NEW JERSEY | NEW YORK

The circles under my eyes were especially unforgiving under the cold fluorescent office bathroom lights. I dug around in my purse and pulled out the concealer I had picked up at the mall the evening before and started spackling the imperfections of my face. I took a look after I was done and wondered if the color looked too yellow. Had Spencer been there, he would have known if "Medium Bisque" was the correct shade for my skin tone. But had he been here, I probably wouldn't have needed to use concealer.

I had just taken out my ponytail and was brushing out my hair when the door opened.

"Well, well, well, where are *we* going? Date with Mr. Peter?" Tina said teasingly, like she always did when she poked fun, but this time it felt sharper and flooded me with irritation.

"No," I said spreading on a dash of Very Berry lip gloss. "I have a meeting."

"At this hour? There must be some serious lookers there. Maybe I should go too. Look at you, all decked out," she said in her breezy way, even after the sabotage, as if she never meant any of it in the first place, as if she'd always been fake.

"Not really—just need to look put-together," I said, not giving in and checking out my eye makeup. The irises of my eyes were darker than usual, deep black holes from which little escaped. "It's not work. Some personal research." I hadn't told Tina about Kerr, and really there was nothing to tell at this point, so I left it at that.

"I see." In my peripheral vision, I could see Tina's right eyebrow inch up and imagined she was almost winking with her left eye. She always made that face when she didn't believe something. I couldn't care less at this point. She was just trying to get to me, to get me to lose balance and take away my job and maybe even Peter if she could.

I made sure my ivory silk charmeuse blouse was neatly tucked into the gray pencil skirt that accentuated my leftover curves. "Gotta go. Late." I made my exit before she had a chance to voice any more of her faux suspicions.

There was no heavy traffic heading into Manhattan, and I got in and parked within an hour. Emotionally, it was a less taxing trip in than the first time I'd met Kerr. Though, when my car went over the slope of the last stretch of highway before the Holland Tunnel and the tip of the skyscrapers shot up into view, the blade of Spencer's death dug into me again with such force that I felt my blood solidify. I shivered. The cars around me moved forward, their drivers going through the motions, facilitating this progress. Was it progress, this life of trivialities, of speeding toward the inevitable, toward nothing? But what choice is there other than to keep on moving, to go forward and pretend, for as many stretches as we can, that we don't know what lies ahead.

I kept my gaze on the horizon, beyond the skyline, on Kerr, into the expanse of a future not obscured by grief, at least not this one, and that promise got me into the city that evening.

With the sun hanging low, the street was cast in shadows. I took out the little sheet of paper and started walking three blocks north to "Sheba," the Ethiopian restaurant Kerr had picked for us to meet at. It was hardly a ten-minute walk from my car, but the balls of my feet were already hurting. I wasn't used to wearing heels, and when I did, on special occasions, I had the suburban luxury of riding in a car and sitting all the way to my destination. But despite knowing I'd be walking, I felt the need to torture myself that evening. I don't think anyone on that street, or Kerr for that matter, cared or even noticed that I appeared to be five foot eleven inches, at a mere three-inch height advantage. But Spencer always said that it's not the height gain that matters, it's that heels make you walk differently, more elegantly.

Kerr was standing outside the restaurant. He was wearing a sports jacket with jeans and an untucked white button-down. Crispy clean, he smiled asymmetrically as soon as our eyes met, exaggerating his cheekbones, and I felt that familiarity and connection that I'd experienced the first time I laid eyes on him on the television screen and again when we'd met. It made me feel faint and delicate. I reached out to shake his hand and my right heel caught in a crack in the ground. My foot wobbled and I lost my balance.

He caught my arm with disarming sweep of a hand. My heart was still in free fall for a beat or two and I could feel my skin ablaze.

"You okay?" He let go of my arm, but the recognizable warmth of his grip seemed to linger for a few more seconds than necessary.

"You're quick." I nodded and pulled myself together and somehow our handshake turned into a hug when he leaned in and wrapped his arms around my shoulders. I closed my eyes and fully allowed myself to feel the closeness of our bodies.

The restaurant was narrow but deep and dotted with small wooden stools arranged around colorful handwoven baskets used as tables. Dim lights, candles, and the warmth of mahogany statues made the room especially cozy. The host seated us in a back corner.

An attractive, tall waitress with dewy dark skin came over and laid a cloth napkin on my lap and offered us drink menus.

I looked at the list of drinks but was unsure if ordering a glass of wine would presume something this wasn't. Was it a business meeting? A date? Something in between?

"Maybe we should get a bottle?" Kerr said, saving me from my alcohol dilemma.

"Sure." I couldn't drink more than a glass or two since I had to drive, but I was too thrilled to complain.

"Is red okay, or would you rather . . ."

"Red is perfect," I said before he had a chance to finish. "Your pick."

He smiled. "Looks like we're on the same page," he said, pointed to something on the menu, and placed our bottle order when the waitress returned. Spencer preferred red too. It made an uncomfortable amount of sense.

"What a cute place," I said, scanning the room, nervous of dead air.

"It's probably the best Ethiopian food you could have outside of the country," he said, with the enunciation that I enjoyed listening to so much.

"Have you been?"

"Just once, I was on my way to South Africa for a conference and I had a layover and decided to extend the stay just to explore."

Explore. Of course, he was the type to explore. "I've always wanted to go to Africa. My best friend spent some time in Tanzania and, come to think of it, in Ethiopia too—Addis Ababa."

"Africa's such a completely different place. If you ever have a chance you should visit. I find that every time I travel somewhere new, especially a place so dissimilar to ours, it opens worlds to me."

Believe you me, I've had worlds opened up to me that you can't even dream of. I nodded in agreement.

The waitress brought over the wine and poured a little for Kerr to taste. Once he nodded approvingly, our glasses were half-crimson. I knew a little alcohol would restart blood flow to my peripheries.

"Thanks for meeting me here," he said over the loud chorus of patron voices and soft music and raised his wineglass. "Cheers."

We locked eyes for a second and clinked glasses. I took a big gulp. It took all I had not to keep staring into his eyes, not to get lost in that green sea.

"So how about you? Have you done much traveling, Emmabelle?" Kerr said.

I stared at him in disbelief. Wide-eyed.

"Emma, are you okay?"

Did he correct himself or am I so desperate to hear what I want to hear? "Yes. Travel, not really, mostly domestic, some conferences and things, and Central America," I said, working hard to string words into a coherent sentence. "But Africa's always been on my list. I guess it's on everyone's list." I smiled, having pulled my thoughts together.

"You'd be surprised how many people are not that curious."

"Actually, you're right. I take that back. I have friends and coworkers who are content with the daily grind, with their once-a-year trips to the Caribbean and their Hondas." I had once put the idea of an African trip to Peter and, when he showed no interest, never brought it up again.

"And you? Are you content?" he asked, looking dead into my eyes, his left eye squinting with his half smile.

"I was, but I don't think I am anymore."

"What changed?"

"It's like what you said about traveling: when your world opens up and you get a glimpse of what could be out there, it's hard to stay in the same structure you fabricated for yourself. If that makes any sense." I decided it was best to leave Spencer out of it for the moment.

"It makes perfect sense." He seemed interested in knowing me, despite that awkward first meeting, or perhaps because of it.

"It's like you're standing at the edge of a cliff, seeing this vast plain of possibilities, and all you have to do is jump." I was revealing too much. More than I wanted to, but it was easy to tell him things that I didn't wish to divulge to everyone else, the extras in my life. Or was it the wine?

"And are you going to jump?"

"When I have the courage."

"Just the fact that you're on the edge and have the eyes to see the possibilities is a sign of bravery."

"I don't yet know where I'd be jumping to."

"Maybe just jump and see where you land," he said.

This guy got me. More than I got me. In the way that Spencer got me. The words going back and forth, like a Ping-Pong ball, seemed to hit their target each time.

He suggested a platter for two to share and I agreed, and so we continued with our chatter. I observed his movements, the random small hairs poking from the edge of his jacket cuff, and his Spencer eyes. After reliving our meeting and reimagining him over and over, he was actually sitting across from me in the flesh. I wanted this night to last forever.

"So the paper I told you about over email." He pulled out a thin stack of papers stapled in the corner and handed them to me. "This is my colleague's work that came out in *The Astrophysical Journal* last week. It's pretty technical, but perhaps something to keep for reference."

"I'm familiar with the journal and made a few copies of several issues from the Rutgers library, but the papers aren't exactly easy to understand." I picked up my glass only to realize I had already finished the wine.

"I'm impressed." He smiled and filled my glass. "Not many people poke into these journals unless they're physicists."

"Don't be. I try to read them but like I said, I don't get far. Sewer equations are much easier."

"The key is not to get too concerned with the equations. Read the abstract, the intro, and the conclusion and you will get the gist. But also, feel free to ask me any questions you have as you read through these."

I smiled back, for a little longer than I probably should have, folded the papers in half, and put them in my purse.

"It's pretty solid work," Kerr said. "As you know, traveling to parallel universes is possible when space-time bends onto itself and forms a loop."

I nodded.

"But to do that would require an enormous amount of energy, energy that's not available to us at the moment, the energy of a star. That's one of the major obstacles to building a time machine. But this work suggests that we wouldn't need this kind of energy to bend time. Imagine a doughnut-shaped vacuum where space-time bends around itself, forming a closed loop. If you were traveling around inside of the doughnut you could keep going to other parts of space-time, to another place."

I was lost. The only doughnut I could imagine was glazed with chocolate and made of, well, dough, but one made of vacuum? It didn't matter. I just wanted to hear him talk, to listen to his comforting voice. That night, what he said was less important. He could read the menu and I'd be lulled into bliss.

"Make sense?" he continued.

"I am a little confused. Does this mean someone could actually travel to another universe?" I asked, going back to my default question.

"The gravitational fields would have to bend in a very specific way, which is still very unlikely. So my understanding is still no, it isn't possible. But in the least it's another bit of info to throw into the mix, and, well, even if the consensus is still no, you know there are people working to understand this option."

"I see," I said, mentally in disarray and unable to tell whether it was the wine or the new theory or the fact that I was sitting in a restaurant with a strange and smart man, one who looked and sounded very much like my dead best friend, and one I was very drawn to.

"Look over it and we could always discuss it later."

I smiled. My hands were now warm and I could sense that my face matched in temperature.

"Can I ask you a question?" he said.

I nodded.

"How did you get so interested in this kind of research? There aren't many people who want to make this their graduate research." His tone was soft and his face devoid of judgment.

I swallowed while trying to think of a decent answer. My brain kept burping the truth into my mouth, but I wouldn't let it get out.

"I took a modern physics class in college and became interested in the concept. You know the bending of time. And then I learned more about black holes and wormholes." I tried to insert some scientific concepts into my explanation to show that I had done my homework. "Recently, I started reading some physics texts that resparked my interest, and I'm hooked on it again and thinking I'd like to study it more."

"Are you thinking of leaving your current job to make a career change?"

"I suppose it all depends on what I find out." *I could be leaving my current world altogether at this point.* "I mean, maybe, if I can do the kind of research I want."

The waitress brought a large tray and placed it on our table. Different meats and vegetable dishes were laid on top of thin and spongy sourdough flatbreads.

"I have a feeling you might have a hard time finding an advisor working on exactly what you want, and even if you did—say I was able to advise you— we'd be hard-pressed to find funding for the project."

"I understand it will be difficult for all the reasons you're mentioning but I'm very determined to make it work, even if I have to work part-time and fund it myself. I just need an advisor."

"Well, I'll see what I can come up with," he said, giving up, as if he was thinking I was hopeless. I wasn't sure if he meant what he can come up with in terms of advisors or if he himself was going to advise and was coming up with funding ideas. But I didn't ask and we didn't chat further about it the rest of the evening. That road had ended, and all I might do by continuing to travel it was lead us to a quick stop.

Instead we talked and ate and laughed, and when he walked me to my car that evening and said goodbye, he held my hand for a moment too long, and for those seconds I felt so happy to be there, with him in my world.

25. Vanished

TOURAN

I wake up just as the first light cracks open the dark sky. I don't move but let my eyes wander around to see if anyone else is up. Mom and Dad are asleep; so are Nima and his parents. It's too early. I sit, wipe my eyes open, push the covers off as quietly as I can, and then stand up, tiptoeing away from my bedding and walking out to the yard. I'm not making a sound. I have to be careful because everything in the world is still quiet. Still sleeping. Even the birds aren't up yet.

Without changing out of my pajamas, I put on my shoes, and then grab the plastic bag I've been hiding behind the large planter of geraniums and walk toward the stream. It's a bit chilly still, and the air hits you like little bits of ice that vanish on skin contact. That's how summer is when you're in the mountains—crisp in the mornings and evenings, warm and sunny in between.

When I get to the stream, I take my sneakers off and roll up my pajama bottoms to step in. The water isn't its usual glistening self but is instead a deep, dark hue, a mirror of the sky. And the temperature matches the cold colors. I bite down on a yelp before it can turn into a scream and submerge both feet. My murky reflection is sinking into the clear water. The currents create lines and grooves on my face, forming an image of an older me. She, with long hair and sullen eyes, is peering back. I reach into the water to touch the reflection, but the ripples blur the image and all I see in the water is good old me.

From the bag still in my hands I take out all the apricot pits, lay them on the dirt next to the water, and flatten the plastic. I bend down and one by one wash each pit, making sure there's no bit of fruit hanging on and no dried saliva left over from when I ate the flesh, then I carefully place each pit on the bag to dry. I'm working as fast as possible so I can get back before anyone gets up and realizes I'm gone. My feet are numb. I look down and see that everything below my ankles is the color of beets. I continue washing, watching the water pull tiny bits of pulp away downstream. I've been saving these the whole summer, carefully stashing them away in my bag and hiding the bag from the eyes of everyone in the house. The past week or so, I've started eating more apricots just to have more pits. I can't wait to see the surprise on Nima's face when he realizes what I've been doing. All the pits are now clean. I step out of the water. When I'm grown-up and have my own house, I'll fill the yard with apricot trees and maybe some jasmines. I want it all to smell like here. Before I put the bag away, I decide to have a taste of that milky, sweet nut. I take a deep and fast breath in and let it out through a smile, put one on a large rock, and smash it with a smaller one. The light brown shell cracks into small fragments, and I start to pull the pieces apart, looking for the prize—the core. But it's empty.

It's as if the almond inside vanished the minute light reached it. I examine the shell with shaky hands. The almond is not on the dirt around the rock either, just some pebbles, leaves, and branches. It's a bad one. I should open another, though I don't want to take away from Nima's stash. But can't help it.

I crack a second one. Empty.

Okay, last one—again unoccupied with a nut. I decide to stop and hope it's a coincidence and that the rest are filled with almonds. They have to be.

To hide it, I pull the bag to an area behind a tree, one Nima and I never go near. I run back to the house, leaving the pits for the sun to dry off, climb back under the covers, stare at the ceiling, and imagine one day living in a big white house surrounded by apricot trees. My husband and I will pick them every summer and crack the shells together. We'll have bowls of almonds all around the house for all our guests. He will have warm honey eyes like Nima. I smile and allow my eyes to close.

26. Smoke Signal

NEW JERSEY

I couldn't stop thinking about Kerr and that tiny moment by the car. His bony hands wrapping around mine. The first boy I kissed in this world was Patrick Denner—he lived three houses away from ours. We were both ten years old and had known each other since we were five, when his family moved to Jersey from Connecticut. He never asked me if he could kiss me. We'd been swimming at the community pool and were sitting on the hot concrete to dry off, our feet dangling in the water, sipping saccharine through the skinny plastic straws of our grape juice boxes when he reached his head over and gave me a kiss on the mouth. He pressed so hard that I got grape juice all over my belly and almost lost my balance and fell back into the water. He then ran away and left me to walk home by myself.

"Anything exciting in there?" Joe asked, looking down.

I glanced up from inside the manhole toward his upper silhouette obscuring the light. "Nope, seems to be okay, the steps are a little corroded but the pipe is in pretty good shape. In fact, I can't imagine these pipes being more than eight or nine years old." I looked around the manhole one more time, a cylinder made of bricks, and started climbing up.

Joe and I had been inspecting the Borough of Shrewsbury's sewer system since morning. We started at 6:00 AM to beat the late July heat. This was our last project before we began the behemoth that was Mayfield Township. We had to complete a full inspection and identify any potential leaks and illegal connections within two weeks.

"Let's smoke this baby up," he said, pulling the smoke machine close to the manhole.

That was one of the more fun parts of our job—being outside and essentially playing with a toy. We put smoke into the manholes and then walked around the street to see where smoke was leaking. If the roof or yard drains suddenly started fuming, we knew that someone had an illegal connection to the sanitary sewer system, meaning extra water was going to the sewer system and being unnecessarily treated at the local plant. We'd write the property owner up and the town would either ask them to undo the connection or fine them. It also helped us identify leaks, through faulty pipes or cracked mains, within the sewer system. Give a couple of engineers a smoke machine and time outside, and you won't find them complaining.

"Nothing here," Joe said, coming back from the north side of the street.

"Yup, all good here too." I walked back to the smoke machine from the south side.

"Let's move on out." I started packing up the gear and Joe put the manhole cover back on and headed to the car. "Ready?"

"Hold on, my pants are ringing." I reached for my cell phone. It was Peter.

"Hey there. How was last night?" He meant my evening with Kerr. I had told Peter that I was meeting a physics professor for some personal research but left out the details. And he never asked.

"Good," I said with a pit in my stomach.

"You out in the field?"

"Yeah, just finishing up a smoke job."

"Listen, I've been meaning to ask you something and was wondering if you want to hang out this evening. I know you said you might go to happy hour with work folks but if you can postpone that, it'd be great."

"Yeah, sure, that'd be no problem." I would have preferred not to miss out on happy hour, hoping to chat with Charlie to make sure he wasn't too annoyed with me. But slightly guilt-ridden about my blissful night with Kerr, I felt I owed Peter the evening.

"I'll see you at your place around six thirty, then. Don't cook—I'll bring pizza."

I headed to the pickup, where Joe was sitting on the tailgate and waiting for me.

"Done socializing? Ready to head back to the office?" he asked and handed me a Gatorade.

"Let's do it. We still need to write our report and it's already nearly 3:40. And I gotta get home on time."

"Date with the mister?" he winked before getting into the driver's seat.

"Something like that." I rolled down the window. Joe and I chatted about our relationships when we were out of the office because we were on jobsites for days at a time, sometimes, and there are only so many topics surrounding sewers—there is the manhole, the pipes, the steps, the smell . . . But really, how much can you say about human waste infrastructure?

"He wants to ask me something," I said quietly, mostly to myself.

"Maybe he's going to propose or ask you to move in with him." He started the car.

The guilt I'd felt turned to horror. A possibility that hadn't occurred to me. "Holy shit. You don't think, do you?"

"I don't know, but why do you look so scared? You are a woman, aren't you?"

"My god, you're sexist."

"I never said I wasn't. How long have you been together, anyway?"

"Close to three years, rounding up that is."

"Well it makes sense, no?" He turned the radio volume down until Tom Petty and the Heartbreakers' "Free Fallin'" became a muted beat. "I mean, aren't you worried about a biological clock or some ticking timer you women think about?"

"You're freaking me the hell out, Joe."

"What? I thought women want more commitment." His words walked straight into my brain, sparking a quick outpouring of chemicals that resulted in frozen fear.

"Shit, why'd you have to put that in my head? Now I'm really scared. What if he does want us to move in together? Shit," I said, feeling my bronchial tubes narrowing, and stuck my head out the window to dry the sweat on my face, hoping the wind would carry the thoughts away.

"Sewer is supposed to flow down there, not out of your mouth, missy." Joe pointed to the street. "Besides, don't you wanna move in with him or marry him?" he said sincerely this time.

"I don't know. Yes, eventually but not now. Ah, shit." I reached back to the small seat in the back and from the pile of papers there grabbed a folded-up map and started fanning myself with it. The window wasn't doing enough cooling and we had no AC in the truck.

"Well, maybe it's nothing. I just guessed. Maybe he wants to ask you why you never want to marry him." Joe started laughing, proud of his little funny. "You women are so damn weird and you say we don't get you."

I stopped listening to him and looked out at the blurred images of houses and lawns going by through the open window. The rest of that afternoon was an impressionistic distortion.

Peter's car was in the parking lot, and I knew he must already have been in the condo. I thought about not going in, about staying in the car or even driving away. But gathered my stuff from the passenger seat and started a slow walk to the door. When I turned the key and stepped in, the bathroom door was closed, and I could hear him washing up. An aroma of freshly baked dough and tomato sauce wafted through the air. I closed the door behind me quietly and paused before putting the keys down on the counter next to his key to my apartment, not wanting to alert him that I was home just yet.

Those moments before he came out seemed so long and so short at once—as if some greater entity stretched time like an elastic band and snapped it right back. And soon the two of us were sitting across from each other on the floor with the round steaming pie between us on the coffee table.

I managed to pull myself together, but caught my hands unsteady when I reached for a slice of my favorite pizza: fresh mozzarella and basil. He was so going to ask me. Otherwise he would've gotten pepperoni, his favorite. I couldn't relax and enjoy the food. All I could think of was my future with Peter—a conventional future in a house with no apricot trees. But what the hell was wrong with me? He had been everything I wanted: sweet and smart and lovely. He had been enough. More than enough, in fact. Yet something just didn't feel right anymore. I needed more time, goddammit. I'd probably marry him if I could have time to think about it and figure things out. I bit into each slice carefully, half expecting to find a ring nestled in the cheese.

"Is something wrong?" Peter asked. "You keep looking at the pizza."

"It's work. We have this big, big project with lots of sewers. Big. Like, huge big." I stopped before I said *big* again.

"I even got them to make it well done. Just the way you like it." He reached over and wiped a little sauce from the corner of my lip with a napkin.

"It's perfect."

"Well, in that case, I guess this is as good a time as any to ask you what I've been meaning to."

I quickly got up from the couch, walked to the kitchen, and grabbed an open bottle of Cabernet sitting on the counter.

"Hold on." I pulled out a couple of regular glasses, the first things I could get my hands on, and hurriedly poured myself half a glass and downed it in a big swallow in the kitchen. I walked back to the living room and handed him a glass and started pouring. "Here you go."

"I've never seen you chug," Peter said, taking a small sip and putting his glass on the coffee table.

"I got thirsty all of a sudden." I sat back across from him on the floor.

"Want me to get you some water?"

I shook my head and this time poured a full glass of wine for myself and took one big sip and tacked on a soft "All good, thanks."

For a moment, Peter slipped into silence and almost frowned at the disruption. I put a hand on his, and his face eased up almost instantly.

"Okay, here goes," Peter started with a speech he had apparently prepared. "I have noticed you've been, understandably, not as happy lately. And I keep thinking what might help cheer you up. And cheer *us* up, really. And I think I have the answer." A winning smile sculpted his fair and chiseled face. Peter was very proud of what he was about to do, wearing a prominent mark of satisfaction on his sleeve. "Oh, wait, where's my bag?"

C'mon, bag, disappear, go away. No one will miss you.

"Wait, I need to use the restroom," I said in a desperate haste.

"Now?" Peter stopped looking around and shot me an abrupt look.

"Yeah, must be the wine."

"Sure, dear," said Peter, always tolerant. Too tolerant.

"Sorry, sweetheart. I'll be right back." Before he had a chance to say anything else, I got up and hurried to the bathroom. Closing the door behind me, I suddenly let myself go and slid down onto the floor, secretly hoping a wormhole would pull me out of this mess. I could just say no. I didn't have to marry, or move in with, Peter yet. Or was this my one chance in life to be with a wonderful human, one who loved me? Is it all that I'd get? I'd decide in the moment. With the help of the wall, I slid my way up to standing, flushed the toilet for effect, and walked back to the living room.

I sat down beside him and used all my might to force my mouth into a smile.

"Lucky for you, I found the bag too." Peter winked and pulled his black messenger bag out from behind the couch.

I swallowed air and nervously looked at his hand reaching in.

"Okay, here goes." He took out an envelope and handed it to me. "I booked us an all-inclusive vacation later this summer to go to Punta Cana. Five days. It's around a weekend so you should easily be able to take three days off."

My hands felt as though they were someone else's appendages, and I let the envelope go and fall gently on my lap. The wires of my brain disentangled.

"Say you'll go?" he said, still waiting for an answer.

"Yes, yes." Relief powered me into motion and I jumped onto Peter's lap. "Of course I'll go." I started kissing him on the mouth and the cheeks.

"Wow, you're happier than I thought."

I nodded in agreement.

"So you like the idea of going to Punta Cana?"

"Where is that?"

"Dominican Republic."

"Sure. I love Dominican Republicans."

Peter laughed out loud, "Dominicans."

"Well, then, I love the Dominican Republicans and Democrats." I really didn't want to go anywhere, but I was so happy this was not a marriage proposal, I would have accepted a trip to Mars. "More wine to celebrate, eh?"

"If I'd known you'd be so happy, I'd have planned it so much sooner!" he said sweetly.

We drank wine and celebrated most of the rest of the night—each of us celebrating something different. But doing it together, nonetheless.

After pizza, I lay my head on the armrest of the couch and put my feet on Peter's thighs.

"You know something? When I was a kid and our family watched television, Andy and I would lie on the carpet and my dad would sit at the end of the sofa, just like I am now, and Mom would put her feet on his lap. He would cup his hands to warm them because they were always cold. They'd both doze off until it was time to go to bed. And I'd think that someday, I want to find someone and be like them. That's all I want, Emma. Everything else I've got."

"And you have it now," I said between quiet sighs.

"I want you to want it too. With Spencer gone, it hasn't been the same, I know. I get it. If I could only erase the pain for you, I would."

"I'm not ready to erase it," I said, retreating my feet from his lap. "What else would I have if that's gone?"

"Happiness." He reached for my feet, but I wasn't giving them up.

"Everything is not happiness." I said quietly. "It's more complicated than just living like the family on *Leave It to Beaver.*"

"This went wrong." He shook his head and moved to the floor and knelt looking up at me. "I miss him too, you know. But I know it's different for you and I don't know what to do."

Neither did I. I kissed his head and held it in my lap. Peter and I were left to figure this one out on our own, without Spencer—a planetary system devoid of its star, in different orbits, living through a continual cycle of inadequate translations and unfortunate misunderstandings.

Whatever was left of the rest of the night was occupied mostly by silence. Tired of my own thoughts, I let my eyes close, and sleep quickly snuck its way in. Peter must have walked me to the bedroom because when I woke up horrified, we were both in bed.

I had dreamed I was the little girl and had taken Spencer to my other world to meet the boy and my family.

I was holding Spencer's hand and walking him through the little yard of the clay orchard house. He was dressed as I had seen him the evening before he died, a pair of dark jeans and a plaid button-down. I walked Spencer into the L-shaped room and started to introduce him to her parents. They stood up from the floor where they were sitting and shook hands with him. I then led him to the balcony to meet the boy, whose back was to us. He was facing the orchard and reading a book. Upon hearing our voices, he turned around and smiled. He stood up and reached for Spencer's hand to shake. But when their hands touched, they both started to become transparent—within a few seconds, when their hands had fully grabbed hold of each other, their fingers faded, followed by the rest of their hands. Their arms and the rest of their bodies, then, slowly disappeared into ether.

I knew this was a dream and not an episode. There was a banality to the dream compared with the vividness of being somewhere in the flesh inside another being's body. There is a flightiness, a light quality to things and a slowness to movements, a knowing that you are in a dream. Like watching a movie.

The birth of a gentle sob woke me. I once had a similar dream about Spencer a few years ago but thought nothing of it. In that dream, I had brought Spencer home to Florida to meet my parents. When we walked through the door, he started to vaporize right into the air. It upset me greatly when I woke up, and I remembered it for a few days but had forgotten about it since. This dream, this disappearance, made me think of that dream. It was so similar, so eerie that I couldn't stop freaking out.

Peter rolled around in bed and said "Shhhhshhh, go back to sleep."

"I am just going for some water." I wiped my tears with the back of my hands and stood up and walked out to the kitchen. It was almost 3:00 AM. I was trembling. I had never made the connection between my dream about Spencer and his death. *This* was a warning.

I started again on that path. Could I have stopped his death? Spencer invited me to go with him the evening he was killed. But I was tired; I had worked outdoors most of the week, and I didn't feel like driving into the city and staying out late. Had I gone, things might have been different. I probably would have complained that I was tired, and we would have left earlier. Or my presence would have pushed a certain molecule left instead of right, and that molecule would have collided with another one, in turn having some kind of domino effect that changed the movement of everything around us, altering the position of each component in that scene, including Spencer and the car.

If only, if only—I went over every single if only.

I sat on the floor of my kitchen trying to think of what the dream meant, if anything—I didn't want any more people to disappear from my life, any of my lives. People died in both of my worlds. I didn't know how long I went over these thoughts, but eventually I walked myself back to bed and fell asleep again.

27. Taste of Summer

TOURAN

"Keep them closed," I say to Nima, leading him down to the water with one hand and keeping a cover over his eyes with the other. We walk past the tall walnut tree behind which we last kissed, our second time, away from the eyes of our parents. I glance up and take a quick mental picture of the tree— its thick dark bark anchored deep into the dirt and leafed branches reaching into the sky like antennas—knowing there are only a few more times I'd see it.

"They're closed," he says. "Where are you taking me?"

"You'll see. Careful, lift your right foot and take a big step. There's a big stone there. Just walk over it." I'm so excited about his present. I'm also a little sad because I know that in a few days we'll be going back to the city, and I won't be able to hold his hand whenever I want or play in the stream anymore.

"Okay, now you can sit on the ground," I say, softly pushing his shoulder down. I wait a few extra seconds before saying anything, to keep that brilliant bubbling feeling going for just a bit longer. "Open up now," I say. A little too loudly.

"This is the water we come to every day. Why did I have to keep my eyes closed?" He looks to the right and then left, his eyes searching the area and landing on me for an answer.

"Because I have a surprise for you." Happiness floods my chest. I sit down next to him and lay my backpack down on the dirt and take out the package I'd made. It looks like a sack, goodies held together with clear cellophane I'd found in the kitchen and tied up at the top with a small piece of rope and a red geranium I'd picked a little earlier and jammed into the tie.

"Whoa, what's this? You got me a present?" Nima's wide-open eyes look like glittering stars under the sunlight.

"Apricot almonds. I've been saving since that day you told me about them. It's for when we leave here, so you can remember the taste of our summer."

"There's so many in here. You must have picked like a bazillion." He takes the bag from me and moves it up and down. "It's pretty heavy!"

"Just a little every day." My face hurts from smiling.

"Should I open it now? Or save it?"

"I think you should save it and each time you miss the stream and the apricot trees, you can have one," I say. "But up to you. It's your present."

"Let's crack a few now. I want to share them with you." He is undoing the tie.

"Okay!" I say excitedly but then remember the other day when I cracked open the empty ones and just like that a pit starts to form inside of me, and this one isn't empty but hard and full of nervousness.

He pulls out a handful, places them on a rock and then smashes them with a smaller rock in one quick move. I almost can't look but can't keep my eyes off them either. Shell pieces fly all around. I look at the rock and quickly look away. But can't keep my gaze away for too long. I can't believe my eyes and rub them to make sure. Not only are there almonds but these are the largest and most perfect tear-shaped ones I've ever seen.

"Whoa, these are gigantic."

"It's like they are bigger than their shells," I say.

"Where did they come from?" He offers me the first one.

"Same place we got the others. Our orchard and the ones around." I put the nut in my palm and feel its smooth and almost polished texture with my other hand's index finger. This is at least twice the size of any we've ever cracked.

"I'm gonna miss this and all the fun stuff we do together." He's looking right into my eyes.

"Even when we did nothing." I lie back in the dirt and he lies back with me, so we're both staring at the sky. I place my almond in the middle of my chest.

"Hey," he holds my hand and swings it up and down. "We'll still see each other. It won't be like now, every day, but we'll visit each other's houses. Oh, and my birthday is next month—I'll invite you."

I get that feeling in my stomach like I did those couple of times we kissed. "I'll definitely come." Nima's never invited me to any of his parties. But now we're closer. "And we can call each other too."

"For sure."

He lets go of my hand and moves his upper body close and gives me a kiss. It's soft and wet. This time I open my mouth a little, like he'd told me to. I never want to leave the orchard. I don't even care that there isn't a pool here. We lie there, next to each other, for a long time, gazing at the clouds that look like they're on some sort of aerial sailing race, they're moving so fast. This time, I reach for his hand. We hold hands for a long time.

28. A Late Summer Afternoon

NEW YORK

Several weeks after his trip proposal, Peter boarded a flight to San Francisco to attend an annual writer's conference as a guest speaker for a few days, and Kerr called and asked to meet again. This time he didn't mention a paper or research and simply asked if I wanted to see him. I did.

We met at the East Seventy-Second Street entrance to Central Park on a late Saturday afternoon. Although it was the third weekend in August, a cold front made the day all kinds of glorious: the sun overexposed everything, green leaves fluttered against a seamless azure backdrop, and a cool breeze blew through the whole city like a soft whisper. Inside the park, on the grass, people sunbathed and dogs played.

We walked on a path past the frolicking with my peripheral vision focused on Kerr. His hand, swinging as he walked, was mere inches from mine. The small distance between us full of possibilities. Then I noticed it, a mole on his ring finger, a small dark brown flattened dot—a harmless detail. But it was in the same place, on the same hand, and I couldn't stop looking at it.

"Thanks for making the trip up again. I would have been happy to come to you," he said. The measured tempo of his voice, the enunciation of his syllables those of Spencer.

"I like getting out of New Jersey," I said. "Puts me farther away from work." I smiled.

"I gather you're not too fond of work?"

"Actually, it's not all that bad. I've just grown a little tired of it lately. It's not as challenging as it was in the beginning."

"Which is why you're interested in a career change?" he asked.

"It's one reason."

"And the others?"

"We'll need some wine for that."

"That could be arranged." He shot over an inviting look.

At the park's boathouse, rowboats were traversing the waters moving around the Lake's water lilies, a living Monet painting. We both stood still and took in the scenery.

"This makes me nostalgic," I said without thinking.

"Did you come here as a child?"

"Not here so much, but I loved, and still love, being around water. How about you?"

He shook his head. "I grew up in California, so there was a lot of ocean. Different kind of water."

Kerr stayed in California until he was eighteen, then made his way to the East Coast to study physics at Princeton University on a scholarship and later attended Columbia for graduate work. His father was a sculptor and his mom a secretary at a dentist's office. It turned out Kerr wasn't always very good in physics. In middle school, he became frustrated with his inability to understand basic concepts in science class and started reading up at the library to help him pass the class. He soon realized this was how he could understand the world around him and started reading popular books by Carl Sagan, John Gribbin, and the like and then became drawn to theoretical physics. By the time he reached high school he knew he wanted to make that his life's work. His only sibling, Helena, had gone on to become a graphic designer and worked as an art director at some ad agency in California, where she lived with a husband and two kids.

"The only scientist in the family? Dinner conversations must be something," I said.

"Same as any other family, I imagine. And you?"

"Oh, my story is boring. Born and bred in Jersey. An only child. Dad's a retired insurance agent, and I had a stay-at-home mom, both of whom moved to the warmer climes of Florida."

"And you stayed."

"I'm not ready for Florida yet. Not sure I'll ever be."

"There are other places."

"Are you trying to get me to move?" My skin was hot. *Who was I flirting with? Didn't he already know my past?*

"Hardly," he smiled. "But I get the feeling you're looking for something."

"I am. But I know for a fact it's not in Florida." I watched a couple struggle with their oars, going nowhere on the water, each paddling in a different direction.

"And the thing you're looking for, what is that?" He turned his head and looked over his shoulder at me. Had I turned my head to meet his gaze, the conversation likely would have gone a different direction right then and there.

"I don't know the what yet but I guess I know the why." I focused my eyes on the nautical duo.

He waited for me to explain.

"Because I don't want to end up in the kind of organized life my parents, my friends' parents, and everyone around them lived. Come home from a job every night, sit at the kitchen table having dinner and watching *Jeopardy*, clear the dishes, and force myself to stay awake until I'm so exhausted that I'm happy to go to bed in hopes of another day that'll be pretty much the same as the last."

"Sounds like most people's lives. And as one grows older and has to deal with the complications of adulthood, it's those quiet moments that are most valuable, don't you think?" The thick summer sun was bouncing off the back of his head, forcing me to squint. "There's something to be said about a peaceful, sedate life," he added, challenging me in a way I hadn't been before.

"I guess, but as a kid you think it'll be different. That somehow your parents didn't get something right but that you will, that you're in some way more clever than them. Then it turns out you really aren't. But something has changed in me and I guess I refuse to not do anything about it. And if it ends up that this is all there is, then at least I know I've made an effort and I can live the routine life knowing so. I feel as though I haven't even tried to escape it. Actually I've probably fallen into this routine a bit sooner than my parents did and now I keep thinking that if today were my last day, would this be the way I want to spend it?"

Kerr was silent, and a mirage of responses seemed to appear in the vacuum of a reply. That he had not yet given up on a woman on the brink of the irrational. That he could take off then and there. Or that he'd really let her ideas percolate in his head to brew into some kind of answer.

"Life doesn't have to end up being a routine," he said. It was a familiar expression, this saying—except it would usually end with the word *Emmabelle*. It was what Spencer would say before he would convince me to go do something new with him, to go to the Philadelphia Fringe Festival, to see a woman pull eggs out of her mouth during an interpretive dance on the street on a stage illuminated by car lights. It was what he would say to get me to call in sick to work and sit in my closet and drink with him because why not, being in a different space alters one's perspective, the way one senses life, he would say.

"But we have to work hard at making sure it isn't. Because no matter what it is we do, it almost always falls into a pattern." He continued and I listened to Spencer's simulacrum, though I kept forcing myself back, reminding myself that this was another being.

"But some people are so happy accepting it as the way it is and even seem to enjoy it. And I'm so jealous of those folks. They follow these predetermined paths without questioning them. But my path? Well, who knows?"

Kerr thought about this for a minute, as if his neurons were emitting pulses and interacting with one another before he processed the information, reconstructed bits of his brain to access relevant info and form a response. "Even when I think I have it figured out, which isn't often, and enjoy the banality of it, something seems to interrupt and make me question my path. And I think that's a good thing, even if it seems like a burden."

For the first time since everything changed, since I began thinking maybe I was no longer cut out for my easy little life in New Jersey, I had the realization this transformation didn't have to be negative. And this person I'd only met three times but seemed to know me from eons ago was the one who made me see it that way. In that moment, I felt wholly happy, without concerns, devoid of dark memories, just there in the park, in the warmth of the day with someone for whom I felt tremendous affection.

The late afternoon slipped away as quickly as a sigh and evening light sprinkled gold glitter over the water's surface. It was a little past 5:30 PM and we walked ourselves out of the park and into the busy streets, where I followed him from block to block until we came to a bar with a large garden surrounded by a brick wall. Pots of terra-cotta filled with white, red, and pink geraniums dotted the top of the wall. It seemed there were geraniums in all of my worlds, sprinkling color whenever I needed it. All was perfect, so much so that I had stopped thinking about why I'd gone there, about my mission of learning about physics and parallel universes and getting closer to a guy who resembled my best friend. We drank sangrias and had appetizers and chatted about life and the weather and more. I listened to him speak, weaving Spencer expressions throughout his sentences. My head was light from the alcohol, from my connection to Kerr, to the ghost of Spencer, from being there. Somewhere in that moment when everything was almost intolerably weightless, he popped the question.

"Emma, tell me again why you contacted me?"

"It wasn't graduate school, at least not initially. I wanted to know about multiverses. To know if it's possible." Maybe it was the sangria, the feeling of bliss or the starkness of his unmasked question, but I didn't want to lie to him.

"I know you wanted to know about alternate universes, but why?"

"*That*, dear physics professor, is a much harder question to answer. I'm not sure you're ready for it."

"Try me."

"Soon." I contemplated pulling out of my purse the photo of Spencer but decided it was creepy. I liked us there and didn't want to change anything, say anything. It was a good place to be, and I wanted to remain in it for as long as I could.

Had he pressed on, I would have told him. But instead he also let us be.

Light faded into darkness, and he invited me back to his place, to have wine and to order food. I said yes, a yes within which surges of delight, uncertainty, and guilt were entangled, and we continued the evening on his couch. Guilt of knowing what I was about to do to Peter and guilt of what I was about to do with Spencer or the idea of Spencer—I was crossing into several forbidden zones but couldn't stop.

"Emma, from the moment you walked into my office I wanted to see you again." He put his hand on mine, his moled ring finger falling gently between two of mine, and the ripening possibility turned into actuality.

I nodded in agreement, my heart aflutter like the leaves in the park. Seconds went by in silence. I looked at the only source of illumination in the room, the small lamp on the side table next to him, lighting his face, a representation of my best friend, enchanted by what was inside his face, the knowledge of all those things I wanted to know and all that I didn't know.

"Can I kiss you?" he asked.

I nodded, too stirred to make out actual words.

Kerr leaned over, took his hand off mine, and slipped it under the flowers of my dress, gently placing it on my thigh. I ran my hand over the back of his neck, a single curl of hair delicately wrapping itself around my index finger. Our lips linked, and I felt a mystery and a familiarity at once. He mapped the insides of my mouth tenderly and deliberately—more so than in the rhythmic routine of anyone else—and I reveled in the slow and purposeful ways he wanted to, or appeared to, know me. It seems all kinds of trite, but it wasn't. It was delicate yet sensational, flighty yet significant. My heart rumbled, and a sudden release of energy—energy that had built up over time to overwhelming proportions—displaced the memories of Peter and Spencer. Worlds broke away and I didn't miss anyone or anything.

After the kiss, back in reality, I pulled away slowly and responded to his earlier query, "I also wanted to see you again, but I have to be honest with you, I need you to know . . ." I said, my voice losing volume with every word.

"You don't have to say anything you don't want to."

"But I need you to know my situation is complicated."

"I know." He sat back.

He knew but I questioned him with my eyes.

"I wasn't born yesterday, Emma, and am well aware there's more to all of this, but the only thing I want to know is if you want to be here. As long as that's the case, I'm glad to be with you. And we could leave it at that." He paused. "For now." His words brushed against my face. His voice, confident and round, blanketed me with reassurances that what I was about to do was not a mistake. Though I was never not going to.

This time I leaned in with my lips. He stood up, pulled me up from the couch, and led me to the dark bedroom. In the doorway, backlit by the living room lamp, I let go of his hand and unbuttoned my dress until I was down to black lace panties, fully conscious of what I was doing. My act of undressing, of exhibitionism, was thoughtful and measured. I wanted and needed to be seen by him, that way, at last, as if my existence were being rerealized.

Kerr stood in the room, his back to the bed. He said nothing, but he saw me and through me. I slipped into his bed and allowed him to slip into my world in a way I hadn't let anyone else.

29. Back to School

TOURAN

Everyone is back in the city. Dad says it's because people can't stay holed up forever away from it all. He says that when the strategic bombing against cities first began a few months back, everyone fled to a cabin in the mountains, a relative's house by the sea, a bungalow in the desert, or just pitched a tent somewhere far from target areas. But after the first few months, people's money ran out, and everyone needed to work, needed to go back to school, and, most important, needed to live. There was only so long that life could be put on hold. So raids became like car accidents and heart attacks; they were just a thing that happened in life. War couldn't stop people from living, and if it did, if we let it, it would win, he says.

It's been a week since Mimi and I started seventh grade. My science teacher, Mr. Artin, my favorite, hasn't come back to school this year. The rumor is he was drafted, just like Mr. Kia, who left at the end of last year. Now we only have one man teacher left in the school, and he's probably too old to go fight. All the young men seem to be gone.

The rock lands on 7. I am hopping to each hand-drawn square on one foot. I make my way to number 8 and pick up the stone and hop back through the court to the start. My classmates are screaming for me, and I love the feeling of being praised with their cheers. One more round and I'll be the winner. I bend down and eye the last square, strategically positioning myself and extending my arm as far as I can without moving my feet into the chalk court, fling my marker, and it lands within the border of square 8. I hop my way around without a hitch and become the day's hopscotch winner. My friends are all around me, congratulating and patting me on the back. Our world needs champions. If everyone were just a little braver, just a little *better* at things, the war would end.

Mimi comes over and we grab our belongings from the ground and leave the schoolyard through the large open door, the only opening in the tall walls that surround our building.

With my light blue bag slung over my right shoulder, I run to race her to the end of the school street. We've been doing that since the third grade, when we first started walking home together. Sometimes, like today, we don't even cue each other to start. We just run. It's almost 1:30 PM. The sun is coming down through the tall plane trees on the sides of the street, making little speckles of light and shadows on the ground.

"That was awesome," she says. "The hopscotch, I mean."

"Makes up for my spelling test this morning."

"You did bad?"

"I think so. I couldn't remember a few of those words and was so mad at myself for not studying harder." Instead of remembering the answers, I got more and more mad. Like the big metal manhole cover in the middle of the street, my head was hissing steam and heat. We make a left onto our street, toward our favorite shop in the neighborhood. It's a little store that carries fancy foreign chocolates and gums and goodies that most of the time we only dream of. Once in a while though, we save up our allowance for a few days and get a chocolate bar or some peppermint drops. It isn't always worth it, because for the same amount we could have bought three or four local candies.

"Hey, my friend just came back from a trip where she had this mint that's so strong you can't even finish it. You have to spit it out even before it all melts in your mouth," Mimi says as we both stop and look through the small window of the shop. There are boxes of chocolate carefully laid out, gigantic lollipops, pink and blue cotton candy hanging from strings, and jars of different colorful goodies. It's torture just looking at all of this.

"That's so cool. I bet I could finish it." I walk away and Mimi follows.

"I doubt it. My friend eats a lot of mints."

"So do I. I am strong when it comes to mints. It's what I do. Actually, I could probably put two or three in my mouth and finish them." *Take that!*

She doesn't look like she believes me. "Nuh-uh!"

"Let's try it." I point to the store with my head.

"Fine. Let's save up and we can test it next week." We start heading toward our houses.

"Deal." I stop and shake her hand. She has no idea who she's dealing with. Not just a hopscotch champ, I'll soon be the mint champ too.

"Okay, see you." She runs to her door, the back of her gray coat flying.

"Byeeeeeeee," I yell. "You'll see I can do it."

Dad is standing outside the yard on the sidewalk with the hose watering the trees in front of our house.

He waves.

"Hi, Daddy," I start running, holding the shoulder strap of the bag in my hand.

"How was school?" He puts the hose down by a tree root and holds out his arms.

I throw my bag on the little strip of grass in front the walls of our yard and jump to hug him.

"It was great. I won in hopscotch."

"Fantastic."

"I'm a champ!"

"That's my girl."

"You know, why can't they get people like me to go to war, to win? Then Mr. Artin and Mr. Kia and the mailman and all those boys can come back?"

"Oh, Lily, there are many different kinds of winning," he says, looking away. "You need to keep winning in school and tests, so you can grow up to do anything you want. That's the best thing you can do."

"I think I want to be an engineer," I say.

"You do? I thought you wanted to be a teacher."

"I did but I want to build all these destroyed buildings back up again," I say. "I can make our city look like how it used to."

"You're a gem, Lily, you know that?" Dad's eyes shine like they do when something makes him happy.

"Do you think I can eat a super strong mint without spitting it out? Mimi says I can't, that they're too strong."

"*That* I don't know," he says, smiling.

"But you believe I can, right? I mean you know I can eat a lot of strong mints."

"I believe it's possible. But you'll have to try it." He picks up my bag and hands it to me. "Mom's waiting for you with lunch. I'll be in when I'm done watering."

I take my bag and head inside.

30. Clarity of Day

NEW YORK

Bathed in morning light, Kerr was tiptoeing out of his bedroom. We caught each other's eyes when he turned to close the door.

"You're awake," he said, already dressed in a T-shirt and jeans, and walked back and gave me a peck on the forehead. My body was warm and jelly under his down comforter, and I had that pitter-patter feeling of proximity to an attractive force. The one I knew was nothing but a rush of chemicals—dopamine, if I remember my one college psychology class correctly—but I couldn't think scientifically then. Instead the rush of stimulants had induced the euphoria of that just barely buzzed feeling, happy and ready to declare love for the person standing before you. A conviction that you will feel that way even after the drug wears off, even when you remember the other commitments you have, the ones you've vowed to love.

"How did you sleep? Seemed like you were having some dream." He sat by me on the bed and ran his finger down the side of my face. On nights that he stayed at my place, Spencer would wake me up by sitting at the edge of the bed and tapping my nose.

"Oh?"

"Didn't seem like a bad dream, so I didn't bother waking you. Figured you might be enjoying wherever you were."

I put my hand on his and grinned: "I don't remember." I sat up.

"Take your time. I'll make us some coffee." He tapped my nose and headed out. I lay back on the pillow, took a look around the bed, the white sheets, blue duvet, and closed my eyes for a moment, letting the scent of sandalwood permeating through the bedding envelop me before getting dressed and heading to the kitchen.

I sat at the small rectangular glossy white table, watching him. His movements were simple. Grab a cup, press the coffee, pour in milk. But he did it all with precision, as if every small move mattered, punctuated by grace. I wanted to stay. It all made sense, then and there, but the gnawing heavy baggage of a life I'd created in Jersey waited for me, and I was aware of how quickly that instant would, and needed to, disappear. Why must there always be something? Why can't it ever just be easy?

"Ms. Emma, you have the face of an old soul." He pulled my chin up with a finger and kissed my mouth, put our coffee mugs on the table, and then sat across from me.

"My soul has aged lately." I smiled, forever making a joke when uncomfortable—something that Spencer repeatedly reminded me not to do. To just take the compliment, to own it. "It's actually gone all gray!"

"How so?" he asked seriously.

"Searching." I looked around the table and saw a box of Altoids next to a salt and pepper shaker set and examined the metal box in my hand—"Curiously Strong Mints."

"For?"

"I don't know. But the process has not left me much wiser."

"Well, it's quite endearing."

"What about you?" I asked. "What are you seeking?" I put down the Altoids box but had a keen urge to open it and pop in a mint.

"Nothing more interesting than anyone else treading through."

"I guess trying to determine the fate of the universe is what everyone is searching for?" I joked and took a sip of the coffee.

"In some way." He smiled and reached for my hand on the table and pulled it to his mouth. I looked at his mole. I stood up. He was still holding my hand under his chin and looked up at me without moving or letting go.

"Did I say something? You aren't leaving, are you?" he said and continued sitting and holding my hand.

"Of course not. But I have to go."

"Not yet," he pleaded and still wouldn't let go of my hand.

"I'll turn into a pumpkin soon." I said. "I'm sorry but I should." I didn't mention Peter, that he'd be back in New Jersey the next day, or the other world, and the original Spencer underground—another young man gone too soon.

"Okay, but on two conditions: Stay for a little bit longer so I can make us breakfast?"

"That's one condition." I was amused.

"Well, you have to say yes to that one before I put forth the other. They are conditional conditions!"

"So complicated, you are!"

"Ahem!"

"Point made." I smiled. "I'll stay for a bit. And the second condition?"

"That you will see me again?"

I started laughing. "This is brilliant, so one of the conditions of my leaving is seeing you again?"

"Uh-huh."

I smiled wide. His genuine interest was obvious, and he made no effort to try and hide it. "Well, I certainly hope to."

"Deal! So eggs or eggs?" He walked over to the fridge.

"I guess I'll have some eggs." I chuckled, feeling radiant—even attractive. It'd been a while since I felt that appealing. Maybe it was the dress or the blushing of my cheeks, but I think it was the subtle tenderness with which he looked at me, a gaze I'd known for years on a different face.

"Your wish is our breakfast!"

"Can I help?" I said.

"No, you sit. I wasn't a very good host and didn't get you any dinner. The least I could do is make you a meal."

"Do you make a lot of breakfasts?" As soon as I said it I knew how that might have sounded.

"You mean for other women?"

"I actually didn't mean that. Sorry, it came out wrong. I meant breakfast, are you a breakfast person? I mean, I'm not. I'll just run out with some coffee, I don't even have eggs in the house. Not even toast, just a coffee, dark, you know, barely . . ."

"Emmabelle, it's fine. Even if you meant something else, I'm fine with it."

The mug slipped out of my fingers and hit the table a few inches below. "Sorry?"

"Really, Emma it's no big deal. I have nothing to hide." He wiped the bit of coffee that I'd spilled with a paper towel.

"Nor should you. I mean, you're a grown man. I really just meant breakfast. My mouth just moved a little too fast."

"So, to answer you, yes, I make breakfast when I can—usually on weekends. And, no, I haven't made breakfast for anyone in months." He had turned his attention to the stove again.

"Really, I don't need to know. I mean, we just met—"

"I know, but still. And we didn't just meet."

"Yeah, but this kind of . . . Anyway, I'm just not a breakfast girl." It was 10:27 AM. In three minutes, Peter was due to speak to an audience of nearly two hundred, some of whom were undoubtedly women, and a few who were bound to be devising schemes to speak to him after his presentation. They would be thinking of what questions to ask, ones that would seem genuine, related to the use of Eastern symbolism in Western literature. Then they'd see Peter again at the conference gala this evening and would later bump into him at the hotel bar, laughing at some silly joke while playing with their hair before touching his shoulder. But Peter, ever devoted to his lukewarm partner—whose every gesture and figure of speech he was familiar with—would excuse himself before anything escalated and make his way to the room and check his voicemails to see if his Emma had left a digital trail of herself and, upon seeing how late it is to call her, would lay his head on the plush pillows of Hotel Nikko and fall asleep.

Kerr smiled, too smart to not recognize my evasion. In all graciousness, he said, "Except today."

"Yes," I said with relief. "Today, I'm a breakfast person."

"Good!" He placed a cut cube of butter in a hot pan, and it started bubbling on contact.

After we ate, I made my way out of his apartment. On the sidewalk a group of kids was cheering. They were gathered around an elaborately chalk-drawn hopscotch court while a boy, not much older than ten, was making his way back. He stopped, bent down, and picked up a rock on the square marked "6" before hopping his way back to the start of the court. His friends patted him on the back and slapped his palms. For the minutes I stood and watched, everything moved slow, as if units of time were spaced apart, each one stretched to infinity. He passed the rock to a little girl. Time snapped back into place and I turned the corner.

Walking down the street to the car I'd left blocks away, I thought of the mess I'd made. Daylight is quite unforgiving. Even so, I knew that I would have, no doubt, repeated the previous night all over again.

31. Prints

TOURAN

Nima's room is a bit of a mess. He has a pile of clothes and a couple of books on the bed, which is hardly made, and a bunch of papers and photos on his desk.

"Sorry." He clears the bed and pulls the blue checked comforter so it's smooth enough to sit on.

"It's okay." *I probably wouldn't clean mine much if Mom didn't make me.* I sit on the bed and watch him make his way to the desk and grab the photos, which is what I've been waiting for all day. To come here and see how our little project turned out.

He sits next to me and hands me the small stack. Of the twelve or so that we took, only about five of them came out okay. The rest are either black or blurry.

"It's because we didn't hold the camera still or I wasn't careful loading it," he says. "I'll throw them out."

"But I like them. They look like dreams." The blurry prints are smears of gray and white and black, turning us and everything around us into strange shapes.

There's one where he tried to jump across a narrow part of the stream and I tried to capture him with his legs in the air. All the photo shows is a dark shadow of Nima, warped into a ghostly figure.

"I'll keep these," I say.

Two are of me pretending to pick an apricot and then one of our feet in the stream lit by a golden sun, his right foot almost touching my left one. "You should keep that one too," he says.

Then there's the silly branch one—that one came out pretty nice also. But Nima wants to have it and I like that he wants a photo of me, even though it's all kinds of ridiculous.

After we leave his house and I get home, I tape the one of our feet on the wall above my desk—it's my favorite and reminds me of the best summer of my life and of my bestest friend. Like me, he also has no sisters or brothers, and we both like cameras and being at the orchard. And our parents are even friends. It's like we have so much in common. It hasn't even been a full day since I last saw him and I miss him already.

In bed, my spelling textbook is on my lap, facedown, and I'm watching the ceiling, thinking of the guy wanting to flog us with his stick. How fast we ran down the hill—running and running, our arms and faces brushing past leaves and branches, through clouds of dirt raised by our feet, with apricots weighting our pockets. Maybe we'll go again next year. Even the thought of it makes me giddy.

I close my eyes and am imagining a future time when we could go back and take photos at the stream, maybe when we're older, in high school even, when a siren goes off. I don't feel like moving. The siren will come and go. It always does. The problem, sadly, is Mom won't.

"Lily, let's go." Here we go. Her voice has a sharp edge.

There's no use arguing so I swing my feet off the bed and start walking to the yard. I don't even bother with shoes. "Let's go, let's go, let's go," she says, shooing me forward. But I'm moving slow. I don't care. What does it matter, anyway? It never hits us. It's silly, this thing we do.

I make it to the basement but don't get under the table. Instead I sit with Mom and Dad. Mom's sitting cross-legged on a chair. She's hunched over and looks nervous. It almost seems like she'll never get used to this. She closes her eyes and taps her red nails on the table without realizing she's doing it. Dad always notices but doesn't say anything. No one ever says anything. Sometimes he puts his hand over hers to stop the tapping. Tonight he doesn't. He's looking out the window. I'm doing the same. Watching the fake shooting stars, flashes of red and white, crisscross the sky. I wonder if making a wish on antiaircraft tracers works. I make one anyway. It's a secret, my wish, to live with Nima again, like we did at the orchard.

Then the sky is dark—no antiaircraft, no flashes, and then *Thud.*

A rumble, vibrations through the air, and a scattering of a flock of birds into the night sky. I scream. Mom jumps too, no longer cross-legged. It sounded too close. Closer and louder than any bomb I've ever heard drop, tugging at the Earth's crust, the table, the kerosene lamp in the corner, us. Maybe this is the time for in case, for the dry bread, the canned goods, for staying here longer than the few usual minutes.

Then, in an instant, everything is calm again. Only darkness exists. We are all still sitting, without words, sounds, or movements. The streetlights come back on, the few cars start moving, and the world is back.

"We can go up." Dad breaks the silence and holds out one hand to me and nudges Mom on the shoulder with the other. We go back to the house and I head to my bed, lie back, and stare beyond the ceiling, trying to imagine a clear blue sky filled with apricot branches, but somehow I can't get back there.

32. Goodbyes

NEW JERSEY

Peter's talk had been a success. Though I tried to focus on him, on us, my thoughts, ever in concentric circles, no matter their original intent, always zeroed in on the same bull's-eye: Kerr. What drew me to the physicist was his familiarity, a quality that I imagine most who cheat don't seek when choosing a subject of indiscretion. Characteristically, they're looking to escape the recognizable and mundane, to uncover a mystery—only to find out that once you open the box, the contents are always the same, even when there are slight variations. But my brand of transgression was attached to a continual accumulation of desire that makes one give in, to disregard the rational and surrender to the emotional. A yearning that began the day I opened my door for Spencer and culminated when Kerr opened his apartment door for me.

And there, on a Tuesday morning, in a cloud of East Brunswick steam under a hot shower, I understood for the first time that together, Spencer, Peter, and I were a structure with three legs, a three-person couple. Take away the one, and Peter and I crumbled—no matter how many times we stood up, we couldn't carry the relationship by ourselves, repeatedly collapsing under its weight. I couldn't imagine that Peter hadn't realized some aspect of this. He likely had but was probably hoping, like I was, that it would work itself out, that we'd be back, that once we got over the grief, it'd all make sense again, that somehow together we'd rise from the ashes. But having the two of them was the only way my relationship with either of them could work. When the fog of the shower cleared, I knew I needed to make a move.

I dressed, left the house, and stopped at a nursery and bought pink petunias and drove to the cemetery where Spencer was, a half hour from the condo. I had never been there. I actually never went to the burial, nor had I visited him since. When he died so suddenly, his parents, who mostly rejected him, wanted a family-only burial. Even though I was his family in so many ways, I wasn't on record. To his parents, I was like everyone else, all his other friends who somehow reminded them he was gay, accessories to some crime he was committing. Afterward, I just couldn't face going there and telling him how sorry I was to have not gone to the city with him, to have not been able to prevent his death, and to face the reality of his being gone: if I saw him in the ground, his death would become a more concrete reality, there would be no going back. Not going allowed me to imagine him to be somewhere, saying something, doing something. I realized that when struggling to make sense of loss, you clutch at any life preserver to save you from sinking into the depths. Not going was the only way I could have survived those months, to save myself from fully disappearing into the shadows. What I hadn't realized is that I had already sunk. Already faded. But that night with Kerr was the hand I needed to pull myself out, and I'd reemerged, even if just a hint.

Out of the car, I swung my legs. Iron rods. I hit them with my fists, hoping to transfer energy from my upper limbs to the lower ones, and tried to shake them out as fast as I could. Though not as crisp or cool, it was a day as beautiful as the one in the park with Kerr. Everything aboveground was alive and thriving, nourished by the morning sun and inhaling the heavy summer air. I looked at the stones laid out in order, marking the beginnings and endpoints of breaths. Car door open and my legs dangling, I didn't think I could move but knew I had to. In some way, I knew every part of the puzzle that made up my life was related, that allowing Spencer to be dead would allow me to continue living, to somehow fix things. Pressing my hands down on the seat, I pushed myself up and then clutched the car doorframe. I closed my eyes, hoping the swirling in my head would quit, that the ground would be kind and stop moving, hoping the nightmare of his absence would magically evaporate.

I took slow, small steps toward his grave. His name was carved on a stone, with dates, a start and a finish. A straight line. A to B. As if time were a linear thing, something we can measure and that is the same everywhere. I placed the flowers on the ground and knelt.

The persistent sun beat on my sweat-drenched face, but a shiver snaked its way through, freezing every tissue on impact. I put my face to the ground and smelled the dampness of the dirt and the greenness of the sparse grass. Rolling to my side, I lay down next to him, detached from the impersonal physical reminders that he was no longer among the living. As desperate as I was to feel something, to accept his death, I couldn't, and he remained suspended in my memory as he always had. The indifferent world moved on around us, but I lay still with him, to show that I hadn't betrayed him.

I don't know how long I lay there, but when I stood up, on some autopilot mode I got into the car and began driving.

Forty-five minutes later I was sitting on a beach in Long Branch. It was a little stretch of sand that was not served by a lifeguard and was therefore never crowded, which is why it was Spencer's favorite bit of the Jersey Shore— though he would never call it by its pedestrian label. Our last time there was in early fall the year before. I, a lover of all things water, was submerged in the ocean, while Spencer sat under the umbrella reading a book.

"You've got to come in," I shouted, walking out of the water, trying to keep from falling as the strong current worked to pull me back in. "September is the warmest the water gets all year. A lot of people don't know that," I said, hoping the last tidbit would convince him.

"I don't do water, wifey. There are creatures in there."

"So what's the point of coming here?" I walked over to him. We'd been through this many times, so even though I asked again, I knew the answer. Still, I never stopped with my ever-failing persuasion tactics.

"This," he said pointing to his book. "And this." He made a sweeping gesture over his face to simulate the salty ocean wind whooshing around him.

"Fair enough." I took a towel from him and wrapped it around myself and sat next to him on the large beach mat. "What are you reading?"

He showed me the cover of the book. *Continental Drift* by Russell Banks.

"Good?"

"Would I read anything that isn't?" Spencer had a way of embellishing himself, his abilities. He liked being the one who knew more about things like books and music; even when he didn't, I let him believe he did. I sensed it somehow made up for the grief he went through with his family about being gay, as if their crime wasn't hating him but simply not having the good taste to accept him as a rarefied, perfected version of themselves. "I'll lend it to you when I'm done, which should be very soon."

I put my head on his lap and lay back.

"Thanks for making my pants wet, darling."

"Spence, don't you wish we could stay here like this forever?"

"Well, now, darling, forever is a long time and as much as I love you, I think we'd both get tired. You'll miss your man and I'll miss my men."

I closed my eyes and Spencer stroked my forehead until I fell asleep.

When I woke up the sun's yoke was dissolving into the ocean and he was close to finishing his book.

I went over the conversation of that day, the feelings, the temperature, the smells, the rawness of the skin above my upper lip from the sun and salt. Our last beach day together. Not only did forever not happen, that experience couldn't even be repeated.

There was a woman with her dog in the distance, obscured by the fog of crashing waves. I stripped down to my underwear and walked to the water. As soon as I was knee-deep, I dove, cocooned in the warm ocean, moving with a wave, up and down and under, coming up for air every few seconds and surrendering myself to the forces around me. I thought of little in those few minutes, not of Spencer, nor of death, Peter, or Kerr, but acknowledged only the ever-changing breath of the ocean. Then, I let myself be carried by the wave, to see where the water would take me. I stopped breathing and allowed my body to go limp and stayed in suspension, losing sense of direction, of time and space. In an uncharted emotional sea, I wanted to be like silence, without mass, without breath. I stayed until I badly wanted to come back up and raised my head out, took a big gulp of air, and looked around, awakened from a deep and lengthy sleep.

Out of the water, I was light but tired. Hungry. Sleepy. I lay back on the cooling sand and slept till the horizon became one with the ocean, before heading back to the car.

When I got home, sometime after eight thirty, and saw Peter was standing by my door, a feeling of dread came over me.

"Where have you been?" He started walking toward me. "I called you about a dozen times on your cell phone and at work."

I pulled my phone out of my purse. I had seven messages, no doubt some from work, which I had ditched. "Sorry. It was on silent and I didn't have reception at the beach. Where's your key?"

"Are you packed?" he said as soon as I got closer and wrapped me in his arms.

"I went to Spencer's grave," I said.

"Oh, why would you do that today of all days?" he said almost snapping.

"I needed to," I said quietly.

"I thought you didn't want to, that it was easier. Let's go inside and get your bags." He took on a softer tone and took my keys from my indifferent hands and walked us in.

"Bags?"

"We have a flight at eleven thirty."

I looked at him blankly.

"Dominican Republic? Remember?" I didn't. I had forgotten about our trip and his plans to take us away, to fix us. "You didn't pack." He sounded weak and almost immediately looked bewildered and confused like the bird that had crashed into my window a few weeks earlier.

"Oh, Peter. I lost track of everything," I said, trying to think of ways to make it better, to pick him up and put him back together. "I never got to say goodbye or . . . I had to do it at some point to acknowledge that he is gone." An army of sobs had begun forming in my chest, ready to march out.

He sat on the sofa and I joined him.

"Maybe things will get better now?"

I nodded a small nod, feeling all the bits of guilt accumulating into a large mass, about not just Kerr but the entire few months of shutting him out of my thoughts and not being the same person he had committed to. "Peter, I haven't been good to you."

"Me neither but it's been rough," he said kindly. "For everyone."

"But still, I was so absorbed in my own things that I forgot how to be us somehow, and we just haven't been . . . I dunno. And it wasn't right and I'm sorry. I just didn't have the tools and maybe I never will." The last part of what came out of my mouth was unplanned—the idea of discussing the future and the prospects of it or the lack of one.

"We will move on and build a life together—buy a house and have children and all of this will be a memory in the past. Now, let's get you packed." He said, ignoring what was transpiring between us.

The earth shifted. The air contracted. A flurry of sadness. "But that's the thing, I don't want that stuff, the house, the children, the life. Or at least I don't think I want it. I'm not even sure I want to stay at this job and do the same things and know what my every single day will look like thirty years into the future." *And I don't know if I want them with you. Not when it's just the two of us.*

"So quit. Find a job you want. There are other firms, other things you can do." He sat on the floor in front of my feet looking up at me. "Where's your suitcase? I'll pack you up quickly. You don't need much, a few dresses, shorts, and a bathing suit," he said, part declaring, part asking.

"I can't go." The words came out without much thought. They had formed themselves and decided this is what needed to be said.

"You can. I don't care what's happened. We can fix it. I will fix it." He stood up. "Let's go."

"I'm not going," I said.

"Emma, what's gotten into you? We've had this planned. The flight is in less than three hours." He was loud. Peter was angry. He was finally losing it with me and he should have and I was glad for it.

I didn't move.

"Let's go." He grabbed a random duffel bag from the living room closet and started down the dark hallway toward the bedroom. I followed him as he walked around in a panic, opening drawers and closets and throwing articles of clothing into it without much consideration as to what they were. I stood by the door, wet-faced, in shock.

"Where's your passport?"

I said nothing.

"Where's your passport?" This time he was yelling. I had never seen him yell.

I pointed to the top drawer of my small oak desk in the corner. He opened it in a fit, seized the small blue book, then grabbed my hand and started to pull me to the front door.

"Peter," I said between sobs. "We can't keep doing this. I can't keep pretending that the two of us are working and you no longer have Spencer to push me off to whenever you feel like it." *Nor can you just manage my emotions to keep us together, even though you know I don't love you in all the right ways.* And just like that, without any preplanning, I told my boyfriend I wanted out.

"You are throwing everything away, Emma, and for what? People die. It happens. You don't break up relationships for it." His grip on my hand was still tight, a little too tight, and we were still by the front door. His face was colored with a rush of blood, no doubt boiling underneath his pale skin.

"It's not just that. You must know that."

He let go of my hand. His back slid down against the front door, and he sat on the doormat, my passport in his other hand.

"Peter, it'll be better for both of us, I promise." I stood by him as he leaned his head into my knees, then squatted down and stroked the blond locks he was hiding under.

"I was going to ask you to marry me, on the trip." He dropped the passport and took a small turquoise box tied with a white bow out of his pants pocket and almost shoved it at me with one hand while pulling at the roots of his hair with the other. "Maybe you're right. I just wasn't ready to let us go."

I didn't take the box and instead gently pushed his hand back to him. The ceiling blew off, the walls toppled, and the last of the life we'd built together flattened. I sat next to him on the floor. He put a hand on my cheek. With splintered hearts, we stayed like that for a long time. Until we had both absorbed what had finally become obvious to us, until the flight had already taken off for the Caribbean.

"Peter?"

He looked up with a defeated face.

I wanted to tell him about Kerr.

I hadn't yet opened my mouth, but he'd already put a finger on my lips and I stopped, deciding at that moment that maybe instead of telling him what would only cause him more hurt, I alone should bear the weight of my disloyalty and so instead filled my eyes once again with the only apology I could offer.

33. Mathematics of Chance

TOURAN

Though I wish I did, I didn't wait to walk home with Mimi today—the streets were especially empty, and between school and home I heard nothing but my own feet hitting the ground, like echoes in a hollow tunnel. I ran home as fast as I could, holding in my hand my math test. I have the highest score of the whole class and I want to show it to Dad. He loves math so much and I know how proud he will be.

"Daddy, Daddy," I start yelling as I wave the piece of paper in the air and push my legs to move faster when I see him on the sidewalk outside our yard's door. "Look here, I got the best score." I'm panting, grasping for all the air I can get into my system between the words.

I stop and hand him the paper. "Math," I blurt out, taking in a big gulp of oxygen. "No mistakes. I had no mistakes on my test," I say, completely out of breath now.

Dad's eyes brighten as they scan the page and then he flips it over to look at the back side. "This was a hard one too, lots of fractions. Good job, Lily." He pats me on the back and gives me a kiss on the cheek. "I knew you could do it. Come on, let's go inside." Something about his voice sounds different. It's not as steady as usual. That voice that I never question, the voice that makes me believe everything he says, that always makes me feel safe like a big encapsulating shell that won't let anything in to hurt me. But now it's uneven, like a train that can't stay on the rails. And he's acting weird. Typically he would go through each problem with me, but this time, he's walking behind me, almost rushing me in.

"You should eat something—your mom made you a snack," he says.

I walk into the foyer, but Dad stays in the yard, clearing the first of the random autumn leaves that have made their way down onto the grass. I throw my bag down on the floor and head to the living room.

"Hi, Mom! I am home." Maybe I can get her more excited about the math test.

She comes out of their bedroom, one of four in our one-story house. Her hair is pulled back tight with an elastic band. Her eyes look tired and smaller than usual, a little puffy, like she has been crying. She is a bit hunched over too. It's unlike her—her posture is always like a fresh yellow pencil.

"What's wrong, Mommy?" I ask, hugging her.

She holds me a little tighter than usual. "Nothing, baby, I didn't sleep well." She lets me go. "What's that in your hand?" she says in an almost collapsing tone.

"It's my test. My math test. Look!" I say very proudly, though I'm unsure whether I should be talking about the test.

"Wow. This is great. I think you deserve those jeans that you've been asking for."

"Really?" I nearly faint.

"Yes, really," she says weakly. "Now, let's go get you something to eat." Those two are hiding something from me.

I stand there and stare at her, waiting for the usual smile, but I get none.

Instead she presses her lips together hard and swallows as if trying to take in some dark secret before it comes out. And then her mouth opens but instead of letting that thing out she says, "Go on."

My lips release a frustrated *okay*, and I kick off my shoes. Then walk over to the bathroom to wash my hands before heading off to the kitchen. All of it lasts a couple of minutes, but somehow it feels longer.

In the kitchen, Mom takes out of the fridge a pitcher of lemonade full of suspended lemon slices and pours some into a glass. I am slowly munching on half a chicken sandwich she put in front of me. She hasn't said why she and Dad are acting strange. Sometimes when they argue, which isn't very often, they both act weird—as though each one is thinking about how to solve a puzzle. But I can't tell if that's what's happening. Mom looks more like she's given up on cracking the code and not like someone trying to find a solution.

"Here's your drink." She puts the tall, clear glass in front of me. "Why are you playing with your food?" There's an edge to her voice.

"I'm not playing. I am eating."

"That's not eating, you're taking a bite and then staring into space. Eat your food and go do your homework." The edge has turned to annoyance.

"I'm eating. Why are you mad at me?"

"Just finish the sandwich and go do your homework," she says, her voice fading, as she walks out of the kitchen.

"Fine." I can feel my eyes flooding. Why is she like this? Suddenly, the pit that started to form in my stomach in the yard gets bigger, and I seem to have no room for the sandwich. But I know I have to eat it, otherwise Mom won't let me out of this forsaken kitchen. I sit and chew, pushing the food down with lemonade. Maybe I can throw some of it out, but know she will find it in the garbage. I wipe a tear from my right cheek and take another bite, wipe another and take another bite, and so on.

I finish the sandwich, walk to my room, sit at my desk, open my bag, and take out my math test and look at my grade with the gold star sticker next to it—a freaking gold star. Guess that's not going on the damn fridge today. I put the piece of paper on my desk and take out my science book and notebook and open to chapter four.

Mom walks into the room before I start.

"Oh, good. You're doing homework." She sits on the bed. Her voice still sounds like it's coming from some faraway place, but at least it's got a kindness to it. "Come here," she says tapping her hand on the bedspread. I walk over and sit next to her. She puts her arms around me and squeezes hard. "I'm sorry about earlier."

I cross my arms and sit in brooding silence.

"You know I love you."

"I love you too." I uncross my arms. *But what's wrong?*

"Now, listen, I want to talk to you," she says in a rickety voice again, like an old house about to crumple. Her face has lost its rosiness too. "But I need you to be strong."

I look up at her and feel like something bad is going to happen. Maybe she and Dad are leaving each other. I'm ready to cry. I nod, trying hard to be tough, even though I have no idea how or why I need to be.

"The other night," her eyes already coated with tears, "when that bomb hit, it landed," tears are now all over her face, dropping onto her lap, "in Nima's neighborhood . . ."

The room starts spinning and all the imaginary branches of apricots on the ceiling close in and darken everything within my vision.

At first all I can do is make sounds that come out as several separated moans, one after another. Then I scream: "What? What? No."

"We still don't know anything," she's taking shallow and broken breaths between what seem like small and soundless sniffles. "They might be fine, but I haven't been able to contact his family."

"We were just there. How could this happen? He gave me those photos just the other day. How could it?" I'm trying to get out of Mom's grip around my shoulders. My limbs feel like they carry no weight, flailing everywhere uncontrollably, about to explode and break free from my body.

She's holding me tighter than ever. "Listen, you need to be strong, for you, for Nima, for your dad and me." She sounds like she's in charge again, as if she has control, as if she can protect me. As if.

"Can we just drive over there? I bet I can find him. He'll be there. I just know it." I get away from her grasp and stand up with a spurt of renewed energy from the thought that we can do something. That somehow we have an option here.

"We can't go there." She rubs her wet face with both hands and takes a long and deep breath—it lasts forever and I can hear my heart beating in the silence. "They have the neighborhood closed off so that they can help anyone who might, who might be," she searches for the last word, staring into a dark place and then snapping back, "in need," she finally says. "We would just get in the way."

"But I know where he would be. He's clever—he'll hide somewhere. At the orchard we had all these hiding places." I am animated, moving in front of her. Trying to give her some of my energy, to get her to move.

"Lily, I need you to be the reasonable girl that you are. You have to trust me. Dad and I will make sure you're okay."

"But I don't care about me. I care about Nima." *Why can't she understand what I'm trying to say?*

"I know. You have to trust us. We will figure it out."

I nod. I nod. I nod an unconvincing nod—what else is there to do?—and out of the corner of my eye fixate on the picture of Nima and me pinned above my desk.

34. Ghost

NEW JERSEY | NEW YORK

'Tis all a Chequer-board of Nights and Days
Where Destiny with Men for Pieces plays:
Hither and thither moves, and mates, and slays,
And one by one back in the Closet lays.

—Omar Khayyam

"He's dead," I said with little expression.

"Spencer?" Dr. Thompson replied.

I didn't look up. I was staring in between and beyond her desk legs into a dark and empty nothingness.

"There was an airstrike." My head bobbed up and down, my gaze on her now. "The boy's house turned into rubble." I went back to looking at the void under the desk. "I've lost him all over again." It was as if I'd regressed to that day, once again and without warning robbed of a love.

"Are you making a parallel because you are reexperiencing loss?"

"I can't stand to go through it again, to lose another best friend."

"Her best friend, anyway," she said.

"It's all me, isn't it? Whatever happiness, whatever loss she experiences,

I experience. So whoever she is, she is a part of me. Both worlds make up my memories. Isn't that what a person is, anyway? A collection of experiences and recollections? Isn't that who you are? So what if it's in two worlds?"

She didn't say anything and instead scribbled, doodled, whatever. I didn't care. The room came back into focus, and I got my stuff together and stood up.

"We still have another . . ." she looked at her watch, "another thirty-five or so minutes."

"Thanks, but I know he can help me." I said.

"Who?"

I extended my hand and shook her delicate one and walked out of her office, for good. In the car, I dialed Kerr's number. When he picked up I didn't let him speak to me in that Spencer-voice of his. I was scared, but this time not of what Kerr thought of me—I was scared that he couldn't help me.

"Hi, it's Emma." I was out of breath.

He was charming even in the way he spoke on the phone: "You must have read my mind because I was planning on calling you later today . . ." His words were round and soft like a down comforter that will lull you to relax.

"I need your help." I cut him off.

"Is everything okay?"

"When can we see each other?" The green digital numbers on the dash-board clock read 6:37 PM. "I'll explain in person."

"Okay, I'm on my way home now," he said. "You can come down now or I can . . ."

"I'll head straight over." I hung up. I didn't want to fall asleep that night without a plan. Time was limited and if there was a chance for me to save him, that night might have been it. I'd lost Spencer once and wasn't about to lose him again.

It didn't take long to get to his apartment. Traffic was going the opposite direction, and it was after hours, but in that daze the fifty-five-minute car ride was more like a slow hike to the top of Mount Everest. New Jersey Turnpike had become an endless road whose sole purpose seemed to instill impatience in me.

He opened the door before I had even gotten up the last step to the landing. The warmth of his lamp—the same one that lit our evening just a few nights ago—highlighted his smile. "How are you?" He gave me a tight hug and a kiss with an almost suspicious gaze.

I walked in and as soon as my face was in the light, he said, "What's wrong?" He put a hand on my shoulder and directed me over to the couch.

I sat and was immediately wrapped by a feeling of hope but still couldn't help what was the start of a mass production of tears.

"Can I get you some water?" he said, sitting next to me with that measured voice again.

I shook my head. "Look, we have to talk."

He nodded with a concern that contained a hint of fear, giving me the go-ahead to continue.

"I have to tell you something, but it's going to sound strange so please bear with me." Why was I saying this? Maybe to him, this was all normal. He would understand. He was a physicist. He was Spencer. He'd know.

"I'm listening," he said, no longer smiling.

"Do you know why I initially contacted you?"

"My charm?" His eyes perked up on a face that had taken on a grayness just seconds before.

"Well, maybe." That almost made me unfurl a little smile. "But I watched that show you were on and I thought you could help me with something." I left out the part about him reminding me of Spencer.

"Right, the research project but then it seemed . . ."

"Right, as you've probably figured, that was a bit of a lie, well not quite.

It *was* a research project of sorts, but not for graduate school. I'm just going to come clean but please let me finish before you say anything because I'm afraid that if you interrupt me at any point, I won't have the courage to finish what I have to say."

"Still nothing to drink?" he said, kindly wanting to help.

I shook my head slowly as if moving through a viscous liquid.

He sat back on the couch and just looked at me, allowing me to continue. So I did, telling him about the recurring and continuous episodes, about how I was in the body of a little girl in a war-stricken setting in a different time period, maybe the eighties, and, and, and. The whole lot of it.

He sat silent for a few too many heartbeats.

So I said the thing one says when it means precisely what you don't want it to mean: "Please don't think I'm crazy."

"Go on."

"At first I thought nothing of them, they were just dreams, and I'd been under stress—my best friend, his name was Spencer, died in a car accident several months ago, so I thought, this is some manifestation of the grieving process. But the dreams felt very real and, though it was horrific at first, I started to feel like I was living in that world, like it was another facet of my life. That one night when I saw the show you were on, it occurred to me that maybe, just maybe, this was some other dimension, a parallel universe, maybe back in time, or another world entirely."

"Oh, Emma, I'm so sorry about your friend. How hard it must have been for you," he said in the most gentle and loving tone I'd ever heard from him and proceeded to wrap his hand around mine. "But as you know and I've said before, that was just a show, very speculative . . ."

"Wait," I said tears starting to form in my eyes again. "You don't know. There are things that happen there that I bring back here with me."

He said nothing and squeezed my hand with his—I fixated on his mole, as though it was there to help me continue.

Then I told him about the other friendship, the raid, that loss, seamlessly crossing back and forth through boundaries of the tangible and unperceivable as if they all belonged in the same sphere.

"I need to find a way to go back and save him. I fear that I lost my best friend here and I could have prevented it but didn't. Now, I have a chance. You have to help me, Kerr. I know you think I'm crazy, and maybe I am." The inside of my head was scrunched up like a paper ball. It occurred to me then that the one photo of Nima was blurry because he had already turned into a ghost. An omen. I should have known then to do something. To have saved him.

Kerr didn't respond in words and instead walked to the kitchen and walked back with an array of helpful items—water, tissues, a glass of bourbon, and put them all in front of me on the coffee table.

I took a tissue and wiped my face. "Please say something."

"I don't know how to respond," he said, mildly annoyed at my push for an answer. "You lost a friend and are understandably under duress. I'm no expert but maybe this is all related and somehow expressing itself in your subconscious?"

"Of course, that's the first thing I thought of," I said. "I have looked at all logical possibilities. Even after seeing a therapist, I don't seem to have other answers. At least an alternate dimension is an explanation—the only thing remotely close to an answer."

"But it really isn't, Emma."

"But you've read the books? Michio Kaku and Brian . . .?"

"As I've said before, what you're proposing is very speculative. You should know that better than anyone. Your job revolves around the practical."

"But what else could it be? What else could it be?" I repeated the phrase quietly, more for myself the second time.

He walked to the kitchen and poured himself a glass of bourbon. "You should have some too." He pointed to the glass in front of me.

I shook my head.

"Might do you good."

I ignored him: "You are my last hope, you've got to believe me." I felt energized, especially animated at the possibility that we'd figure this one out. There had to be a way.

"I cannot believe something that defies logic. That defies science," he said with conviction, leaving no room for doubt.

Our heated exchange quickly turned into silence. With no response, I felt myself go limp, picked up and examined the bourbon in my hand and took a sip, trying to think what else I could do, but I was stuck in a vacuum with no ideas to hold on to.

Kerr sat next to me. "Okay, assume that I believe all of it, which I don't. What can I even do? It's not possible. Think about it all . . . if you . . ."

"I've been thinking about it and reading about it and analyzing it for longer than I care to admit. I have no idea what it is or what it could be. And you know something, at this point I don't think I care anymore. Whatever it is— alternate reality, imagination, dream, subconscious—I have been given a second chance to save my, or *a*, best friend and to save her from heartache, and I need to do something."

"Look, I'm sorry, really sorry, but your best friend is gone." His face had switched to concern again, which was better than apprehension.

"Here, yes, but not in the other world."

He sighed. "Suppose you're right: suppose you are traveling to some alternate universe or other world or what have you. And suppose this popular rendition of physics works. If it were even possible that you could go back, if you change something, you might ruin the order of that world, a bigger disaster could happen because you made this change." He took a swig from his glass. "I can't believe I'm even saying this."

"Don't say that," I said, practically begging him.

"Okay. But does that make sense to you?" he said. "And you yourself just said you have no control over what happens in that world. How then can you change anything?"

"I don't know. That's why I need help. I mean, even in physics, the Newtonian is predetermined but the quantum, the world of the very small, is all about probabilities. You can't determine things."

"Well, yes, but how . . ."

I cut him off. "Even if it seems predetermined in that world, what about free will within those constraints? Are we all just pawns in some mastermind's chess game, just there to be played? I never had a chance to undo anything here in this world but what if this is the universe's way of giving me another chance?"

"Another chance at saving a boy in a dream?" he said, frustrated and stern. He no longer reminded me of Spencer.

"Whatever—dream, world, life. If it gives me a chance at happiness again, a chance at saving a life, tell me why I shouldn't take it?" I said.

"Because it's not real and you can't change anything and even if you could, even if I believed all this, which I really have a hard time doing, you shouldn't. You don't even know how you get there or what these dream things are. And honestly, at this point, you just have to assume these are dreams." He was clearly irritated.

"Okay. Let's assume they are dreams. I still want to save him." I didn't know how else to plead to him.

"Even if I wholeheartedly believed you, I don't know what I could do. If you tell me how I can help you, I'll try."

"I don't even know." I resigned and closed my drained and tired eyes for a long time, and unwillingly fell asleep.

·

When I woke up, it was morning. I was on the couch with a pillow under my head and a blanket over me. It was after ten, and I realized I was still in New York and not at work. Kerr was sitting at the desk in the living room, drinking coffee and reading the paper.

"You're awake." He looked up without smiling. I couldn't tell if it was all over between us already.

The more conscious I became, the more I realized I'd fallen asleep without a plan. I began panicking, my heart drumming erratically and my armpits getting sticky. But soon I realized that I hadn't traveled to the other world the previous night. Maybe I still had a chance.

"I should call into work."

He handed me a cup of coffee and my phone but didn't say anything. I sat up and took both from him. He went back to his desk. I called Charlie—I was running out of excuses. He picked up after the third ring.

"Charlie, it's Emma. I'm so sorry but I'm not feeling well and can't come in. I should have called earlier . . ."

"You had to be out in the field this morning, Emma." Charlie was angry and almost yelling in a quiet voice.

I had forgotten that I had scheduled my whole crew to work all day in Mayfield.

"I asked Tina to take over since she knows the project." *And since you never seem to be here, physically or otherwise,* was the subtext of what he said.

"Right. I'll be sure to take over again starting tomorrow."

"That won't be necessary. I'm putting Tina on Mayfield. Come see me when you're back in the office. We should go over a few things."

I hung up, holding the phone in my hand and resting my head on it.

"Everything okay?" Kerr asked.

"I think I'm about to lose my job, or just did."

"I'm sorry." He sounded uninterested.

It was coming, I wanted to say something but the words thickened in my throat. I couldn't linger on it too long, however. Time was limited on the other end.

I drank about half the cup until I was able to fully recap the previous evening, stood up from the couch, and made my way to the desk. "I'm sorry about last night. I realize it's all too much, too strange . . ."

"Emma." This time he cut me off, his eyes gliding up from the newspaper to meet mine. "The dinner and the other evening, was that all you just wanting to get physics help from me?"

"No." Though I should have known this was coming, I didn't and wasn't ready for it. "There was something about you even when I saw you on that show, something that made me pick you to contact." *You look and sound like a love of my life.* "And when I did, I felt alive for the first time in a long time. Saturday, well, that was me wanting to be with you. I'd wanted to tell you all of this but how does one do that? Each time I saw you everything felt so familiar and good and right that I didn't want to ruin it." I was tired of keeping secrets, all the way back to loving Spencer, and had gone for broke, knowing all I had in this world was either already gone or vanishing— Peter, the job, and now Kerr. Maybe this was the part when he would confess too, say he was Spencer back from the grave in another body. Or that he was Spencer's way of giving me a sign to indicate he was okay. But with a clarity that I hadn't felt before, I knew that wasn't the case. "I understand if you don't want to see me anymore." My last statement sounded more like a question.

He didn't respond.

I hadn't even told him about Peter. My god, what a mess. "Probably best if I head out." I put on my shoes and grabbed my purse.

"Wait."

I turned around, relieved.

"Sit for a minute." He got up and gave me his chair. I did as I was told. He sat on the floor and faced me quietly for a long time before he began to speak again. "You have to realize you are shaking the foundation of all my beliefs and I can't pretend like I can just go along with it."

"I don't expect you to." I let out an *I have given up* sigh. "In fact, I never expected to believe any of this myself."

"Let me finish. Why are you working so hard to rationalize it all?"

"I don't understand."

"Why won't you just accept the inexplicability of your dreams as something that science or logic doesn't need to explain?" He studied my face for a reaction.

I didn't know the answer. Why didn't I? Was it because they were so strange that I couldn't recognize them as dreams or that I desperately wanted to believe them to be something they weren't?

"Maybe they just are what they are," said the man whose life was based on explaining the world through logic and science.

"Maybe." Knots untangled and cages in which my thoughts were stuck magically opened.

The river is moving.

The blackbird must be flying.

Spencer liked these two lines of the Stevens poem, and the words assembled themselves in my head of their own accord and, though I never quite understood their meaning, for the first time they made sense.

That night in bed, back in my condo, I stayed up late into the darkness, fighting the urge that I had any power to change a place that didn't exist at all. Though I was skeptical, I still didn't want to risk falling asleep and missing a chance, if there were any way, to save the boy—even if he was only an elusive intruder into the shorting circuitry of my brain. My chest was tight with suspense but also pulsated quickly—up and down, up and down—from anticipation, the thought of potential, of a second possibility even if only in my mind's eye.

If I could go back to that night, I could convince her parents to go over to his house, but then they could also be killed. Maybe have them come over to Lily's house. Maybe warn them, tell them what's about to happen. But would Lily even know what's about to come? How could she? What's the point, anyway—everyone dies at the end. Even if she saves him, he will die again someday. But he was too young and too close. We, delicate beings in the hands of fate, will do anything to hang on to living, no matter where and how we fit in, because life is, in every facet—its deaths, wars, mundaneness, and colors—a pointless yet magical thing.

Every few minutes, my tired eyes would give up for milliseconds and I'd catch myself, continuing with my musings, trying to put together a plan. With everything but my thoughts in utter stillness, the kitchen clock alerted me to every passing moment. Ticktock. Ticktock. Tick—

I got out of bed and made my way to the living room, pacing the small space, trying to send a mental message to Spencer: *My Spencer, I've forever loved you. I'm sorry I didn't go with you that night. Maybe you'd be here if I had, but even if not, I wish I were with you. I failed you, I failed us. But I'm going to make things right again. And whatever happens, I love you loads.*

Over by the answering machine, I listened to his message one more time and, with the press of a large red button, forever erased the voice, the last trace, of my best friend, finally letting him go, allowing him to exist in some other realm, to be dead.

Then I made my way to the bathroom, looked at my reflection, and saw a woman, frail and withered by loss but for the first time in a while also full of hope, smile back at me—like a little girl with a plan, about to do something mischievous, about to turn the world on its head.

I went back to bed and closed my eyes, letting the deepest of all sleeps take over.

35. Prints II

TOURAN

Nima's room is a bit of a mess. He has a pile of clothes and a couple of books on the bed, which is hardly made, and a bunch of papers and photos on his desk.

"Sorry." He clears the bed and pulls the blue checked comforter so it's smooth enough to sit on.

"It's okay." *I probably wouldn't clean mine much if Mom didn't make me.* I sit on the bed and watch him make his way to the desk and grab the photos, which is what I've been waiting for all day. To come here and see how our little project turned out.

He sits next to me and hands me the small stack. Of the twelve or so that we took, only about five of them came out okay. The rest are either black or blurry.

"It's because we didn't hold the camera still or I wasn't careful loading it," he says. "I'll throw them out."

"But I like them. They look like dreams." The blurry prints are smears of gray and white and black, turning us and everything around us into strange shapes.

There's one where he tried to jump across a narrow part of the stream and I tried to capture him with his legs in the air. All the photo shows is a dark shadow of Nima, warped into a ghostly figure.

"I'll keep these," I say.

Two are of me pretending to pick an apricot and then one of our feet in the stream lit by a golden sun, his right foot almost touching my left one. "You should keep that one too," he says.

Then there's the silly branch one—that one came out pretty nice also. But Nima wants to have it and I like that he wants a photo of me, even though it's all kinds of ridiculous.

After we leave his house and I get home, I tape the one of our feet on the wall above my desk—it's my favorite and reminds me of the best summer of my life and of my bestest friend. Like me, he also has no sisters or brothers, and we both like cameras and being at the orchard. And our parents are even friends. It's like we have so much in common. It hasn't even been a full day since I last saw him and I miss him already.

In bed, my spelling textbook is on my lap, facedown, and the stack of photos is next to me. My eyes fall on the top one. It's the one of me with an apricot. I can taste the sweet juices and even the creamy almonds inside. I put that photo underneath the rest and the blurry one of Nima is on top now. A frosty and heavy air takes over my room. An uncontrollable shiver blooms. Nima looks like a ghost. It's like it's not him but some version of him that isn't there anymore. It's Nima without a body, just a shadow of the boy I know, a phantom. I look at the photo for so long that I'm looking through it into empty space. It's a darkness I'm not familiar with, it's hollow, as if nothing exists there, as if nothing comes out of it. I close my eyes to avoid looking at the photo when a siren goes off. The lights are cut and everything darkens. I don't feel like moving. The siren will come and go. It always does. The problem is Mom won't.

"Lily, let's go." Her voice has a sharp edge.

I swing my feet off the bed and, still shivering, start walking to the yard. I don't even bother with shoes. "Let's go, let's go, let's go," she says, shooing me forward, making a motion with her hands that is trying to hurry me, her arms waving under the faint light from the sliver of the moon. But I'm moving slow.

I push through the thick fog of night and make my way to the basement stairs with what seems like extra effort. The air is heavy. Suffocating. I make it to the basement but don't get under the table. Instead I sit with Mom and Dad. Mom's sitting cross-legged on the chair. She's hunched over and looks nervous. It almost seems like she'll never get used to this. She closes her eyes and taps her fingers on the table without realizing she's doing it. Dad always notices but doesn't say anything. No one ever says anything. Sometimes he puts his hand over hers to stop the tapping. Tonight he doesn't. He's looking out the window. I'm doing the same. Watching the fake shooting stars, flashes of red and white, crisscross the sky, I wonder if making a wish on antiaircraft tracers works. I make one anyway. It's a secret, my wish, to live with Nima again, like we did at the orchard.

The antiaircraft seem to go on forever tonight. I hate them. But more than hating them, I hate when they end and a bomb drops and someone dies. So many people have died so far, and all the men are going off to fight. Soon it'll just be women and older men, and they will just have to wait their turn to get bombed. How many ghosts are floating above our darkened city? My hands start shaking. I'm not cold. Not scared. Just trembling. I want to make it stop but don't know how. And then, I don't know why but without saying anything I start running up the basement stairs as fast as I can. Mom and Dad are yelling at me to stop but I can't. It's like a force is making me. I'm moving faster than I ever thought possible, like a weightless shadow. By the time Dad is at the top of the basement stairs, I'm in the house running to my room.

"Lily, have you lost your mind?" he says from the front door, his voice getting closer by the time he finishes his sentence.

I can hardly see anything but I know my room so well that it's easy to make my way to the bed, where I last left the photos. Sweating but still shaking, I feel for them on the bed. When my clammy hands find the stack, I take the top shadowy photo of Nima and start ripping it as fast as I can, shredding it—to destroy his ghost so it can't exist in the real world, so there's only room for Nima—and then furiously step on the small pieces of the picture.

I let out a mixture of a scream and other sounds that make no sense—a language of their own, one that's violent and defiant. I am all rage, and it feels as if my entire body will soon explode like a bomb of its own. Then I grab my doll off the bed: "It's gonna be okay, Emma." I clutch her to my chest and stroke her long hair.

Dad enters the room and without saying anything grabs and scoops me and Emma into his arms and heads out toward the safety of the basement. I don't struggle anymore and am no longer shaking. I look up. Instead of Dad's it's the face of a young man I don't know but whose arms I feel safe in. My agitation turns to a stillness so calm that I couldn't imagine it seconds ago. He carries me to the yard and puts me down at the top of the stairs to the basement. I reach for his hand and he holds it for a few seconds. Looking at me with his brilliant green eyes, he smiles and motions to me to go down. We let our hands go, and his slim shadow disappears into the moonlit night. Watching the jewel-studded sky through the basement window, I know that Nima is safe, even when I hear the thud of the bomb drop.

36. Blank Canvas

NEW JERSEY

It was a little past eleven when I woke up on Friday morning. I hadn't slept in that long since college. The late morning light accented floating dust particles in the air with amber warmth. Mesmerized, I watched them shift lazily in their lava lamp–like ways, the only moving parts of the room. The stillness of the morning was like everything had stopped because all that had needed to happen already had. Now everything could relax, at least for a day. It took me a few minutes to realize what had transpired—only when my eyes landed on the picture of Spencer and me on the nightstand did my briefly vacant mind fill with the realization I'd been waiting for, and I let out a shriek of pleasure and threw the covers off, skipping out of bed, into the living room, my white nightgown still too large, dancing behind me.

I pulled open the curtains, letting the outside in, and thought of the girl who had done what seemed to be the impossible with a kind of courage I never had. Defying what we all wish to defy, the inexorability of fate. How, then, can we say we are just pawns in the hands of destiny? That there's a wheel in which we're stuck, involuntarily moving inside its gears, to its turning whims?

Perhaps I was the mastermind of her world, perhaps it was fate and I pulled the strings in her reality, but I refused to believe in this predeterminism, this fatalism, in which every decision, every outcome, every thought, every death was already inscribed and could not be altered. Because if I did, if I believed that everything was fated, what then was left of living?

The light on the answering machine was blinking fast—many calls through which I'd surprisingly slept. Most were likely from work. It hardly mattered if it was work, no one counted on me anymore. I had lost the one thing I'd worked so many years for. I pressed play anyway.

Emma, I've been trying to reach you, Tina's distressed voice came from the white box. *I wanted you to know I spoke with Charlie and told him the report thing was my fault. I also had a chat with Joe and he explained to Charlie how you're the only person with knowledge of Mayfield. Um . . . I wish you were home. Anyway, give me a ca—* The phone rang, interrupting the tail end of her message. It was Kerr's number so I picked up.

"So glad I finally caught you," he said.

"Finally?"

"I called twice, an hour ago and about fifteen minutes ago." It sounded like he was outside. Sounds of cars whizzing by and chatter of people in the background. "Can we talk?"

"I haven't had my coffee yet."

"I meant coming over, can I see you in person? I just finished class and can grab a car and drive over in a bit."

I agreed, happy to share with him what I knew now with certainty.

Sitting on the balcony floor I sipped on coffee and listened to Bob Marley's "One Love." I could feel Spencer sitting with me, singing along, and intermittently complaining about the disheveled state of my balcony.

Dear heart, why are these pots so gross, there's standing water in this one. And where have all the flowers gone? Sweet Jesus and Mary, you need to have pretty things in life. If you don't take care of yourself and your surroundings you'll soon become unsightly too, ladycakes.

I stood up and one by one turned the pots upside down over the railing, getting rid of the soil and dirty water, and carefully stacked each one on top of the next. I looked over to what had been a little geranium earlier in the season. It had grown and flourished all on its own, despite my lack of care. I watered it, its lemony fragrance lightly spreading through the air.

There was a definiteness to the act of cleaning the balcony, like a sweet goodbye but an even sweeter beginning. It was the last time Spencer and I would be together like that, and I savored it, taking in every smell, every caress of the outside, every word I heard and imagined him say, every memory, every wild thought.

Back inside I tidied up the living room, picked up random coffee mugs and dishes and loaded up the dishwasher, and went through the mail that had spread all over the kitchen island.

By the time Kerr showed up, I had showered, dressed, and late afternoon had set in.

"So this is where the magic happens," Kerr said as soon as he walked in.

"I guess you could say that! Welcome to my little suburban life." I led him to the living room.

"Suburban, maybe, but not boring." He sat on the sofa, scanning the surroundings.

"Can I get you something to drink?"

"From that smile, I assume things are okay?" he said, ignoring my pleasantries. I sensed a tenderness in his demeanor that I thought would have slipped away since we last met.

"I think so." I almost elaborated but decided that it was best I stayed silent. "I have a feeling my link to that world is gone. Perhaps that whole world is even gone. Poof." I handed him a glass of water and sat next to him.

"Oh?"

"Maybe it's still going on, maybe it's gone. Maybe the sole purpose of the other world was for it to save me, for my mind to fix itself. Maybe I set it up and then destroyed it."

"In your head?"

"Does it matter? The understanding of every reality occurs in the head so why do we need some physical evidence to believe that something really exists?"

"Because both you and I are scientists and we need empirical evidence?" he said, not unkindly.

"Last I checked you were a theoretical physicist." I raised both eyebrows.

"Touché."

"Listen, I can sit here and try my hardest to convince you that my life has always been all kinds of normal. Maybe we were all meant to be sewer engineers one way or another. But I now have a taste of what's possible. It's like I've been handed a blank canvas and blank canvases hold the potential to have anything painted on them."

"And what does this mean, practically?"

I thought about his question.

"In terms of your future, I mean," he added for clarity.

I shrugged: "I've just been enjoying the idea that the molecules of air seem more spaced apart, making it easier to move through, to breathe in."

"I'm happy for you, Emma," he said politely.

"But?" I realized I wasn't sure why he was there. We hadn't touched or kissed, not even an exchange of a hello hug. My eyes landed on his hand to locate his mole, that sign of familiarity, but I couldn't find it. I looked again and even took his hand in mine to further examine. Nothing. In fact his voice had lost its Spencer ways too. A knot of sorts untied, and something in me relaxed.

"But nothing. I hope this feeling continues for you." There was a crease between his eyebrows that I hadn't seen before. He looked less like Spencer with furrowed brows.

"Kerr, I'm sorry I pulled you into this the way I did. The truth probably lies somewhere in the fact that I was drawn to you for many reasons—physics being just one of them, though I latched on to it as if it were the only one. And maybe it wasn't fair but in the end, I'm happy to have met you no matter what sparked it. You are the unexpected find in this whole thing."

Silence.

And then finally he said, "I have not, in my mind, settled why or how any of this happened. But I'm not opposed to the idea of possibilities."

"That's all the universe can offer us anyway, right—its grandest gift, promises?"

That was the last we spoke of the dreams, the episodes, the other world.

After Kerr left that night, I lay alone in bed, thinking of blue skies. Of tomorrow.

Outside, gentle rain blanketed East Brunswick roofs. Wet, just-yellowing leaves somersaulted down onto the ground. The moon sliver moved eastward. Inside, tucked under a warm comforter, eyes shut, I fell asleep under the shadow of a thousand apricot branches bearing floating yellow orbs like little suns.

When it gets dark

there will be more stars

than you've ever seen before.

Try to remember

the names of constellations

you once knew by heart.

Recite yourself to sleep

on a groundsheet of detailed maps.

Someone will find you.

—Esther Morgan

Acknowledgments

It takes a universe, and a generous one at that, to raise a book. I'm indebted to my agent, Lori Galvin, for her sharp editorial eye, patience, kindness, and belief in this project; to her colleagues at Aevitas Creative Management, especially Maggie Cooper and Esmond Harmsworth for their thoughtful feedback and Michelle Brower for connecting me to Lori.

Many thanks to my publisher Will Evans for his support and enthusiasm, Serena Reiser for her care with copyedits, Jill Meyers for coordinating and Marina Drukman for creating the gorgeous cover, Kirby Gann for typesetting, and Sara Balabanlilar and Walker Rutter-Bowman for helping this book find its readers.

Sanderia Faye, it was my great fortune to find you sitting at that banquet. A thousand thanks for advocating this project and giving it your attention, hours, and considered feedback.

Sarah Cypher, you are a story sorcerer and I'm grateful for all you've done to make this book better. Sarah Russo, I'm lucky to have you and Robin Wane in my corner.

To Fayre Makeig, thank you for reading this manuscript in the eleventh hour and for your generosity time and again. Thanks to Alan Lightman for his encouragement when I was just finding my way into the writing world and his graciousness since, an example by which I hope to live.

Justen and Sara Ahren: Nearly every good thing that has happened with my creative writing can be traced back to Noepe Center for the Literary Arts and I'm eternally grateful to you. Thank you to Shari Goldhagen and Karen Braziller, whose workshops helped shape the early drafts of the manuscript. To Les Standiford and Marina Pruna of Writers in Paradise, thanks for believing in this book at just the right time. Much gratitude to Mat Johnson and the Tin House Workshop for giving me the writing boost I needed to keep going.

Thanks to Maaneli Derakhshani and Matthew O'Dowd for helping me ensure the physics bits were sound and free of errors, even if highly speculative.

I'm grateful to my friends Chris Brandt and the very missed Linda Gregg, who through poetry and with utter kindness taught me to strive for exactness in language.

Thanks to my generous community of writers that includes Georgia Clark, M. Elizabeth Lee, Laura Catherine Brown, Brian Platzer, Katie Peyton Hofstadter, Rebecca Nison, Nan Byrne, Sweta Vikram, J Andy Kane, Lisa Preston, Joshua Korenblat, Vikram Paralkar, Rae Delbianco, and Vadim Prokhorov (to name just a few), with special gratitude to Amy Poeppel, Deborah Stoll, and Jack Sonni, who are on speed dial and always pick up.

Thank you to friends, near and far, for being the best cheering squad and to neighbors, present and past, for the much-needed hallway breaks and comradery.

To Foster, the sweetest and much-missed kitty, thanks for being a constant companion during the writing of this book. Thank you to Andrew Bird, whose music helped me through many revisions and who continues to be an inspiration.

Thanks to the adoring Rhoades family, especially Terri, Lisa, and Gene, for your encouragement and enthusiasm for this book.

To my siblings, Katayoun and Afshin; their spouses, Mohsen and Katayoun; and my nephews, Omeed and Saba—your love, support, and friendship is the world to me. Thanks to my father, Houshang, whose place is forever empty, for instilling in me an affinity for literature, science, and humor and to my mother, Hamdam, who champions and loves without limits and who, by example, teaches me to create. None of this would be possible without my partner, Anthony, who believes in me even when I don't and whose art and dedication to it inspire me every day.

Sara Goudarzi's work has appeared in the *New York Times, Scientific American, National Geographic News, The Adirondack Review* and *Drunken Boat,* among others. She is the author of *Leila's Day at the Pool* and *Amazing Animals* from Scholastic Inc. Sara has taught writing at NYU and is a 2017 Writers in Paradise Les Standiford fellow and a *Tin House* alumna. Born in Tehran, she grew up in Iran, Kenya, and the U.S., and currently lives in Brooklyn.

Thank you all
for your support.
We do this for you,
and could not do
it without you.

DEEP
VELLUM

PARTNERS

pixel ||| texel

EMBREY FAMILY
FOUNDATION

ADDITIONAL DONORS, CONT'D

Mark Haber

Mary Cline

Maynard Thomson

Michael Reklis

Mike Soto

Mokhtar Ramadan

Nikki & Dennis Gibson

Patrick Kukucka

Patrick Kutcher

Rev. Elizabeth & Neil Moseley

Richard Meyer

Scott & Katy Nimmons

Sherry Perry

Sydneyann Binion

Stephen Harding

Stephen Williamson

Susan Carp

Susan Ernst

Theater Jones

Tim Perttula

Tony Thomson

SUBSCRIBERS

Ned Russin

Michael Binkley

Michael Schneiderman

Aviya Kushner

Kenneth McClain

Eugenie Cha

Stephen Fuller

Joseph Rebella

Brian Matthew Kim

Anthony Brown

Michael Lighty

Erin Kubatzky

Shelby Vincent

Margaret Terwey

Ben Fountain

Caroline West

Ryan Todd

Gina Rios

Caitlin Jans

Ian Robinson

Elena Rush

Courtney Sheedy

Elif Ağanoğlu

Laura Gee

Valerie Boyd

Brian Bell

AVAILABLE NOW FROM DEEP VELLUM

FORTHCOMING FROM DEEP VELLUM

SHANE ANDERSON · *After the Oracle* · USA

MARIO BELLATIN · *Beauty Salon* · translated by David Shook · MEXICO

MIRCEA CĂRTĂRESCU · *Solenoid*
translated by Sean Cotter · ROMANIA

LEYLÂ ERBIL · *A Strange Woman*
translated by Nermin Menemencioğlu & Amy Marie Spangler· TURKEY

RADNA FABIAS · *Habitus* · translated by David Colmer · CURAÇAO/NETHERLANDS

SARA GOUDARZI · *The Almond in the Apricot* · USA

GYULA JENEI · *Always Different* · translated by Diana Senechal · HUNGARY

UZMA ASLAM KHAN • *The Miraculous True History of Nomi Ali* • PAKISTAN

SONG LIN · *The Gleaner Song: Selected Poems* · translated by Dong Li · CHINA

TEDI LÓPEZ MILLS · *The Book of Explanations* · translated by Robin Myers · MEXICO

JUNG YOUNG MOON · *Arriving in a Thick Fog*
translated by Mah Eunji and Jeffrey Karvonen · SOUTH KOREA

FISTON MWANZA MUJILA · *The Villain's Dance,* translated by Roland Glasser · *The River in the Belly:
Selected Poems,* translated by Bret Maney · DEMOCRATIC REPUBLIC OF CONGO

LUDMILLA PETRUSHEVSKAYA · *Kidnapped: A Crime Story,* translated by Marian Schwartz · *The New
Adventures of Helen: Magical Tales,* translated by Jane Bugaeva · RUSSIA

SERGIO PITOL · *The Love Parade* · translated by G. B. Henson · MEXICO

MANON STEFAN ROS · *The Blue Book of Nebo* · WALES

JIM SCHUTZE · *The Accommodation* · USA

SOPHIA TERAZAWA · *Winter Phoenix: Testimonies in Verse* · POLAND

BOB TRAMMELL · *Jack Ruby & the Origins of the Avant-Garde in Dallas & Other Stories* · USA

BENJAMIN VILLEGAS · *ELPASO: A Punk Story* · translated by Jay Noden · MEXICO